# HERE-AFTER

JULIE HOLLAND

hearts and minds art

# CHAPTER ONE

---

'SOLD!'

The crowd jostled, like seagulls in a head wind. The smack of the gavel into the auctioneer's palm was an anticlimax; a whack onto a wooden podium would have been more befitting the sale of such a well-known local property at 66 Ferryman Road. Under-bidders craned their necks, trying to spy who had purchased Binalong, and why. After all, the old girl had worn a few different shingles over time.

*Well, Abigail, you've done it now. You've bought an old building based purely on nostalgia and emptiness of heart.*

A shiver ran down Abigail Croucher's body in defiance of the warm spring day in South Melbourne. Like a leaking hose, the chill trickled along her limbs to her fingertips and toes. A black butterfly swooped in figure eights in front of her face, eager for her attention.

Strangers' murmurs of congratulation wafted around her like the butterfly as the estate agent's assistant click-clacked across the sidewalk, Pearl Lustre teeth sparkling behind a smile of victory. A double handclasp, then a gentle push from the agent, and Abigail teetered on the building's threshold. She took a hesitant breath and stepped inside. A whoosh of air, a random breeze out of nowhere, urged her forward. Flurries of blossoms from nearby trees whispered around her feet to sneak in with her, then parted like a filmy pink cloud as if in floral welcome.

The auctioneer held out his gold pen with a grin and a flourish. His eyes said otherwise – unspoken 'I hope she has the money' and 'why would someone in her middle years want to commit to this place' – reached her as though he had actually spoken the smug words.

Abigail couldn't blame him. In Australia, bidders weren't required to supply pre-auction financial documents. Her active wear admittedly was made from fine Italian microfibres that had cost more than she cared to admit, but it still presented as a T-shirt over tights. Yes, she had registered her name to bid but that had been after a couple of self-administered chardonnays, and it didn't mean anything. Not really. She had intended to go to the auction out of curiosity. Her bank card felt warm tucked inside her bra.

The heavy front door glided closed behind her. It was early afternoon and the edges of the grey room hovered behind a hazy glow of light. Abigail couldn't quite make out where the beam was coming from but noted it was thick with the dust their footsteps had awoken. The particles swirled around her then settled, the light changing to a dull yellow fluoro as extra overhead lights were turned on. It brought with it a stark reality.

She had inspected the property only once before the auction; enough for old hopes to raise their hands again and for memories to fizz expectantly over the following weeks. She wondered how many more of the building's now apparent shortcomings had been camouflaged by her expectations. The building beckoned, and she couldn't let it go. Not because of the past, but because of her future. Did she really believe that?

Abigail glanced at the paintings and sculptures which were perched around the space, witnessing her return. They were of various sizes, standards and points of completion.

"An artists' co-operative is renting the room but they only have another month on their lease with no option. They'd vacate if you didn't want them to renew," the agent informed her. The notion of encouraging local artists was appealing, so Abigail pushed the possibility to the side for the moment.

'Registered bidder number eight. Abigail Croucher,' the assistant announced, holding out a chair for her to take a seat.

At the mention of her name Abigail felt a little trip in the air, the hint of a simmer and buzz. She shivered and wished she'd brought a jacket.

Oblivious, the agent pointed to Purchaser to Sign Here, turned the contract pages and pointed again and again. With each tip of the pen, a tinny ringing in Abigail's ears grew more insistent. She shook her head. It wasn't unpleasant. In fact, the humming sensation gave her a peaceful sense of being elsewhere – like floating above her body as she had once seen in a movie death scene. She signed for the purchase and transferred the deposit for Binalong; this building that had played such an important role in her life.

Abigail glanced around the room, willing the shadows to relinquish their hold on history, but her own pinballing thoughts were being bombarded by purchase formalities and real estate small talk about the history of the area. She'd heard it all before.

'I'm sorry, what did you say?' Embarrassed, realising they were waiting for her to respond to something they'd said, she turned back to the agents.

They were looking at her, heads cocked to the side like sideshow clowns waiting for balls to be popped into their mouths. Business cards were pressed into her hand, with details on the collection of the keys once settlement had gone through.

'We'll be starting the auction for the cottage at number sixty-four next door in about five minutes if you'd like to stay and see who your new neighbours are,' the agent said.

She was surprised the vendor's agent hadn't checked their records of interested parties for both properties, but wanted to remember this day as a positive step forward, not one pock-marked by negativity. She glanced at the floor and noticed a white feather, all alone, at the base of her chair. She gathered it up, smoothed its creamy barbs and rotated it to and fro between her fingers as she was ushered outside. She found a quiet spot by the cottage's front fence and waited.

'Hello, Abigail.'

She hadn't seen Jane for months. 'Jane! Gosh, what are you doing here?'

'I'm being nosy, probably like half the crowd. What about you?'

Jane obviously didn't realise she had been the winning bidder, so Abigail waved away the question, not wanting to go into details. 'It's not far from home and I was out walking.'

'How are things? Are your boys here for Christmas?'

'Gosh, I haven't started thinking about Christmas yet, but no, I think they'll stay in London with their dad. Oh, they're starting the auction.'

Abigail edged closer to the cottage. She ran the feather along the front fence, sensing a gentle hum tingle through her fingers. She gazed through the cottage's open front door and listened to the sales pitch again. The competition amongst bidders was fierce, but any tension reached only the edges of Abigail's thoughts. She knew it was 'right as rain', as her late dad would have said, when she held the feather higher and with a quick nod became the final bidder. A small smile tweaked the corners of her mouth as she blinked away unbidden tears.

Once again Abigail was ushered into the building by a circle of arms as though paparazzi were about to swoop. In reality the onlookers, laden with environmental bags full of market produce, were happy to drift away to whatever was next on their Saturday agenda. Attending auctions and checking out sale prices was, after all, a long-held

Melbourne pastime, with expert opinions exchanged during every dinner party.

Out of the corner of her eye, Abigail caught Jane giving her a quick wave goodbye, accompanied by raised eyebrows.

The agents slapped each other on the back. No doubt they, and the single vendor for both properties, were thrilled with the results.

'Well, we won't need the feather you're clutching for a quill pen,' the auctioneer joked. 'I guess you know the procedure by now.'

The front room of her second purchase was bare and beautiful, with only a single chandelier twinkling in the afternoon light. Little rainbow prisms flitted around the walls. Abigail smiled graciously as she turned her attention to the documents. Somewhere between the previous signing and this moment she had lost the ringing in her ears.

'I believe you are already in the area. If you haven't already sold ...,' the agent probed.

'I'll keep you in mind,' Abigail replied, completing the sentence. 'If that's all I'm needed for, I'll head home now.'

As the convoy of agents' sleek BMWs drove away down the street, Abigail crossed the alleyway alongside Binalong and propped herself on the low stone wall opposite her indulgences on Ferryman Road.

# CHAPTER TWO

THE STIFF FEATHER trembled as Abigail eased its sides into a gentle peak. She shuffled her feet, sending up little plumes of dirt. She knew she was procrastinating, wasting time before studying the faded building in front of her; to feel something in response to the fact that she had just purchased the building where their restaurant, Grappa, was to be. Without looking, she knew the mouldy brick-work under a dirty festoon said Binalong. It had always been a joke between Luca and herself:

'Binalong-time since a great art show.'

'Binalong-time since we both dared to dream this big.'

It had been at Binalong Gallery that they had first met. 'Binalong-time since I met a girl like you,' Luca had joked. Abigail had laughed, nearly choking on a piece of finger food, but he had her attention.

And he had kept it for the next six-plus years. Until twenty-two months ago. Not that she was counting the months, weeks and minutes, but so much had been unresolved between them. And now it was too late.

A young couple stopped to read the agent's signs, nodding at the matching Sold stickers. The shadows lengthened and a crisp coolness descended on the typical late afternoon in Melbourne. Abigail was surprised she wasn't feeling more anxious; after all, she had just spent a good portion of her inheritance on a sentimental whim. And now that she was appraising it, she did wonder at the size of the task she had committed to.

Binalong wasn't crumbling; it had passed all of the necessary building inspections for commercial or residential use. However, the terrace house definitely had seen better days.

The building was quite imposing, towering over the corner of Ferryman Road and the wide alleyway, its footprint extending right out onto the front and side concrete sidewalks. It wasn't a beautiful construction, more like an ugly duckling of a huge brick box. Certainly nothing like those that appear in *Architectural Digest* or even Melbourne style magazines. It was from the Victorian era apparently, like many others in the sought-after historic suburb.

Two storeys of old-style architecture that offered only rendered and raw brown brick. Brick, brick, brick! However, she liked how the wide wooden front door cut across the corner, as though covering all angles – not wanting to miss anything that happened in either direction. The front wall was flat from top to pavement, interrupted only by a rectangular window on the first level and a small ground floor window. They had been blacked out, presumably for security. The only other colour visible was in the rampant graffiti along the mottled alleyway wall.

Abigail's eye strayed away from the corner to No. 64, which shared a common wall with Binalong. It was a narrow two-storey residence, or cottage as the real estate brochure described; Abigail had sensed the copywriter had never been to the Hamptons. Flush with the front wall of No. 66 ran No. 64's cute curlicue iron front fence, choked by a passionfruit vine. Its rusty little gate seemed to beg to be opened, beckoning the visitor to take a few paces along the concrete pathway to the narrow front porch. The red brick cottage boasted a freshly painted glossy emerald door, a window coloured in by an internal blind pulled low, and a straggly front garden.

The terrace had been modernised and repainted throughout, although Abigail had observed during the inspection that 'paint over the spider webs' was more accurate. Cream-vanilla bricks sunrayed the front door and windows. Three bulky chimneys jutted from the slate roof. Abigail frowned, recalling only two chimney shafts across both buildings. She made a mental note to do a recount at some time.

'I see it's sold.'

Abigail jumped at the raspy voice. She eased around to see an elderly woman, dressed from head to toe in black, nodding at the agent's board. Thick grey strands were pulled tightly into a bun, although later Abigail wouldn't be able to recall exactly what her hair had looked like. She achieved a towering presence despite her posture being somewhat hunched.

'Guess it'll be knocked down for apartments or another fancy restaurant.' The woman sniffed, eyeing Abigail.

'Oh no, I don't imagine so,' Abigail replied, sensing the woman was waiting for her reaction. She suddenly felt quite proud to admit to ownership. 'Actually ...'

'Well, all I can say is Patricia is not going to be happy. They'll be out on their shell-pink ear, no doubt.'

She stared at Abigail, her alert blue eyes in contrast to the other aged parts of her body. 'Then again, Binalong-time since someone really cared about the old girl.'

Abigail started, too slow with a reply. It struck her as odd that not only had she used that phrase, but she had given Abigail a healthy wink before shuffling away.

The woman's unsolicited chat, however, didn't surprise Abigail. She had found that living in South Melbourne was the same as living in many other inner-city suburbs. It nurtured a strong sense of community. Many of the residents had lived their whole lives in their beloved homes. It was only when residents passed on that properties became available for sale, most of the houses now snapped up by developers.

Until the auction, an uncertainty had lingered about No. 64. Abigail hadn't been one hundred percent sure if the cottage was what she wanted or needed. But then she had felt inexplicably drawn through its front door, and she knew that no one else should be so close to Binalong.

She wondered who Patricia could be, wishing she had a notebook or phone to jot down ideas and points to follow up. 'Chimney and Patricia, chimney and Patricia,' she chanted to herself.

Abigail had expected Binalong in particular to have attracted a higher reserve, and she only hoped she hadn't missed anything prohibitive in the contracts. There was no cooling off period, but the agent would send the papers to her solicitor to double-check that there had been full disclosure.

A slight tremor rippled through her heart. She took several deep breaths, knowing the attack was brought on by a fear of the unknown. The earlier sense of peace had deserted her, but then she recalled an inspiring phrase she had read once: 'Remember that the minute you take your first step into the life of your dreams, the first to greet you there will be fear. Nod. Keep walking.'

Abigail nodded, and reached for the underlying excitement she knew was within her.

A sudden gust of wind stirred around the dusty gutter, tossing leaves and flowers and pollen against her. It was unusually quiet, and for a moment she felt as if something grand and dangerous was about to happen; but the air settled, a cyclist rode by, a woman's laugh floated on the breeze and all was normal. She recalled the utter calmness that had cocooned her as the pen flew across the contracts of purchase for the properties. It had been wonderful, as if someone was guiding her, reassuring her that this was the path she should tread.

Yes, it was a lot of money, but she knew she could afford it. She had decided to offer the space to the artists rent-free until their lease expired and then they would have to vacate.

Since Lucas's death, her life had changed into something jagged and incomplete. But now, at last, she just knew with all her being that this was the way to repair it. Her stomach settled with the comforting weight of purpose.

'Thank you, Dad,' she sighed, blowing a kiss to the heavens.

Binalong would offer her future a gentle touchstone to the past. To Luca.

---

SCANNING *the gathering crowd through a chink in the grimy, painted window, I suddenly see her.*

*Her thick auburn hair has grown. I guess it would reach to her shoulders when released from the clips pulling it back from her beautiful face. The afternoon sun catches the blonde highlights.*

*My mind wanders as the exhibitionist auctioneer begins his overinflated spiel. Members of the crowd chat, some move from foot to foot with impatience while others hold their faces up to the thin rays of sunlight. I yearn to be able to do the same, to feel the soft breeze. Literally. I ache for touch on my skin, to see a look of lust to be cast my way. But I swear at myself, cursing, telling myself to get a grip, and turn my focus back to the street. To Abby.*

*She rises to her feet with an expression I remember so well. Fierce determination. I don't know if she means to buy* the building, but I know she is destined to. That's partly why I am here, to witness it. I am happy for her, I guess. I send a jet butterfly as my hug of congratulations. My eyes close as I imagine it is me caressing her hair – how magical that would be. She brushes it aside.

Binalong is knocked down to her and they usher her inside. I move into position in one corner of the downstairs studio room, trying to control my excitement at being so close to her, but wary of casting any light or vibration that she may sense. Not that, for an instant, she would understand what she was experiencing.

Her trusting face furrows with a small frown. I am a silent witness as she signs, as she moves one step closer to reclaiming a chink of her past. Once more I waver in my purpose. Should I be here? What right do I have to enter her life again, even if it's to set a record straight? The lights flicker at my agitation, but none of the group notices. Abby shakes her head and glances curiously around the walls. Perhaps she does pick up on my presence. My heart sinks as she leaves the room, but thankfully my carefully placed feather is between her fingers.

Outside, she seems distracted as a woman engages her in conversation. And then she surprises me. She plays the game of a good auction and steps in right on cue to buy the terrace house next door. I can tell she's satisfied; a job well done.

But now she looks so alone, sitting on the stone wall opposite. I shudder as I see her speak to the familiar woman who passes here most days. The old lady in black makes me uneasy but I don't know why. I can't remember if I recognise her from 'then' or 'now'. The woman disappears down the street at last and suddenly Abigail looks up, staring straight at me. Her eyes are the colour of hazelnut shells, but it is her unwavering focus that has me edging away from the window. I catch my own stupidity: Apparently she can't see me until I want her to! I move back to the window and watch her scan along the buildings, taking in every curve, crack and brick.

I am pleased to see a smile cross her fine face. I only wish I had been the one responsible.

# CHAPTER THREE

EVERY STEP ECHOED Abigail's increasing joy as she sprinted the couple of blocks to her house. Nigella, the five-year-old Airedale, greeted her with her normal bouncing expectation of a hug, food and a night in.

The first person Abigail would share her news with would be her close friend, Steph. Abigail had a quick turn-around shower, changed her clothes then told Nigella the bad news.

'Sorry, girl. A pat and a doggie treat is all I have time for. But I won't be late.'

Don Carmelo Restaurant was a local favourite so Abigail was relieved to find a parking space so quickly. Gino, the owner, welcomed her with wide hugs and double kisses and ushered her through the bustling crowd to the table before hurrying off to fetch a glass of her favourite Shiraz.

Steph stood and gathered Abigail in for a hug, then

quickly whispered, 'Jane and Paul were sitting at the next table so they decided to join us.'

Abigail hadn't seen Jane for months, and now they'd crossed paths twice in one day. She glanced across the table to where Jane sat with her husband, Paul, their hands entwined. A bottle of Chianti was already open in front of them. She sent them a smile and greeting before sliding into her seat but cursed silently that it wasn't just Steph and herself.

The tantalising aromas of heavy Italian casseroles, fresh herb and tomato sauces and olive pizza reminded Abigail she hadn't eaten all day; she was starving. 'Eat a horse and chase the jockey' had been one of her dad's sayings. If one good thing had come out of her marriage to an Italian, it was a renewed appreciation for good hearty food.

After the waitress had given them a quick review of the specials, they ordered their meals. Abigail settled back in her chair, finally feeling a wave of calm take over.

'What did you get up to today, Abby?' Steph asked.

Abigail flicked her eyes around the table. Jane obviously hadn't mentioned running into her at the auction.

'I went to an auction and purchased a property.' Abigail raised her glass in mock salute.

Steph's reaction was all she had hoped for as she let out a whoop and clinked her glass with Abigail's. 'You bought something? Well done, where? It's good that you're moving on to, you know, somewhere without so many memories.'

'Well, I'm not. I mean I might. I don't have to yet, but I can sell my current house if I need to free up some more money.' Abigail never lied about her wealth to her friends, but she was always careful not to be flippant about it either. She was all too aware of possible underlying jealousies even from those closest to her. 'I bought a lovely terrace house. It doesn't need a lot of work, just the kitchen to be updated and new life breathed into it. I'd love your input though, Steph.'

'Of course,' Steph replied.

'As for the memories you mentioned, I bought the old gallery. You know, Binalong. On Ferryman?'

Jane gasped. 'You bought it as well? It's next to the terrace she bought,' she informed Steph, as though Abigail wasn't sitting there.

'That old dump?' Paul added, shaking his head.

'Wow. Well. That's ambitious, Abby. I mean ... gosh.' Steph's smile failed to conceal her surprise.

Abigail's face must have betrayed her disappointment. Ever the peacemaker, Steph jumped to her feet, raced around and embraced her. 'Good on you, Abby. Sorry about my stupid comment about memories and all that.'

'So, what are your plans? I didn't go through it, but is it sound?' Jane asked.

Abigail took a deep breath. 'Look, I know it's a little unexpected. I surprised myself, really. But it just felt right. Yes, it is sound but a little rundown. I'm not sure what I'll do with it yet. There is room for accommodation upstairs.'

Abigail knew she was justifying herself. She was thankful when Gino brought their meals and the topic was put to the side. Abigail buried her nose in her spinach, zucchini and pine nut linguine and pretended to follow Jane's story about one of her children.

The conversation soon turned back to Abigail. 'You know,' Steph said, 'it's a shame that Guy and Steve are going to be in France until next year. They would have loved to help with the refurb of your building.'

'I'm sure they would,' Abigail agreed. 'Actually, I'll email them some photos and maybe they could send me some ideas for the interior. It's Victorian but the ground level has been opened up a fair bit. Maybe I can knock through the common wall to extend it even more. Do you remember when it was first renovated to become an art gallery? When Luca and I met?'

The elephant in the room had trumpeted. Luca. Abigail appreciated that not one of her friends would ever wish that Luca had died, particularly so tragically; but she was also aware that they had never really warmed to him. When a dinner was planned, Luca would often be busy, so it became a girls' night or Abby went solo.

And now her friends were silent, intent on their dinner, obviously not wanting to rock the boat or resurrect old grievances. They gazed into their pasta, shifted in their seats, swilled their wine. Anything but look her in the eye.

'This is delicious,' Steph said.

Jane and Paul nodded.

Abigail broke the uncomfortable silence that had resettled over the table.

'You know Luca and I always loved that building. It would have been perfect as a restaurant. We tried and tried to buy it over the years.' She pressed on. 'It's ironic isn't it, that it's come on the market only two years after Luca died? Like it was waiting. Like it was sitting there, saying to itself,

"No, let's just string them out. Can't have too many dreams come true for this couple.'"

'Or maybe it was waiting for proper finance rather than being lobbied around for contributions,' Paul muttered.

Steph glanced at Abigail, while Jane sent her husband a 'don't go there' frown.

'What do you mean by that, Paul?' Abigail asked. Something in her stomach – or was it her heart – had leapfrogged over any excitement that was nestling there.

Paul held up his hands as if in a truce, but his strange half-smile was evidence that he wasn't sorry. That he was keeping something back.

Abigail continued to stare at him. 'Paul?'

Abigail heard her voice rising, reaching nearby tables, but she didn't care. She stabbed at her linguine. She could see the frown on Gino's face and knew he would be beside her shortly, trying to restore order. She looked from one face to the next around the table but couldn't dampen her annoyance. They were supposed to be her friends, to support her no matter what.

Jane leant over. 'It's okay, Abigail. You don't have to get upset. Paul didn't mean anything by his comment.'

Paul shrugged. 'Oh, I don't know. It always seemed to me that everyone held Luca on too high a pedestal. Yes, the guy had plans and a big personality, but his ambitions did tend to come with unwelcome expectations. I'm sorry he died, Abigail, but ...'

Abigail stood as she pushed her chair back, the wooden legs scraping on the concrete floor. 'I would have thought you'd be pleased for me. I know Luca wasn't your favourite person in the world, but he was still my husband.'

'Honey, of course we're pleased for you,' Steph said gently. 'We're just hoping you haven't taken on too much, that's all. None of us is twenty anymore.'

Steph's placating tone didn't go unnoticed with Abigail. 'For God's sake, we're not even sixty. Why shouldn't I get stuck into something that's going to excite me?'

'Abby, sit down. Finish your meal,' Jane pleaded.

But Abigail couldn't, she just couldn't. She had felt like the glittery ball on New Year's Eve, so full of hope for the future. But now, she was falling, plummeting, as anger and disappointment rolled together in her stomach. She didn't have time to be surprised by her reaction, she just needed to leave the confines of the table and the restaurant for some fresh air. To her enormous relief, no one tried to stop her as she spun to leave the restaurant.

Gino's hand waved away her money as he gently placed his hand on her arm. 'Bella, I don't know what just happened, but are you all right to get home?'

Abigail nodded curtly. She seemed to be constantly apologising to Gino. First, after Luca had made his opinion clear that Don Carmelo's menu was 'bland Aussie-Italian', then when Luca and Gino had words about how Sicilian stuffed sardines should be prepared. Abigail's innocent comment to Luca, that his mother was from Northern Italy so how would he know, hadn't helped. They had never returned as a couple, much to Abigail's embarrassment. And now she, not Luca, had disrupted his business.

The cool evening air spiked through her light clothing

as she walked briskly to her car. Annoyance simmered around her edges. She could have gone home, opened a bottle of wine and drowned her sorrows, but there were still too many memories of Luca ready to ambush her there. Paul's comment had certainly found its mark. Instead she drove the short distance to the Port Melbourne foreshore, parked under a streetlight in the carpark and locked her doors. She needed to shut out the nagging world. Joggers and dog walkers were taking advantage of the clear night, and Abigail watched them absently.

She drew her legs up across the front seat, snuggling against the hard door, and gazed out over the bay. It was swathed in moonlight, as if a gap in the clouds had let through a glimpse of Heaven. *Heaven.* Was that where Luca was? Could he see her? She exhaled a long breath and tried to centre herself. Where had she read that your physical appearance in Heaven is from when you were happiest – would that have been during their marriage for Luca? She wished she knew. The low waves were mesmerising as they whooshed up the sand, foamy bubbles popping as they receded back to the depths. Again and again.

'Life gose on' was scrawled on the side of a disused surf club in an optimistic purple paint. Normally the typo would have itched at Abigail's eye for detail, but in that moment she couldn't care less.

What an elegant retreat it would have been if she had brought her wineglass with her from the restaurant. To slip and swerve around diners, glass held high in salute to her exit – much more theatrical than stumbling between tables like a fool. In hindsight, she wondered whether, as embarrassment had crept in, it had been her fault that the conversation had taken such a turn for the worse. But the argument, if that is what it was, had happened so quickly and she couldn't really remember how it had all panned out. One thing was patently clear – her friends were not impressed with her decision to purchase Binalong. No doubt Jane would have filled in Steph by now on how the auction had panned out. Abigail wasn't stupid and knew, deep down, that they suspected she was just clinging to the memory of her late husband.

But buying Binalong and establishing Grappa Restaurant and Bar had been her dream too. It would have given her the opportunity of picking up a paintbrush again, urged on by the excitement of sharing the challenge with Luca and his grand vision. They had bounced ideas off each other for 'their space', wherever it eventuated, the hope that Binalong would come on the market only fuelling their ambition.

Luca's mother's family held a legendary reputation in the Italian restaurant world. However, over time, with changes in the industry and different demands from the public, patronage had started to wane. When Sofia had warned that the popularity of white tablecloth fine dining wasn't as strong as it once was, Luca had shrugged his broad shoulders and said his intentions for his business were more present day anyway. It was a restless single-mindedness that would rear up many times.

Luca's reaction to Abigail's sketches for large mural works had warmed her heart.

'They are amazing, Abby,' he had enthused in true

Luca style. 'I agree that you should paint some murals throughout the restaurant. I think sultry pieces: dark rustic tables overladen with produce, gigantic piles of fruit in colours of faded autumn, fishmongers hawking against a paint-splattered marketplace. That would be perfect.' The ideas were endless. But then everything changed.

They had been on the threshold of staging an ambitious pitch for funding while waiting for a suitable property. Luca had travelled back and forth connecting with possible backers and liaising with family members in Italy. Liam Cleary, his friend and contact in the banking industry, was looking for potential commercial investors for them as well. Luca had said it was in the bag.

Abigail had presumed that working on the project together would bring them closer together. It was a dream inching slowly toward reality, but also a dream that ignited unsettling conflict between them. Luca had finally divulged that he intended to use subtle black and white moving images of Italian landscapes against the walls. Abigail's murals had been casually shelved by her husband and he refused to discuss it further. She had worked on the designs for weeks and was both hurt and mystified by his late admission. Then he had suddenly cooled on the whole project.

'It's not the right time,' Luca had blustered without any clarification. Abigail could tell he was just stalling.

'What? What do you mean? We'll find another venue if Binalong doesn't eventuate,' Abigail had reasoned.

'Luca. Perhaps if you cut back on some of the more extravagant areas. You know, take a more modest approach.

We could look for a smaller, less expensive space,' she had suggested, but Luca had walked out on the discussion. She had presumed, amidst the secrecy, that any potential backing from Italy hadn't been as firm as he had promised her.

Abigail had been embarrassed to learn he had tried crowdfunding the project with little success. Now Paul's comments came back to her, sticking in her throat.

Her husband had bounced back with typical enthusiasm. Abigail kept reminding herself that his optimism was one of the traits she had fallen in love with. He had done a backflip, smothering her with attention and pleas for forgiveness and urged her to reconsider approaching her mother to access the Arpels' family fortune.

'You can access the Trust,' Luca had pushed.

'Maybe. I ...'

'Just do it, Abigail. Do I have to do everything?'

His words had stung as they were thrown into the mix along with his many inferences about her moneyed upbringing. If he had been honest with her from the beginning, she may have tried to access her funds, but his actions had cut deeply into her trust.

Going over it all again wasn't helpful, particularly when she was alone, curled up in her car by the beach. Sniffing, Abigail fumbled in the glovebox for a pack of tissues. Car service receipts, pens and out-of-date tubes of sunscreen scattered onto the floor. She left them where they fell, surprised at her untidiness. As the car windows started to fog, she eased them down then put them up again. She wanted to breathe in the salty air but couldn't bring herself to let in the world, even a few centimetres of it. The moon had disappeared, and the night closed over Heaven's door.

When Luca died, they hadn't been getting along well in their relationship. It still distressed Abigail to acknowledge their final six months – truthfully, one year – had been so volatile. He had been hiding something else from her, she was sure of it, but he had scoffed when she enquired if perhaps he was ill. Isolation and abandonment had settled over her life.

She had thought there would be time to sort things out, had backed away from serious confrontation on so many occasions. But something wasn't right – she could sense it. Luca worked so hard, she couldn't see how he would have time for an affair. Abigail had even secretly met Luca's mate, Liam, to try and prise information out of him. To no avail. And then the accident, and grief.

'Life gose on', however you spell it. Yes, it must.

# CHAPTER FOUR

AS ABBY APPROACHES THE BUILDING, *I grin with such anticipation that I'm sure I must be glowing. She stops on the corner, squinting up at the windows. Her swaying body is a sure sign of nervousness. She has always done that – whenever things weren't right in her world.*

*That momentary glimpse of shyness, of being unsure, was one of the things I loved about her. On the one hand she is someone who chooses to back away from confrontation, yet she has such inner strength. Of course, her upbringing gave her all the social graces needed in this world, but to my knowledge she has never used her name to get ahead or to score points. Mention her name in any social or business circle and you will be greeted with exclamations of praise and respect. Many a time she was there for me, a grand sounding board when I needed someone. To be sure, her self-belief and love of life had started to waver during the last stage of the marriage though.*

*Perhaps she has regained her passion and determination. She must know the challenges ahead of her with this place, both emotionally and physically.*

*I know what she's doing here but I suddenly realise that I don't have a vast clue how I'm going to catch her attention. I know I want to rush to her side, to say how can I help, as I had in the past. I can talk to her, but how will I appear to her? Will I be able to touch her, hug her? If she brought a notebook, could I physically write a message? I hear the key in the lock, but don't venture down.*

---

HANDS ON HIPS, Abigail stood in the centre of Binalong's front room. Easels supporting half-finished works leaned quietly against the walls. She could hear voices drifting from the kitchen, so she presumed that was why the front door had been unlocked and that the co-op members would be opening soon. Abigail quelled a sneeze, unable to fathom how they could paint amongst so much dust.

As if on cue, the front door flew open and two women strode in, laden with fruit and foliage. The pair looked like Carmen Miranda on wheels but couldn't be more opposite in personal appearance. The bearer of most of the fruit was small and mousey, with grey dungarees over a matching T-shirt, worn Birkenstock sandals, and fragile hair hauled back in a ponytail. The other woman, the one speaking loudly as if her friend had lost her earpiece, was a vision of vibrant colour via a flowing neck-to-ankles caftan. Her orange topknot was piled high around a fluoro headband; large spectacles of a similar colour slid down her nose as she rambled on.

They both stopped short as they saw Abigail. A lemon toppled from the fruit pile and rolled across the floor, leaving behind a wobbly snail trail.

'Hi, I'm Abigail.' When no response came, she continued. 'I guess you're from the artists' group. I was hoping you'd be here today. I wasn't sure which days you came.'

'Hello, I'm Sandy.' The smaller woman timidly looked sideways. 'And this is Patricia. And, yes, we are from the Binalong Artists' Co-op.'

Abigail sucked in a breath. Calling themselves the Binalong group, as though they belonged there, would make her conversation tricky. Particularly if this was *the* Patricia.

'And why are you here?' Patricia asked before turning away, heavy eyebrows arched. 'Put all the props over there, Sandy. The students will be here soon.'

'I've come to take a look around the property. I'm the new owner.'

'Are you now?' Patricia smirked. 'Well, no doubt we will need to discuss the terms of our lease. It's due to expire soon.'

Sandy stepped forward, her hand extended. 'Lovely to meet you. Perhaps you'd like to stay and watch. We have a still life class this morning. And then, of course, a cup of tea and cake whilst Patricia does her wonderful appraisals of the artists' work.'

Abigail glanced to Patricia for her reaction to the invitation and was met with a steely gaze.

'I'm sure Abigail isn't interested in art, Sandy.'

'Why would you think that?' Abigail asked with a teasing smile, sensing the rise of her inner Don't-Mess-With-Me. The stubborn one, not the one who shirked confrontation. She immediately rethought her rent-free offer if this was to be Patricia's attitude.

The three women jumped as a loud bang from upstairs echoed around them.

'Goodness, what could that be?' Sandy clutched at her T-shirt.

Half a dozen women bustled in. Instantly the tense atmosphere softened to one of chatter as they happily greeted each other and set up for their session. Abigail quietly backed off.

THE FRONT GALLERY, where Patricia and her clan of followers were ensconced, was familiar to Abigail. It had been where she and Luca had met at the opening night of a Binalong exhibition. Her friends had decided to take in the abstract exhibition before heading off for dinner, but Abigail had stayed behind, more interested in the cheeky Italian she had encountered than any form of degustation. She could still picture him leaning casually against the mantel, chatting with his friend but with eyes only for her.

They had returned to the gallery many times for various exhibitions. Now she couldn't help but feel sad at the loss of its vibrancy; it seemed to be biding its time, waiting for someone to love it, to inject it with great purpose and lively voices. She glanced over her shoulder as she made her way to the back of the ground floor, certain she would catch Patricia watching her. Guessing Abigail's traitorous eviction plans. But Patricia was busy directing one of the artists to 'express more dimension' in her still life.

A pokey bathroom appeared on Abigail's right, then a small kitchen. Mugs and plates of sliced cake stretched across the countertop, but everything was as clean as a whistle. A storeroom and narrow back door were locked, so she retraced her steps to the stairway. No doubt she wasn't legally supposed to roam the building until she had been given the keys, but she just couldn't wait to take herself through it again.

An uneasy feeling of being watched hung over her as she approached the steep staircase. A coolness whispered across her face as she started the climb. She wondered if an upstairs window had been left ajar. Abigail skipped up the stairs, surprised at her rapid heartbeat. She clung to the railing, pausing to catch her breath. The breeze didn't strengthen, nor did it abate. It had a tinge of something, a scent. Peppermint. Abigail smiled, recalling their friend who always had a box of Tic Tacs in his pocket. 'Ready for the next kiss,' he'd joked, and everyone knew that wouldn't be far off.

But then, in the end, had he been a true friend to Luca and to her? So many unanswered questions, she reminded herself for the hundredth time.

*Damn it.* The ringing in her head had returned. Promising herself to get fit, she continued to the landing.

When Abigail had done her research on Binalong, she had found that No. 66 was being promoted as an ideal two-level space to offer exhibitions and events. No. 64 shared the common wall, and behind the emerald front door was a fully restored house. It had been used as an Airbnb by the previous owners, with Binalong the rather unsuccessful commercial arm.

She knew that the upper level of Binalong comprised a spacious front bedroom and bathroom, another storeroom at the top of the stairs and an additional kitchen at the back. It all made sense when you considered how the plumbing would mirror that below. She went straight ahead but all the kitchen windows were closed; in fact, they were painted shut. As was the small bathroom window, the only vent a stretch of wire grilling clogged with debris. She could only presume the breeze she'd felt was an irregular draught from under the storeroom door.

The front bedroom beckoned. Abigail strolled along the corridor, running her finger along the plaster wall. Her heart rate had slowed a little, but the ringing persisted. Sounds of shifting easels and laughter from below filtered up the stairs. Abigail couldn't imagine what the bump had been that had startled them earlier, as there was no furniture at all in any of the upstairs rooms. Perhaps there was a resident possum somewhere. She was relieved not to find any droppings, and there was no rodent-type smell; only the increasingly stronger fragrance of peppermint.

She crossed her arms, shivering as she walked into the

room. The windows, roughly blackened and painted shut, still allowed shafts of light through in places as if a knife had sliced through fabric. The space around her ankles seemed to spin – had someone fled at her approach, leaving air to slowly whirl, then settle?

Even in this bare state the room had such a wonderful, mysterious quality. It seemed to tug at Abigail. *Luca*. Memories of him and their plans reared violently, turning into soggy regret. Slowly she turned, picturing her murals on all the uneven surfaces; the possibilities that never became reality. She tried to remind herself that he hadn't wanted her to work on these walls anyway; he had let her down. Two levels of great Italian dining and bar space, and the opportunity to host wonderful celebrations had never eventuated.

Her eyes rested on a rectangular piece of ironwork. If that had been the bump she had heard as it toppled to the floor, she didn't know what had caused it to fall. Rusted tendrils of ivy intertwined around each other, flakes lying dead on the floor as though autumn had come and gone decades ago.

The room began to blur. Her imagined paintings spun around and around, the sepias and coppers melting into one mass, like the boy in the story who turned to butter after being chased around a tree by tigers. The light flickered. Abigail held her hand out, her clammy palm flat against the wall. Her knees buckled and she slowly slid to the floor.

I HADN'T ENJOYED HEARING *the way that Patricia had spoken to Abigail, and was as surprised as anyone when the metal piece had fallen at my bidding. I wish I knew more about this whole bloody situation and how to work it. I could always charm, cajole and get my way in my earth life with no effort at all, but now I'm ignorant. In no man's land.*

*I start to panic as Abby races up the stairs. She darts around at the other end of the floor, then slows as she approaches my room. I stand, pressed as best I can against one wall. I open my mouth as she walks through the door, ready to explain but, of course, she doesn't see me. She seems to be cold. It breaks my heart to see her expression, so expectant yet sorrowful, and the quickness of her breath seems unnatural.*

*Ha, who is the unnatural one here, I joke, when I should be concentrating on keeping calm and not projecting my thoughts or emotions. That much I do know – that there would be consequences from not keeping myself in check. And there are; the central ceiling light blinks on then off and the room takes on a chilled air, that even I can detect. She looks puzzled. But worse still, Abby turns ashen and clutches the wall, then slowly she slides to the floor.*

*She is only out for a moment, but I use that time. Every nano-second of it. I squat in front of her, relieved in the knowledge that she is okay, although her breathing is very shallow. She sniffs as if catching a scent in the air then gasps as I run my finger, uselessly, down her face. What I wouldn't give for her to open her eyes, to tilt her head and smile cheekily as she used to do. I could help her to her feet and we could hug like old times.*

'Oh, Abby, I miss you so much,' I whisper to her, sighing. My breath catches her hair and it wisps around her face. Again, she sniffs the air, then opens her eyes. Her brow crinkles tentatively, as though she's not sure whether she has a reason to or not.

I jump back and wait.

She sits straight against the wall, blinking, and takes in a deep, faltering breath. She squints around the room as if she's looking for something and frowns when she doesn't find it. Slowly she pulls her knees to her chest and drops her forehead. Her deep cries are muffled, but if I could take each heartbreaking sob and do away with it, I would. I am embarrassed to acknowledge that many people would be surprised and suspicious to see me so full of compassion, but Abby always seemed to bring out my good side. Which is why I'm here, I guess. I yearn to gather her into my arms and comfort her. To explain and make things right. It has been another step forward in my quest just to see her, and to learn a little more about my so-called abilities. I'm sure she senses something too.

But I have to wait for the right time, and somehow I know this isn't it.

---

ABIGAIL'S BREATH shuddered as she opened her eyes. Finding herself slumped on the floor, she tried to remember the last time she had fainted – it must have been many years ago, when she was pregnant. She touched her cheek, ready to brush away a memory that lingered there but found only sweaty strands of hair. Vaguely she accepted that the peppermint scent must be from some sort of cleaner.

When Luca had died everyone earnestly told her to move on as they had waved airily towards the horizon. But it was all so hard. For months Abigail's nightmares had been graphic – images of days with Luca turning to ash as they slid away from her, through a curtain, into an urn and then scattered in a surging sea. Luca had hated water, feared rivers and swimming, but that was what she dreamt night after night. Meditation, counselling, long walks then longer walks had helped, but Abigail couldn't move on, not totally. She had loved Luca and had known something wasn't right, as if there were words and explanations mysteriously floating around her, then darting like an elf out of sight again. She had just kept putting one heavy foot in front of the other.

She wasn't sure how long she sat on the floor but finally she knew she had to move or be found frozen to the wall. How could her body be layered with heat and cold at the same time? She turned onto all fours, hoisted her body upright then shambled down the hallway. As she slowly descended the stairs, hoping that Patricia's group hadn't heard her cries, her body settled and her heart slowed. By the time she tiptoed out the front door into the comforting sunshine she felt semi-normal. She glanced back up at the building.

Binalong – what was it about this building that affected her so much, caused her heart to race, for her mind to go to mush? Enough time had passed since Luca's death and she had resigned herself to a life without him and all his secrets. But now, this block of bricks and mortar was triggering her unresolved questions. She would have to come to grips with whether she was prepared to plough on or put the property back on the market, then walk away forever.

# CHAPTER FIVE

'DARLING! When are you coming to visit your mother?'

Abigail heard the familiar veiled accusation in the question. 'Mum ...'

'Now next week is good for me, except for when I volunteer at the gallery on Tuesday. And there's mah-jong at Hillary Baxter's on Wednesday ...'

'Mum,' Abigail called into the phone. Really, trying to focus her mother's attention was like trying to catch bubbles in a stiff breeze – some popped, a couple stayed and the rest just floated away.

'I'm just pointing out the importance of keeping busy, Abigail. Don't keep locking yourself away down there. It's just an hour's flight to Sydney. Why don't you take yourself back to London to see those two gorgeous sons of yours. I appreciate it's been a couple of years now since dear Luca died, but I'm telling you the pain remains forever when a partner passes.'

*Here we go.* 'I know, Mum. Dad died so long ago, but I still miss him every day.'

'Really?'

'Of course. I'll always remember your stories of your childhood, of your family's joy when you met Dad, how proud they were that you married a junior accountant. How hard he worked, but he always had time for his children. He was a wonderful man.' She mentally added 'with a bucketful of patience' to her father's qualities.

It was family folklore that when the engineering company Allan had worked with had faltered, he had risked everything and bought it at a base-level price. The following years had seen continued growth and profits far beyond his initial expectations. Audrey, however, had always known she was destined for greatness and had even ensured her family's top ranking by naming her children, Adam and Abigail, with an A – 'So as to be always at the top of the list, sweethearts.' Whenever someone had enquired if there was a family connection to the exclusive European Van Cleef and Arpels jewellery company she would smile shyly. In truth any extended association to anyone only went to the Arpels of the outer Sydney suburbs. Abigail had often wondered if her mother's actions had been desperate attempts to shrug off her poor upbringing.

The months following Allan Arpels's collapse from a heart attack was the only time Abigail could remember her mother letting down her guard. Audrey had phoned her and her brother at all hours, confiding in them the fear she was experiencing for the first time in her life, the realisation she had loved her husband with all her heart and soul. When he died, Audrey, Adam and Abigail Arpels had been left heartbroken and wealthy.

'Are you still there, Abigail? You need to keep busy.'

'Yes, Mum, but you will recall that I always wanted to have a larger role in the company. And I do spend a lot of time with my philanthropy projects.'

It was an old argument but one Abigail would never give up on. Even though her father had constantly told her how capable she was, how he knew she could achieve great things for herself and those in need, he also warned her of his succession planning. His will, reinforced by her mother's opinions, had made it abundantly clear that Adam would take up the reins of the company. He was, after all, the male of the family. Abigail was under no illusion that her brother had been instrumental in that decision too.

It had been a double-edged sword which left Abigail unsure of where she stood; a strange feeling to, for the first time, flounder in her goals. So, she chose the good life. She decided to take her grief and fresh university degree overseas, had travelled widely but not escaped the deep pit of loss left by her adored father's death. On her return to Australia years later, Abigail's professional frustrations still simmering, she had sought out the philanthropy arm of the business. This time she refused to be ignored, and her ability to make a difference had proved immensely satisfying. Over time, Audrey had got on with her life by throwing herself into Sydney's elite circle of widows.

'Mum. Listen. I'm ringing to tell you that I have bought

a building.' Abigail rolled her head, easing the stiffness in her neck.

'Oh, a new house. That's wonderful. Memories of Luca must be in every corner of your home.'

'Well, it's more than a house. It's a building. Two actually. I mean, they're structurally fine but there are things I need to do. I'm not quite sure what yet. But, there you go,' Abigail said firmly.

'Oh, Abigail. Have you ...'

'I am perfectly capable of making my own decisions. Why do I need to remind you that I'm an adult? Have been for a long time.' It had become her mantra over the years, as much a reinforcement for her as a directive to her family. Abigail tried not to regret her words as the silence from her mother dragged on.

Finally, with a sigh, Audrey replied. 'Well I'm not sure what you mean by a building, so please send me a photo. I have to dash. Stevie is here for my massage. Ciao.'

Abigail grimaced at her mother's adopted Italian. Audrey had adored Luca and in turn, Luca had loved the attention Audrey had lavished on him and had gone to great lengths to nurture it. At times Abigail had been suspicious of his true motives but grateful for his efforts. Audrey had no idea of the troubles that had lurked beneath the surface of her daughter's marriage. But then she had never asked either.

A FEW HOURS LATER, Abigail received the anticipated call from Adam.

'The Arpels gossip line is obviously working,' she said, cautious of Adam's reasons for contacting her.

'Well, what did you expect? I have been sent in to rescue you from any silly document signing you may have undertaken without our solicitors' advice. I hear you've bought a new house.'

Abigail sighed. 'No, Adam. I have bought a building and a cottage. It may become my home as well, but I'm still deciding what to do. And yes, I have sent Dan the contracts to okay. I'm surprised he hasn't told you.'

'Ah, we are very strict about confidentiality in the family business, you know.

Abigail raised her eyes to the heavens in a silent thank you to Dan. She was still wary of Adam's intentions though; fully aware she had been kept in the dark on many family decisions over the years.

'Where are the building and cottage then?' he further probed.

*Here we go.*

'In South Melbourne, not far from my house,' Abigail replied vaguely.

'And? Come on, Abigail, spill the beans. I can tell you're holding back.'

'It's Binalong. I've bought Binalong.' Abigail could picture her brother in his large corner office, having made time to ring her only on their mother's plea. He would now be putting down his onyx pen, tossing his glasses onto the desk, pushing back the leather swivel chair and rubbing his eyes. Half his mind would be elsewhere, on some Arpels business endeavour.

'Binalong. That rings a bell. Oh, not that gallery.' When Adam didn't receive an answer, he continued. 'You bought a whole building? Why?'

'Why not? Really, Adam, there's no beating around the bush with you, is there.' She stopped short of adding '... your darling wife's habit of speaking first and thinking later is rubbing off.' Abigail had never particularly liked or trusted the social-climbing Georgia. Georgia prided her position as the boss's wife and would never relinquish an iota of the privileges that came with it, particularly to his sister. Abigail was sure the feeling was reciprocated, with the sisters-in-law only crossing paths when she made an effort to see her niece, Scarlet.

'A few reasons, I guess, not least being that it finally came on the market. It might inspire me to paint again. Maybe. And there's a link to Luca without it being too solid a link. It will be mine, not ours, which I always presumed would be a bad thing, but the more I think about it, it just seems the right thing. People keep telling me to move out of the house, so I guess that will happen too in time if the cottage next door feels right.'

She stopped, surprised that she had shared so much with her brother. And surprised she was voicing thoughts that had bounced around her mind for some time. She knew she had to stop running from the past without ignoring it, and this could be the answer.

'You know what? It's actually nice to have something just for me,' she said firmly.

'Well, you know that I'm no great believer in listening to other people. You're a smart woman, well, pretty smart. A little smart ...'

Abigail smiled. She sensed his jokes about their places within the family hierarchy were to humour her and that he was more than happy to be sitting in the corner office, in control. But if push came to shove, and her brother displayed any sign of weakness, she was sure Georgia would be in that office in a flash, whispering in his ear to refocus and probably sticking pins in her Abigail doll. Abigail didn't have long to wait for Adam to revert to his normal self.

'Having said that, if you need any help with the money side of things, just let me know. I presume it's coming out of Dad's inheritance, so all good there.'

Ah yes, the old 'Abigail needs to be careful' tack. Bitterness had hardened the wedge between them when Adam had warned her against Luca's attempts at accessing her Trust Fund. His caustic opinion of Luca had never been far from the surface. The physical distance between her family in Sydney and her home with Luca in Melbourne had suited Abigail just fine.

# CHAPTER SIX

ONCE THE SETTLEMENTS had been made, Abigail became the proud owner of 64-66 Ferryman Road. She was itching to spend time in the properties, to take hundreds of photos for her mood board and to start filling in her journal with ideas. She didn't want to rush into changing anything, but more to wander, to feel, to leave herself open to a myriad of options. Not for a moment did she take for granted how lucky she was to be able to live in one house whilst renovating another – there would be no mattresses on the floor nor flaky plaster in takeaway meals.

Her friends had regrouped after her emotional exit from Don Carmelo's. Steph had called in to see her shortly after.

'I'm so sorry, Abby, but truthfully we are on your side. You know that, don't you?' Steph had anxiously clutched her friend's hands.

'Yes, of course,' Abigail had replied, still disappointed by their reactions, but firm in her knowledge that Steph would always have her back. 'You were the one who gathered me up after Luca's accident, administered strong cups of tea or a brandy, with a caring ear and a hug thrown in. You commiserated but set me straight when I got all melancholy.'

Steph gave her hands a squeeze.

'It was the strangest thing, actually,' Abigail revealed. 'When I was signing the contract, it was as though I ... well, I don't know, really. It was as though I wasn't alone, as if someone was there watching over me to make sure it all went well. I felt centred and calm.'

'Well, you're hardly the flight-of-fancy type, Abigail, despite Audrey.' Steph laughed.

'Do you think Luca may have been there with me, Steph?' Abigail whispered.

Steph glanced away, frowning, and Abigail realised how silly she was sounding.

'Of course not.' Abigail flicked away her comment. 'I'm just anxious that I've done the right thing.' Which wasn't true – Abigail knew with every beat of her heart that buying Binalong was exactly what she had been meant to do. Any earlier second-guessing on her actions had been firmly dismissed.

Steph nodded, grinning. 'We'll have to call you The Property Tycoon soon. I can't wait to see them. Good on you, Abby.'

Steph gave her friend a big hug before leaving. 'Promise you'll call me when we can go through the properties together.'

Abigail decided that it would be easier to think of the

two buildings as just one purchase; it might help take away some of the unnerving relevance that Luca and her past seemed to be playing in her future. The cottage would be the welcome balance.

---

THEY HAD BOUGHT the existing home soon after their wedding. Its generous size was quite deceptive from the street, but they had still undertaken renovations. Abigail had insisted on adding an upstairs study plus bedrooms and en suites to accommodate visitors. Luca would not let go of his notion of a wine cellar and the kitchen became a state-of-the-art hub that looked onto an expanded open-plan living zone. The long central hallway was perfect for a row of their own photos of Italy, offset against the floor of French oak boards. Abigail devoted weeks to creating a stunning trompe l'oeil of a lush flower garden in soft shades of mint, wheat and rose that formed a backdrop to the stairwell.

The rear outdoor terrace handled Melbourne's erratic weather with a louvered roof that closed automatically. Soon after its installation, they had stood beneath it at the first sign of rain, giggling with anticipation. They had argued over more greenery vs an outdoor kitchen, but Abigail's dream garden with water features had won out. She loved every stone and leaf that had gone into its construction.

Over the last several months, she had replaced the hallway photos with several original paintings from her collection; had allowed the garden to spread its tendrils a little further. They were small, concerted steps to moving on.

Cradling a mug of strong coffee to ward off the cool breeze, Abigail wandered out into the courtyard. Nigella plopped across her feet. Soothed by the tinkling water in her fountain, she settled into a deep garden chair and checked her watch. It was the perfect time to call her boys, who should be getting ready for their day.

Martin and Abigail had met in London. She had been working for an art historian at the time, after university and her father's death. She loved her work and had jumped at the chance to work as a consultant on an arthouse coffee-table book. Within the first half-hour of meeting her contact, Martin, at the publishing house, they had both agreed on how unappealing and dry the book was and had absconded to a nearby pub. Between chapters on William Blake and Lucian Freud, they had fallen in love and had married soon after, settling in London. Her late twenties saw the arrival of Scott and then James; 'the boys' who brought tremendous joy to her life every day despite the oceans between them.

Once again, Abigail thanked whoever had invented WhatsApp as her eldest son's cheeky face popped up on her screen.

'Scott, I know it's early but at least I have a chance of catching you both. How are you?' Abigail had to make a conscious effort not to shout into the phone, but the sight of her boys always excited her. She missed them terribly.

Scott turned and yelled into the background. 'Hey,

Jamie. Come here, Mum's calling.'

Abigail used the moment to slant the phone, trying to get her best angle, but she never seemed able to lose the 'needs more makeup and a chin lift look' with video calls.

Suddenly James photobombed his brother. She smiled, aware they kept the screen shot tight so she couldn't witness their messy apartment.

'Hi, Jamie. Now boys, I just wanted to let you know something exciting. I've bought a property, two terraces, actually. It's near to me here in South Melbourne. I have to renovate a little after I've worked out what to do but they're great. I'll send you photos.'

'Wow. Good on you, Mum,' Scott exclaimed.

'Are you moving out of your house?' James was always the one to pick up on any dips and rises of her emotions and she knew where he was heading with his question.

'Maybe,' she replied. 'I don't feel any urgency to move on from here. But this new space will be a great option when I do. It's two buildings with a common wall, so I can maybe live in one side and use the other for ... I'm not sure what yet. But there will be room for you to stay of course.'

She saw him give a little smile of satisfaction that his mum was okay.

'How's your father?' she asked diplomatically, taking a sip of coffee. She had never discussed Martin's tendency to try to rule the world, or indulge in too much wine. As long as it didn't adversely affect her sons' lives, she would keep her opinions to herself.

'Oh, he's great. Christine too,' Scott answered. 'They're talking about a trip out to Australia soon. Christine is supposed to be reporting on some Slow Food Trail, whatever that is.'

Abigail nodded. Christine's career as a celebrated UK chef had appealed to the boys from the start. 'Celebrity and food together. Sweet!' they had joked.

'Christine is looking for an assistant,' James blurted out. 'She reckons I'd be good at it.'

'Really?' Abigail tried to keep the stab of jealousy out of her tone. 'I mean, of course you'd be wonderful, but does your Hotel Management degree cover what you need?' *You're clutching at straws, Abigail.*

'The business side does. And Scott reckons that his, and of course Dad's, publishing contacts would help Christine's production of a cookbook too.'

Martin, whilst never showing any culinary interest during their marriage, had thrown himself behind Christine's career with gusto. She presumed the celebrity side of things was the attraction for him, and he would relish having control over publishing her cookbooks. And now it seemed her boys' futures were being gathered like moths around her BBQ flame.

'Well, there you go.' Abigail hoped her forced smile from the other side of the globe wasn't obvious. She waited for a heartbeat. 'Does that mean you're rethinking about moving to Australia for a while?'

The boys glanced at each other. 'Not sure yet, Mum,' James replied diplomatically.

Scott and James quickly brought their mother up to date about life in London, then headed off to work. Abigail's coffee mug sat cold and neglected by her side.

The joy of speaking with the boys had passed with their escape to their day, leaving her flat. She felt decidedly on the outside, removed from her boys' lives. She was so proud of them and the decisions they made, but after the phone call she questioned what role she had played. They had lived apart for so long, all because she had succumbed to the Arpels family demands.

Could she blame the Audrey influence? Probably not, but it had been the catalyst for Abigail returning to Australia. Time apart from Martin had been a bonus. Admittedly her mother had been very sick and Abigail had happily flown home to help her, but weeks had turned into months, making the prospect of a quick return to London unlikely. When Abigail learnt that Audrey's condition had actually stabilised and that she was making endless doctor and scan appointments for no good reason, Abigail had insisted on returning to the UK.

Audrey's reaction still sent shivers down Abigail's spine.

'But you're my daughter, Abigail. You are supposed to be here, to care for me! Who knows what might happen next.'

'Mum, the doctor says you are perfectly fine. You just have to keep on your meds. You already have every helper under the sun, and I need to get back to London. Heavens, I'm a mother too and I need to return to the boys.'

'Nonsense. They do perfectly fine without you.'

Daggers couldn't have carved a deeper wound in her heart than those words. 'Adam's here anyway. And Georgia, I guess.'

Audrey had slunk lower into her chaise and whispered, 'Well, I do think you are being incredibly selfish. You know that Adam works very hard for the company which you obviously don't appreciate, Abigail. And Georgia is busy running their household.'

'Running between spa treatments, more likely,' Abigail had muttered, but Audrey was already dabbing her eyes and gazing out the conservatory window at her view of Sydney Harbour.

Once back in London, Abigail was surprised to find that her sons were in fact carrying on with their busy lives. Her absence hadn't caused a ripple, apparently. When one of Melbourne's small museums had beckoned with an advisory contract, they had backed her, announcing they were off travelling through Europe together anyway. When their travelling came to an end, the boys had taken up great jobs and stayed in London, with Abigail and Martin speaking only when they needed to discuss their sons. A future in Australia had been discussed at one stage, but one thing had led to another and time had drifted by. She had remained in Australia, in Melbourne, much to Audrey's dismay. Then Abigail met Luca.

Frequent return visits, as well as taking the boys on mini holidays around Britain, had been her all too brief, but happy, 'Mum fix'. Sometimes Luca had joined them with his own side trips to Italy to visit his mother.

Abigail scratched Nigella's head. 'You never stop being a mother, nor lose all the niggling guilt that comes with it, my girl. Come on, we'll put the kettle back on.'

# CHAPTER SEVEN

'I'LL MEET YOU THERE, ABBY,' Steph said. 'I have to drop off some props to a client in Clarendon Street first.'

'Okay, no hurry.' Abigail grabbed her Ferryman Road keys. The agent had joked about prison keys as he had passed over the clanking bunch – all different sizes and shapes threaded onto a large brass ring. She couldn't wait to see which mysterious key matched which door. Armed with her wish journal she set off up the street, hoping the painting group wasn't ensconced in Binalong that morning. At least the agent had assured her that Patricia, or Sandy more likely, had to collect and return the front door key from their office for every session.

After the unsettling episode in the upstairs room on her previous visit, Abigail intended to go through No. 64 first and work her way back to the other building. There was just something about that bedroom that jangled her nerves. What it was, she couldn't possibly put into words, but wondering about it had kept her awake on more than one night. And the strange thing was, although she had at first been upset by the experience, on reflection she was surprised to feel okay with it, almost peaceful.

64 Ferryman Road sat back from the footpath, behind an iron fence. Abigail had pictured herself unlatching the little front gate, strolling up onto the narrow porch, putting the key in the lock and announcing her arrival to the empty rooms inside. But it wasn't to be.

'Oh no!' She almost dropped the keys as she raced to the gate. Water was pouring through it and, from the steady stream gushing down the gutter towards the drain it looked as if it had been going for some time. Images of broken pipes, water cascading down the internal stairs and mould forevermore bombarded her mind. Abigail flung open the gate and splashed inside the small yard, readying her front door key.

Then two things happened at once: First, Abigail registered that the water wasn't coming from her house but a sprinkler in her neighbour's yard. Its arcing waterfall, complete with shimmering rainbow, seemed to be stuck on her side of the low fence, drowning her front yard. The second was even more irritating. As she flicked her attention over the fence to the house at No. 62, its front door opened. A fellow dressed only in loose track pants casually wandered out like a sleepy Cheshire cat. Open-mouthed, Abigail watched him limber and stretch as he bent effortlessly forward to place his hands flat on his deck.

'Hey! Could you please turn off your sprinkler? It's flooding my garden,' Abigail yelled. She screwed up her face, squinting through the fine spray.

Her neighbour nonchalantly lifted his head, leaving his body curved in a U that Abigail couldn't remember ever having been able to achieve. His eyes flicked calmly from her to the offending sprinkler. Easing out of his stretch, he skipped down his steps and quickly turned off the tap.

'Sorry. It must have got stuck.'

'No kidding!' She diverted her gaze from his tanned chest to the sprinkler head, now drip-dripping onto his dry lawn. 'It's a bit of an outdated way to water your garden, isn't it? Why don't you put in a drip system or something?'

He gave a lopsided grin. Barefoot, he covered the few steps to the fence where he stopped and crossed his arms, piercing Abigail with a gaze from eyes the colour of coffee beans.

She raised her eyebrows, flicking her hand towards the soggy ground. She felt a trickle of water run down her cheek and sit on her chin, ready to plop onto her chest.

'It actually won't do it any harm,' he replied. 'It should soak in pretty well. But I'm not happy about how much must have gone down the drain. What a waste.'

'Exactly.' Abigail gently lifted one foot then the other, trying to keep her canvas shoes out of the wettest patches.

He leant over the fence, his hand outstretched. 'I'm Jack.'

Abigail had been misled by his flexibility. It appeared her neighbour was older than she had first thought, possibly late fifties. Short, slicked-back wavy chestnut-coloured hair framed an open 'share a joke with me' face. A faint scent of lime, soap or shampoo, told her he must have just stepped from the shower.

She placed her palm in his firm grip and nodded. 'I'm Abigail.'

He didn't take his eyes from her, except to glance at the wet earth around her feet.

The ripples of a tense conversation drifted across the fence as a blonde woman walked out to the deck. 'I said no, Rose. I don't care. Just a minute then. Jack, can you speak with Rose?'

Abigail saw the woman hold the cell phone aloft in Jack's direction. She quickly placed it on the deck, turned and let the screen door slam behind her.

'Uh oh. Daughter trouble.' Jack frowned. 'I'll catch you later.'

Abigail sighed and tiptoed back across the lawn. She couldn't help but notice the ground was pretty well drained of water as her cheeky neighbour had predicted, plus the concrete path did appear to be cleaner where the water had washed across it.

Abigail liked the way the cottage's narrow front deck dropped to a garden bed, then to a square of lawn bordered by the path on one side, a low row of near-dead bushes along the neighbouring fence and the rampant vine across the front. Similar gardens in the area boasted bushy rhododendrons and camellias, or neatly trimmed box hedges; others were filled in with English cottage garden plants, lavender, roses, and annuals. Abigail couldn't decide on a favourite, but she knew her new garden would include bulbs. The idea of renewal, of a plant suddenly bursting from the ground and reaching for the light then flowering anew every year, held a lot of appeal. She was surprised that none were pushing up their heads now that it was spring, but really had no idea. She couldn't even keep an African violet alive.

She was just thinking the yard was what Audrey would call pocket handkerchief size, her mother's dressing room being larger than this little plot, when Abigail heard the gate unlatch.

Steph tiptoed up the wet path. 'What's happened here? It looks like you've had your own personal cloudburst just above you.'

Abigail laughed. Only Steph could be that visual. 'Not such a little cloud, and more like a hippie neighbour with a dodgy sprinkler.'

'Hippies? In South Melbourne? They must be trading in marijuana to afford to live here then.' Steph hugged Abigail. 'How are you, darl?'

'Good, apart from wet feet. Thanks for coming, Steph. I know this building has been renovated pretty well, but I'd still like your feedback, and I'll definitely need some ideas for next door. Did you want to go for a coffee first?' Abigail knew she was stalling before taking the next step.

'No. Let's get to it. Gosh, I feel like I should be carrying you over the threshold or something.' Steph grinned as they turned toward the emerald-green door.

Abigail took a deep breath as she slipped off her soggy shoes and stepped through the entry into the hallway. She couldn't help pausing, waiting for the ringing in her ears, to feel faint, to get a chill. Nothing. But then she was yet to experience anything unusual in the cottage.

'This is gorgeous, Abby.' Steph had strolled a few steps

through the first doorway into the front bedroom. She stood in the centre, slowly turning circles as she took in its dimensions, its floorboards, the open fireplace. Tugging on the long window blind, she let it roll up to welcome sunlight and reveal the room's character.

'I love the height of these windows,' Steph said. 'Imagine wispy, slate-grey curtains falling from a black rod. And you could get some shelving custom-built for either side of the fireplace. I'm presuming there's central heating as well. That chandelier is divine and surprisingly it's not at all kitsch.' She eased open the bathroom door. 'Fabulous large en suite. Someone has done a nice job of renovating this building. It just needs another coat of paint and an injection of decorating flair.'

Abigail's head was spinning with ideas now that she had another creative mind to bounce off. She started to plot where her furniture could go and made a note to look up a chimney sweep and consider the built-in cabinetry. She smiled as Steph oohed and aahed and nodded her approval as they moved through to the large living room and back kitchen, laundry and bathroom. They clicked lights on and off and tested taps as they moved from room to room. Everything seemed to be working perfectly.

'There's only an attic upstairs,' Abigail said. 'Hopefully it's been cleaned out since I was last here. It was full of junk.'

'I hope not,' Steph replied, as they climbed the stairs. 'Imagine what treasures you might uncover. Just like in one of those *American Pickers* shows. She paused. 'Oh, it looks like our priceless discovery isn't to be, damn it.'

The large space sat empty. Abigail sighed with disappointment now that her friend had planted the seed of discovering the old and mysterious.

'Bring that bunch of keys over here and let's see what's behind this door,' Steph beckoned. 'It's probably just a shallow cupboard.'

One by one Abigail tried the keys in the lock. 'You know, I don't remember this door when I went through the property. But there were so many boxes piled high in here, I must have missed it. Nope, none of these fit. I'll have to ask the agent if he has any others.'

Steph gave the brass doorknob another shake but couldn't budge it.

They made their way back down the stairs and out the front door. Abigail gave a little skip and smiled to herself as the door clicked behind them – somewhere between the chandelier and walking outside she had come to a decision. The cottage had seemed to settle around her in welcome, protecting her from a past that lurked just a few blocks away. It had nudged her at every step, promising happiness. She would sell her house.

***

'OH, GAWD.' Steph stood in Binalong's large front room, her hands-on-hips stance an indication she didn't have the same enthusiasm she had for next door. 'This isn't how I remembered it at all. But hey, what an amazing space! What are you thinking of doing with it?'

Abigail turned away. The now familiar tingling sensation was strengthening, making her sway slightly. She quickly came up with the perfect excuse not to venture farther. 'Oh, I've left my journal next door. You go ahead and I'll dash back for it.'

Steph was already heading up the stairs as Abigail let herself out the front door and took a deep, calming breath. She couldn't think straight; it was like trying to stir stars through mud. Anyway, her journal was essential and she headed for the cottage. She nudged open the gate with her hip, glancing at the remaining damp patches of the garden. Head down and searching for the right key, Abigail tripped up the front step of No. 64. Palms outstretched, she slammed down onto her right knee.

Swearing like a sailor, she rolled over in time to see her neighbour effortlessly side-jump the fence, land on the one remaining living plant, and rush to her side. Abigail winced, unsure whether it was due to the ache pulsing from her leg or the demise of her stunted Daphne. She looked up into concerned brown eyes which were charmingly crinkled at the side.

'Are you okay?' Jack didn't seem to know where to put his outstretched arms. They tried the air either side of her leg, then moved to her shoulders, then dropped. Spying the ring of keys, which had been flung to the end of the deck, he retrieved them in two easy strides and stood above her.

'Is it your knee?'

She nodded, trying not to clench her teeth, then was stunned to see him turn and disappear over the fence. Abigail rubbed her palms together, forgetting they had taken the brunt of her fall. Splinters and dirt embedded themselves further into the bloody scrapes. Tears pricked her eyes as she reached into her pocket for her phone.

As she was texting Steph, her neighbour reappeared, through the gate this time, clutching a bag of ice and what looked like a bag of lollies. He knelt next to Abigail, obviously noting her red eyes but sensibly not mentioning it. 'I thought you might like a Turkish Delight,' he mumbled.

*Turkish Delight?* Abigail smiled weakly at his efforts. 'As opposed to a bullet to bite on?' Abigail's attempt to cover her embarrassment fell flat as Jack focused on her injury.

'Can you roll your jeans up? Do you think they'll fit over your knee? I mean, I'm sure they will but ...'

As Abigail rolled her pant leg above her injured knee, she noted the pleasant lime fragrance remained around him, that the track pants had been changed to loose jeans and a Rolling Stones Tour T-shirt hid his torso.

'Jack. From next door, remember?' he prompted as he gently folded the bag around her knee. He took it away, emptied some of the ice, flattened the bag and rewrapped it.

Abigail nodded, watching the discarded cubes melt across the deck. 'I don't think this side of the fence needs any more water,' she said. She could have kicked herself – if her sore leg had permitted – when his response was just to raise his eyebrows.

'Sorry, we didn't have a proper ice pack.'

'It's okay. My friend is next door. She can take me home,' Abigail said, just as Steph came through the gate.

She stopped short at seeing Abigail propped on the

step, Jack leaning over her with one hand on her exposed leg.

'Steph, thank heavens. I fell and landed rather heavily on my knee.'

Steph raced to her side, smiling at Abigail's neighbour. 'Hi, I'm Abby's friend, Stephanie.'

'Hi. Jack. The iceman. From next door.'

As they started to laugh Abigail attempted to stand, unable to see any joke in the situation. The pack of Turkish Delights dropped from her lap.

'Steph, can you take me home, please? Now.'

'Oh, of course. Come on. Jack, you take one side and I'll take this side.' Together they hoisted Abigail between them, the bag of ice sliding from her knee to dangle around her ankle. Abigail shook herself free from her neighbour's firm hold, although she had to admit having his strong body pressed next to hers had been an unexpected comfort.

'I think I'll be fine from here,' she said, embarrassment taking over from gratitude. Abigail held onto Steph as they staggered down the path and, side-on, through the swinging gate.

Steph settled Abigail into the car, then waved to Jack as she skirted to the driver's side. She pushed the button to slide Abigail's window down and giggled. 'Now say thank you to the nice hippie, Abigail.'

Abigail mouthed to her neighbour as he clicked her gate shut then gave him a little goodbye flutter of her fingers.

'Ugh, well that was awkward.' She sighed as the car drove away. 'I don't know what's going on with me lately. I don't seem to be able to walk a straight line without falling over, with or without wet shoes. I do appreciate you coming today, Steph. And don't give me that 'well, well, well' look – my neighbour is married. Or something. Anyway, there is a very pretty blonde in there with him, plus a daughter somewhere, so I'm not interested, okay?'

'Gotcha.' Steph nodded. 'But my friend, in reference to said neighbour, I was looking out for me, not you. Now, to the doctor or home and couch with more ice?'

'Home and ice. With a long gin and tonic on the side,' Abigail replied.

# CHAPTER EIGHT

THE *CLICKITY-CLACK-WHOOSH* of the Melbourne tram gently lulled Abigail as it headed into the city. She settled against the window and idly watched the sites go by: the cosmopolitan villages brimming with cafés, groups of young pram-jogging mums, the old cottages in various states of repair and the new apartments that had replaced those that hadn't survived.

Her injured knee only gave a slight twinge as she gingerly stepped down from the tram at Federation Square. Her neighbour's bag of ice had seemed to have helped, as the swelling had decreased with each day, but it was still an awkward amble across the expansive bluestone courtyard. A little stab of remorse jabbed like a needle as she recalled how abrupt she had been with Jack. She considered taking a bottle of wine as a thank you, but then there was the cursed broken sprinkler and the blonde woman. It would be best to keep her distance. The decision was made in under ten seconds.

She was looking forward to catching up with Kate. They had first met in London; two excited Australian girls with shiny new Art History degrees. Together they had bluffed their way through exclusive openings and exhibitions, industry lectures and auctions. Abigail had landed the job with an art historian and Kate had relished a stint with the Tate network. Together they had holidayed around the breathtaking museums and throbbing bars of France until Abigail had met Martin, but their friendship had remained firm.

Kate had dated Adam for a few months after returning from London, but the relationship hadn't lasted after she followed her friend to Melbourne. Abigail hadn't been surprised, recognising Kate as too caring, too genuine for Adam. Georgia, on the other hand! Most people had seen Adam as a single, wealthy socialite who could effortlessly put together fabulous parties, but Abigail also knew the other side of her brother. He was a man driven to build a successful business, with a partner's needs coming a long way behind the office.

Kate and her long-time boyfriend Freddie both knew all the ins and outs of Abigail and Luca, the marriage, their dreams for Luca's restaurant. Now, Abigail was tempted to wander through the Ian Potter Centre where Kate worked and check out their latest exhibitions, but she knew her knee wasn't up to it. She still had to manage to walk up the Collins Street hill for her appointment with the architect, although another tram ride looked to be a better option. A shaded table beckoned, which was perfect on such a balmy, warm day. She relaxed back into a seat under the market umbrella and watched dozens of schoolchildren as they chatted and filled out their city visit surveys.

'Sorry I'm late.' Kate put a flustered kiss on Abigail's cheeks then flopped into the opposite seat.

'No problem. I knew it was a possibility,' Abigail replied. 'So, how is the incredibly demanding Mrs Drysdale?' It had always been a quiet joke between the friends that Kate's boss at the gallery shared the surname of Russell Drysdale, a respected Australian painter, and they had allocated many of his paintings' titles to her quirks.

'Stressing about the next exhibition like "A Road with Rocks".' Kate laughed. 'But that's what I'm there for, I guess; to take the flack and check all the details. I ordered our coffees on the way out, with mini muffins. So, how are things in AA's world?'

Kate's rambling conversations always warmed Abigail's heart and she loved the way her friend called her Abigail Arpels like old times. Kate was always so positive and had carried Abigail up on her bubble of happiness on many occasions.

Their coffees and coconut muffins arrived. 'I wonder how many muffins we have consumed over the decades. It must be hundreds, and a gazillion calories,' Kate said. 'How come I ended up as a barrel on legs and you're still slim?'

Abigail laughed as she clutched her waistline. 'Hardly! You don't know how much lurks under this shirt.'

She took a sip of coffee and looked to her friend. 'Guess what. I bought Binalong.'

Kate's mouth dropped open. 'That's fabulous, Abby. Is it just as you remembered it?' Only a bite of her muffin stalled her eager inquisition.

Abigail replied quickly. 'Yes, it is amazing, and it is a little different from how I remembered. In fact, it seems different every time I go there, but all good.' She didn't mention her hesitation about the upstairs bedroom, mainly because she had no idea how to explain it.

'And I've only just decided to sell my house and move into No. 64 which is next door and also mine, but I'm not sure when exactly.'

'You bought next door as well? I hope it's already renovated.'

'Yes, I want to make a few changes in the kitchen, and the gardens need work. Binalong is a different matter. I need to think about whether I renovate and rent it out as a commercial space, or renovate and do something myself.'

'Like what? Do you mean a business?'

Abigail waited for a question about the Binalong-Luca link, but none came. Nor had Kate blinked an eye about her friend purchasing two properties next to each other, which Abigail was grateful for. She never had to explain anything to Kate, whether it was how she had struggled dealing with Luca's death, her tenuous relationship with Audrey, or why she had bought two properties on a Saturday whim. Old friends just get it – they know when to offer help, give help whether it's asked for or not, or allow space.

'I'm not sure. Probably not. I don't know enough about anything, really, except art history, and that's not going to work. We'll see.'

'Nonsense. You can do anything you set your mind to. Heavens, you oversee all those important trusts, remember? Well, if I can help, I'm there. Payment is a dinner at Don Carmelo's.'

Abigail placed her hand on top of Kate's and gave it a squeeze.

'We'll have to go cap in hand, I'm afraid.' Abigail winced. 'The delightful Paul baited me the other night and like a fool I rose to it. What is it about that man?'

'Forget about it. Who cares what he says. I wonder what Luca would think about you finally buying Binalong without him. I reckon he'd be a little peeved. Unlike Liam.' Kate sent Abigail a quick wink.

Abigail frowned. 'What do you mean, "unlike Liam"?'

'Oh, come on, Abigail. You must know how much he adored you and he had the utmost confidence in you.' Kate wiggled her finger. 'Don't wave me away like that. It's true. I can tell you that for certain, even though it's way past its use by date. Rest their souls.'

'Did he say something to you?'

Kate nodded. 'Not that he needed to say anything. But, it was at your wedding. You and Luca were dancing under all those divine little lights. It was incredibly romantic I might add but Liam was looking all forlorn. Anyway, I asked him if he was jealous.'

'Kate!'

Kate shrugged. 'It must have been the champagne speaking. Liam said, "Of course, I want my friend back." I presumed he meant Luca but then he said, "I want my friend, Abby, back." He was very misty-eyed, but then I saw that he couldn't take his eyes off you. Surely you knew that, Abby.'

'No, not really. He was always there for me, but as a friend.' Abigail's heart softened as all the good times they had shared tumbled back into her memory.

They sat in silence for a moment, watching the crowds around them. Tourists leaned backwards taking photographs of the centre's impressive tiled façade, visitors watched a Victorian Tourism documentary on the big screen, grey-suited businessmen hurried by with cell phones pressed to their ears, and the students assembled for their next task.

'Do you know what I thought of the other day?' Abigail ventured. 'That time we stayed in the monastery in Brittany and ...'

'Heavens yes, excuse the pun,' Kate interrupted. 'Our souls never got cleansed but we nearly froze to death. And it had that odd smell ...'

'Peppermint, wasn't it?' Abigail asked.

'Peppermint? No, it wasn't peppermint. Just a sort of musty concoction, like dead bedbugs. Definitely not peppermint. But we thought it was haunted because we had read that haunted places are cold.' She stopped short, slapping her hand on the table. 'Good lord, your place isn't haunted, is it?'

'No, of course not,' Abigail insisted. 'I just thought I recognised something about ...'

Kate's phone erupted, and with raised eyebrows at Abigail, she answered. 'Kate speaking.' She listened for a moment. 'Yes, okay, I'll come and access it for you.' Rising to her feet, she turned to Abigail. '"The Drover's Wife" needs me.'

# CHAPTER NINE

THE GRAFFITI that was spray painted along Binalong's side wall distracted Abigail from her purpose. She actually didn't mind the geometric images created by Plop and wondered if that was the same artist responsible for the misspelt message along the foreshore. The short alley formed a dead-end at a newly created little park, with a single bench sitting in the middle. Although the park wasn't nearly as lush as the private garden in *Notting Hill*, and there certainly hadn't been any graffiti, the setting reminded Abigail of the movie and the bench that bore the inscription: *For June who loved this garden. From Jacob who sat beside her every day.* It had made her cry when Julia Roberts had read the words aloud.

She slumped onto the seat. Nigella nudged her hand, either in sympathy or as a request for a run.

'Not today. Not here, old girl. I couldn't catch you if you take off.' She leaned over to rub the dog's ears. Nigella stiffened, a low growl rumbling in her throat.

'Do you think she understands you?' asked a now familiar voice.

Abigail glanced across to the old lady who had spoken to her the day of the auction. She couldn't imagine where on earth she had materialised from.

Trying to brush away her surprise, Abigail gave a false little laugh, which obviously didn't fool the woman if her piercing gaze was any indication. 'Of course. Nigella is very clever.'

'Oh, I'm sure. Never think your voice isn't being heard by someone, my dear. If you have something to say, or questions to ask, you must do just that. Have a nice day,' the woman replied in her raspy tone. She swivelled in different directions like a creaking old weathervane, seemingly unsure which way to go. Finally, she turned and shuffled away around the corner.

The woman's sudden appearance had broken the quiet moment Abigail had indulged in, sitting alone on June and Jacob's bench. Her appearance, not to mention her brief comments, still seemed odd. Had she been trying to make a point about something? Abigail tugged on the lead. 'Come on, Nigella, let's go cause havoc in the art class.'

BINALONG'S DOOR appeared to be locked. Abigail frowned. She was sure that the art group was due that morning so she hadn't brought her keys. Muffled laughter came from inside. She knocked again. Nothing. Abigail banged harder.

It was a few moments later when the key turned and the door inched open. Sandy jumped back as Abigail pushed the door and took a tentative step into the entrance, trying to drag Nigella behind her.

Sandy's mouth formed a little O as they moved past her, Nigella giving a woof of greeting. 'I don't know that a dog ...' she began, before Patricia's voice boomed from the front room.

'Who let a dog in here? Sandy, what's going on?'

'It's, um, it's ...' Sandy shuffled off toward the artists, Abigail's name apparently evading her.

'Why is the door locked?' Abigail asked, but the *why* became very obvious as she walked farther into the room.

In the middle of the circle of easels was Patricia, reclined on a gold chaise lounge. At least an entire bolt of lolly-pink satin swathed her voluptuous body. She gasped, dragging her toga-style covering farther up her cleavage. Pink chubby feet now poked out the end, revealing a dolphin tattoo on each ankle. Anger, recognition, then embarrassment flicked across her face like flip cards.

Abigail gasped. 'You're doing a life-drawing session.' She glanced left and right at the attempts to capture Patricia à la Rubens. 'These aren't bad,' she mumbled for something to say, then registering the silence and the charcoals raised mid-sketch, she turned back to Patricia. Sandy draped a woollen shawl around Patricia's alabaster shoulders and went to stand at her easel.

'I do apologise for interrupting your class. I just wanted to have a chat, but I'll leave you to it.' Abigail tugged at

Nigella to draw her away from the pile of grapes that were spilling over and around the silent Patricia.

As they paused at the base of the stairs, Nigella vibrated with a low growl. She peered upwards. But Abigail needed to keep going. Her stomach ached from the laugh she was desperately trying to hold in. She gently clicked the front door closed, then, without thinking, skipped the short distance to No. 64. Without keys, she sat on the front step, Nigella propped between her legs for a pat.

'Oh, wasn't that funny. I'm so lucky I didn't barge in on a totally naked Patricia. What a shame Kate wasn't there. She would have been in hysterics.'

'I presume you're talking to the dog.'

Nigella leapt to her feet, pulling the lead from Abigail's hand.

'Here, girl,' Jack called, tapping the fence. Nigella jumped her two front paws onto the fence and leant in, relishing the attention and ear rub from their neighbour.

'That's the second time today I've been asked that and the third time we've met in my front yard,' said Abigail, unsure why she had made such in inane comment. She shrugged. Her neighbour didn't seem to be listening anyway. 'Her name's Nigella.'

Jack nodded, glancing across at Abigail. 'Abigail, right? Are you feeling okay?'

Perhaps he had heard her.

'How's the knee?' he clarified.

'Oh, it's fine now. Thank you again for the ice.' Abigail stood and dusted off her backside, then took the few steps to the fence to untangle the lead from Nigella's back legs. She sensed that Jack was treading carefully, having experienced her prickly side. She watched his strong hands massaging Nigella's head. They were workman's hands, hardened and brown. Her eyes strayed up to his face, to pursed lips aimed at Nigella and challenging eyes aimed at her. She quickly looked away and reached for her totally squashed Daphne bush. She pulled it out and tossed it aside.

'You'll be pleased to know the sprinkler is fixed, so no more floods,' he offered. 'Are you the new owner?'

When she hesitated, he hurried on. 'I'm not prying. It's just that I'm new in the area too and don't quite know the history of our neighbours.'

So it is 'our', not 'my', Abigail thought, unexpectedly disappointed.

'Yes, I bought it at auction a few weeks back. I've just been next door to speak with the artist group that works there but, well, they were busy. Next thing I knew I found my way in here, with my dog but without keys.'

'It's a lovely old building. Did you buy the corner building too? Is that in good condition?'

'It's not bad, but I will do a few things to it. Nothing major. I'm too impatient to put up with endless council objections. Nigella, stop!' The dog had started to lick her neighbour's hand, urging him for more attention.

'Well, if you need any equipment, check with me first. I'm a landscape architect and dabble a bit with hands-on gardening as well.' He faced his palm to Abigail and gave a deep chuckle. 'Oh wait, why are you giving me that "you're kidding" look? Just because I over-watered your garden?'

Abigail laughed. 'Well, I have to admit that anything to do with gardening wasn't top of my list for your vocation.' Abigail glanced behind her neighbour. He said he'd just arrived, didn't he? Maybe that accounted for his own garden's unkempt condition.

Without taking his eyes from her, his handsome face eased into a smile. 'So you don't think this garden should go on my resume?'

'Oh, Jack, I wasn't ...'

'Yes. You were,' he interrupted, eyes twinkling. 'But that's okay. I agree wholeheartedly. It's about to be a work in progress, so we'll be on the tools together. Remember, if you need garden advice, I'm your man.' He gave Nigella a last pat, turned and strolled back into his house.

Abigail watched his retreating back, trying to summarise him in her mind. He seemed to be easy-going, plus what's not to like about someone who welcomed animals? Gardening would explain his slightly weathered appearance, and there was more than a flash of intelligent humour behind those attractive eyes. All in all, probably a handy person to have living next door, particularly if he was offering to help.

Abigail headed home as late afternoon lights began to pop on in homes, bathing porticos and paths in a warm glow. She glanced into windows as she passed, seeing children at desks and parents tidying up after the day. Music popped into the air as front doors were opened then shut for the evening. Her mind looped back to the old lady, and she wondered if she lived behind one of these doors and what her story was.

Abigail was suddenly overwhelmed by a yearning to be strolling with someone, to feel a warm hand clasped in her own. She had become accustomed to focusing on the projects ahead of her and making her own decisions, to building a façade to the world. She had tried so hard to make the most of each day with gratitude for her life. But the shadow of loneliness had a way of sneaking back into her soul, unwanted but there just the same.

As Abigail turned into her own dark house, she decided another face-to-face conversation with the artists' co-op wasn't on her agenda and that she would send an email to them that night, advising their use of Binalong had to come to an end. It was time.

---

I NEED *to move things along. And then what? I'm not totally sure, but it is annoying me no end to see Abby at a distance and not be able to communicate directly with her.*

*The artists distracted her this afternoon when I am sure she was here to work out what exactly happened when she fainted in this room. My purpose here is to help her – my heart's desire is the same.*

*From the first moment I met her donkey's years ago, I was captivated; she reminded me of my wonderful mother which sounds completely weird, but not in a matronly or Freudian way. It was her warmth, her inclusion of others, her ability to trust that drew me to her, although that last* quality probably was her undoing. And now I wander these halls, the walls binding me to a mission I don't fully understand. Nor do I have much confidence in its conclusion. But if there is anyone who will stop and listen to me, no matter how unusual the circumstances, it is the lovely Abby. She could always make the improbable believable, which may help my difficult quest.

There is some kerfuffle downstairs with a lot of laughter from the artists, but I have no interest. Amateur art has never even raised my eyebrow, although I was won over by Abby's vast murals; there was something naive and enveloping about them. But she wasn't out to win over the world, and as a collector I preferred the eminent in everything. A Kandinsky would light my passion any day.

She must have forgotten her keys and wasn't happy about being locked out, judging by the surge of impatience I felt rush up the stairs. Then a shift. I sensed her soften; was that a giggle? I was sure she would climb the stairs at any moment, and I was preparing a welcome into my space. But before too long she left, in a much better mood than when she arrived. It was the opposite for me – her arrival brought joy, then stubborn disappointment as I heard her tug at her dog to leave. Nigella knew.

## CHAPTER TEN

LARGE ARCHITECTURAL PLANS of No. 64 and 66 Ferryman Road were spread across Abigail's dining table. All morning she had pored over every angle of each building and had decided that her priority was to focus on selling her house and moving into the renovated cottage. She had heard the excitement in her own voice as she recounted her ideas to Kate during a phone call.

'Well, Abby, I must say my heart is happy to hear your voice so full of enthusiasm and passion for something. I know I've missed it, so you must have too,' Kate had said. 'Go for it.'

As the front door buzzer sounded, Abigail quickly placed a book on each corner of the plans and hurried down the hallway. Steph was standing on her doorstep, two coffees on a takeaway tray in one hand and a paper bag in the other.

'Two pastries from that new little bakery around the corner, Maison de something,' she announced as she wandered through to the kitchen. 'Great, you got the plans.'

The morning sun shot a beam of light through the high windows, casting an almost ethereal pointer onto the paper like a scene out of *The Da Vinci Code*. Abigail leaned in to see its destination. The upstairs bedroom in Binalong. She shivered. If the beam had suddenly burnt a hole where it landed, she wouldn't have been in the least surprised. It had to be just a coincidence. She quickly sat down, her mind racing.

'So, I've been thinking ...' Steph began, unaware of her friend's reaction.

'Oh, wait a sec. That reminds me about the chimneys,' Abigail exclaimed, jumping to her feet again. 'There are three stacks through the roof, but I know of only two fire-places. Well, four with two apiece when you look at both the upstairs and the downstairs. The cottage has one in the front bedroom with the chimney extending through the attic, and Binalong has one in the bottom gallery that extends through the upstairs bedroom. But where does that third stack come down?' She flicked the plan for No. 64 onto the top of the pile, cutting the ray of light, and ran her finger over the layout. Steph popped the coffees out of the tray, handing one to Abigail.

'There it is. Oh, okay, it's in that space I don't have a key for which tells us it isn't a cupboard. I asked the agent and he reckons if he ever had a key, it would be on the ring, which isn't very helpful. I'll have to break in – how dramatic!'

Steph gave her a thumbs up before proceeding with her

own idea. 'I've been thinking about the entire building and, after the kitchen and bathroom updates, why not just paint it throughout in a fairly neutral tone to keep it light. You don't have to stay true to Victorian influences so something like cream or buttermilk would be amazing. You've already got the all-clear that the building is sound, so there's no major structural work to be done and all the plumbing and electrics are fine. The outside needs a good sandblast to take off the dirt and mould. You can get the upstairs chandelier cleaned and all the chimneys swept so you don't burn up any possums.'

'Ew. But you're right. I've been thinking the same thing because I just can't get my head around what to do with it, you know? That would give me a great base to work from.' Abigail's voice faltered. 'I've waited so long for Binalong, and now I have it, I'm lost. Maybe I just wanted it because Luca did. Could I be that stupid?'

Steph put a comforting hand on her friend's arm. 'Oh, Abby. No. I understand why you'd have those creeping doubts, but it's not like you went after it the week or months after Luca died. You waited for it to come on the market. That it was what you wanted. You said yourself you loved the property, its age and general je ne sais quoi, and on the auction day it felt right. Sometimes things are just meant to happen in their own time.'

Steph tore open the pastry bag and licked the glaze from her thumb. 'The use will come to you. But if you start neutral then you can add even more atmosphere and character later. If you open a store, you can paint one of your amazing murals throughout to tie in with whatever that is, and use the upstairs for storage. If you rent it out, the tenant may need something specific. It's all very exciting.'

Abigail's shoulders relaxed. Steph's clear-cut comments sat well in her usually ordered thinking process. Abigail couldn't say why she was so contrary lately: one minute she was confident in her new direction, the next she was querying every move. It was as if she was a cork riding the peaks and troughs of wave after wave, waiting for something or someone to pluck her to shore.

'I got a reply from Guy and Steve, did I tell you? They are over the moon about the property and haven't stopped filling my inbox with images from cobblestone villages all around France. They really are divine, but I still want clean Australian lines too. I've started an additional journal and have printed out images of my favourites ...'

'Of course you have! No really, that's good.' Steph smiled. 'Isn't that what Pinterest is for though?'

'I am going back to the old ways. A touchy-feely visual diary with ideas, sketches and images. It's a work in progress for both buildings; there are so many amazing options out there. Too many really, but you must see that all the time in your line of work.'

Steph nodded.

Abigail sipped her coffee as they both gazed at the plans. She had the funds to contract as many workers as she needed to keep a tight timeline, whilst keeping a firm hand on overseeing the works. She just had to start. She shook off the feeling of being alone, the wish for a partner to share her dreams. At least she had a good friend at her table and a landscape architect on call.

THE AFTERNOON GREW grey with a light sprinkling of rain. Abigail left Nigella at home, rolled up the plans and drove to Ferryman Road. Parking was at a premium in the area, with many of the locals relying on their Resident's Permit, but Abigail managed to find a parking space a few houses along from the properties. She couldn't help but glance towards Jack's house, but all was quiet.

She had intentions of jemmying open the mysterious door-with-no-key in the cottage, but first she wanted and needed to confront something else.

As Abigail walked closer to Binalong, she could see an A4 sheet of paper was glued to Binalong's window. It informed readers that:

*"Unfortunately, the Binalong Artists Co-operative has experienced an END OF LEASE EVICTION. Future space for this important creative group is being sought. If anyone can help, or would like to sign an objection, please contact Patricia urgently."*

End of lease eviction? A small smile escaped Abigail's lips. The artists' co-op, or more particularly Patricia, had replied promptly to her friendly but firm email with an abrupt paragraph. They apparently felt very disappointed to have to move on, particularly as they had taken great pains to adopt Binalong's name. A silly notion from the beginning considering their short lease, Abigail felt. They also asserted that a certain degree of 'respect and assistance' for the local art scene would have been appreciated – Abigail had prickled at the inference but chose to ignore it.

She was sure that once the renovations began, Patricia would have been very vocal in objecting to the disturbance.

The possibility of mentoring emerging artists had been playing around in that part of Abigail's brain which wanted to help her community, but she had no firm plans. She had funded many not-for-profit projects over the years but had always been careful about the *what* and *who*, dedicated to directing the money to the worthiest recipients. Many years back, pre-Luca, Adam had insisted they both attend a Philanthropic Brains Trust conference in New York. It had been wonderful networking with fellow participants who were in a position to contribute in varying degrees to a wide variety of projects. The siblings had been way down the list of wealth indicators, but Abigail had learnt so much about how to use her still sizeable inheritance for the benefit of others.

Abigail couldn't explain why, but she had never mentioned the experience to Luca; it had only come to light when Audrey had made a reference to the conference and praised Adam's involvement, flicking away Abigail's attendance as a mere notetaker. Luca had waved his arms around, inferring she had not tried hard enough to find backers for Grappa. An all-out row had followed as Abigail tried to explain the different but necessary aims of philanthropy, but Luca just couldn't see it.

Her finger twitched over a flapping corner of the notice, tempted to rip it down, but she dropped her hand and entered. She brushed away the dusting of raindrops that had nestled in her hair and on her shoulders. With a sigh of relief she saw that, apart from a couple of wayward charcoal stubs, the artists had left the room and kitchen vacant and clean. She moved on.

The building waited patiently, silent except for the tap-tapping of her screwdriver against the stair railing. She stood gazing upward.

Slowly Abigail climbed the stairs, trying to keep her breathing level and slow. Her heart beat against her chest, screaming to get out, as she concentrated on each step. She paused on the landing, waiting for a breeze to wisp around her. Nothing came.

As she turned towards the front bedroom, she felt the air shift and chill. She crept on, her eyes scanning the way ahead. A 5c piece sat squarely in her stride. Surprised, she picked it up, rubbed it between two fingers then tossed it lightly against the wall. Perhaps the artists had taken a look around and dropped it. A floorboard creaked as she approached the door-way. Unconsciously she gripped the roll of plans in both hands like a baseball bat, holding it in front of her with the screwdriver as if waiting for the first pitch of a baseball game. Her nervous humming broke the silence, although she was unsure why the line 'Hello darkness, my old friend' from Simon and Garfunkel's 'The Sound of Silence' song was the answer.

She tiptoed into the room, aware of a subtle vibration buffeting her. She couldn't see it, but she could feel it with all her being. Abigail switched on the light, a warm companion on a dull day. It flickered then stayed, as sheets of rain suddenly spiked the window. In the back of her mind rose concerns of leaking window frames, of seeping water, flooded gardens, of Jack. She dragged her thoughts back to being present in the room with the faint scent of peppermint which, curiously, she had expected. Abigail placed the items on the floor against the wall and clutched her hands. Her wedding band, worn on a gold chain, felt red hot against her chest.

Abigail strained to empty her mind, to steady and open herself, as she had read about during the grieving process. She had taken on mountains of advice from books and friends after Luca died, like a scientist consumed by an experiment. Like them, her efforts met with varying success. Now, she remembered she hadn't turned her phone off. The random thought was nagging and intrusive, but she pushed it back down. The pressure in the room started to build and cool. Closing her eyes, she breathed deeply, trying to conjure images of what might be transpiring in the room She sensed the light flickering and dying, the rain on hold as if time was standing still. Abigail summoned all her courage and planted her feet wider apart, trying desperately for a more solid connection to her world.

---

SHE'S *at the base of the stairs and I can feel her nervousness; her swaying gives her away every time. You would think that after all that has passed, I would have my patter word-perfect, that I would be upfront in all I have to explain. But I'm standing here with a thumping heart, still unsure. A 'deal with the devil' has been made as they say, or more accurately a 'deal with a conscience', to return and be with her fleetingly.*

*I turn my thoughts to memories to fill in the time it takes her to stroll the corridor. It feels like hours.*

*We met right here, in this building that she has now bought in a romantic effort to, what? Revisit old times, own the past once again, try to move on?*

*We had such fun together. Who knew it wouldn't continue forever and ever. Amen. I knew her sons too, initially meeting them when we were in London; before I travelled farther north, we got together for dinner in a swanky Mayfair restaurant. She was so proud of them, showing them off like a mother hen, and they were in fact deadly boys. Ha, she didn't like that word but I told her it meant 'brilliant.' They were sons I would have liked to have had. Unfortunately, I ruined the night by drinking too much, talking too loudly and trying to chat up the blonde front-of-house.*

*I'm anxious about raising Francesca's name, unsure of how much Abby knows. And afterward, will she still want to stay here or get rid of this building that could now be more of a blister than a salve? Does it matter? But my deal has been done and I must see it through.*

*But none of us are perfect, are we? As the Irish proverb says: A man may live after losing his life, but not after losing his honour. I am here to explain, because she blames me for the car accident that night. You can't change the past, but sometimes, given the chance, you can help decipher it. I only hope she lets me in.*

*Only a few minutes have passed but so many memories*

have fought for their own time in my head. Do they know they'll soon be gone forever?

She walks into my world.

I smile, watching her trying to focus. It appears she's been reading too many self-help books on how to just be.

# CHAPTER ELEVEN

ABIGAIL TOOK a deep breath and opened her eyes. Her lids flickered in surprise and disappointment at the empty room. She had steeled herself for a different outcome, had convinced her soul that something in this room was a link to Luca, to what had actually happened that ghastly night.

Despite their problems and her suspicions of him having an affair, she had still expected him to always be with her. Blame the historian in her and a mending heart, but she still sought answers; to tick all the boxes of discovery. However, her grieving had lost the razor-sharp shards that once stabbed her when she least expected it.

'You idiot, Abigail.' Her shaking voice echoed around the room as she picked up the rolled plans and moved to the window. As she gazed out, tears welled like balloons, squeezing out and plopping onto her chest. It didn't register that the window was the same painted one she had noticed on an earlier visit. It was now clean, allowing a literal window to the outside world.

'You made a mountain out of a draught, a faulty chandelier and the smell of bloody mint cleaner.' She squeezed her eyes shut.

'Oh, I don't know. It sometimes took a bloody effort to get your attention, Abby,' came a soft voice behind her.

Abigail spun around, paper scattering across the floor. 'What? What is going on? Luca?'

Hiccups of fear coursed through her body, but she still couldn't see anyone. She fought a wave of nausea, not wanting to pass out again. She forced herself to take deep breaths. In. Out. Abigail fumbled for a tissue she knew wasn't there, reached for her cell, but let it go. The tightness in the room had changed; it was thick and comforting like cotton wool. The light flickered again but stayed on, and peppermint wisped gently around her nose.

One more time, she forced herself to close her eyes, then slowly open them.

And there he was.

Abigail thrust her hands out in front of her in protest and stumbled back onto the wall. 'Liam! Oh my God. Liam. What ...'

Liam Cleary stepped toward her, halted by the look of horror on Abigail's face, her terrified eyes wide and unbelieving.

'Jesus, Mary and Joseph, what did I expect? You're disappointed it's me, aren't you?'

It only took seconds but in that short time Abigail witnessed looks of anticipation, joy, then disappointment flash across his face. Amongst all the other thoughts swirling like a tornado through her mind, she realised Kate had been right. Liam had loved her.

Her eyes flicked to the door in search of an escape. She opened her mouth but no words formed. He looked exactly as he had in life. Abigail tried again: 'Liam. I am struggling here. You're dead. You died with Luca. I know you did. What am I feeling, what am I seeing? And why am I not beyond freaking out, for heaven's sake?'

Liam nodded. 'I'm glad you feel safe.'

'I wouldn't go that far. What is happening?'

'I don't know ...'

'You don't know?' Abigail whispered shakily, as a myriad of prickling sensations and questions bombarded her at once.

'I mean, it was my choice to come back.'

'Why? How? From ... from where?' Abigail looked around the room and out of the window as if the answer would present itself any moment. It would be a giant floating map with arrows, perhaps, or a perfect scene of a meadow with flowers and a stream like those on sympathy cards. She heard her heartbeat bouncing off every wall and back at her.

Liam paused. The surrounding tension was as taut as a cello string. 'I'm here to see you. The *how* I'm not so sure about.'

'Why to see me? Where's Luca?' Abigail started to pant. 'Are you reincarnated? I mean, I can see you. Whole. Like a real person in real clothes. With a human voice.'

'I have a spiritual presence, not a fleshed physical body.

You can see me when I choose. I only wish I was a real person in real clothes, as you put it.'

'Oh,' Abigail gasped, clutching her chest. 'Are you here to take me?'

'What? No, Abby, no. I ...'

'Then you're a ..., a ... manifestation.' She threw the words at him like defensive blocks of wood. Her eyes narrowed. 'Just a manifestation of someone I used to know. Something otherworldly and fake.'

Liam winced.

'Why am I even talking to you?' Abigail felt a thickness in her throat; she hoped she wasn't about to be sick.

'Then how do I know things?' Liam said. 'How is it I know exactly what happened to cause the accident or ...'

'Stop. Just stop!' Abigail put her hands over her ears, shaking.

'Abby ...' Liam reached out, but Abigail shrank away from him as far as she could. He was entirely too close for her comfort.

Anger built and surged through her without warning. Gone was any interest in trying to understand what she was experiencing. Here was another thing to taunt her, another black hole she had to balance precariously on the edge of. She feared that grief had raised its ugly head again and was sending her mad.

Liam watched as she covered her face with her hands and puffed short, sharp breaths through her fingers, then one long exhausted one.

'Okay. This is from my past,' she told herself firmly,

remembering the process from a relaxation class. Slowly she skirted around Liam toward the door.

She turned her back to the room, to Liam, then continued with her affirmation: 'My mind is putting you in a box. A white box with a white ribbon. I am tying the bow. Yes, I'm tying the bow and moving the box out of sight. It's on a cloud, being taken away on a stiff breeze, never to be seen or felt by me again.'

Her trembling hand flicked into the air beside her as though sending the cloud on its way.

Silence.

With long strides Abigail made it down the corridor to the top of the stairs without looking back. The coin glinted against the wall where she had tossed it, unnoticed. She descended the stairs two at a time then slammed the front door behind her, the sudden stab of daylight surprising her. She tried to blink away its bright reality. Her knee shook in protest and she nearly slid on the wet footpath. Her pace slowed to a fast walk, although her heart still raced like an overwound toy.

As she shakily opened the car door, Abigail remembered the plans still lying abandoned on the floor upstairs. They would have to stay there for the moment. Her denial turned to panic at the thought of going through that ridiculous charade each time she entered Binalong.

'HELLO?'

Abigail jumped, suddenly aware of someone tapping

gently on the car window. How long had she been sitting in the car, its engine idling? Her hand was shaking as she slowly pressed the window down.

'Are you okay? I saw you running and you look a bit distressed. You're Abigail, aren't you?'

'Yes, and you're my blonde neighbour,' Abigail replied before thinking. 'I'm sorry, that was rude.' Her fingertips beat spasmodically against the steering wheel. 'I just got a fright, that's all.'

'Well, maybe it's a good time to introduce ourselves properly. Why don't you come in for a strong cup of tea?'

'Oh, no I ...'

'Please, Abigail, you are as white as a sheet. Either you need to sit quietly in your car until you're okay to drive, or come and have a tea with me. I might even have cake.'

Abigail certainly was in no mood for meeting anyone new or making small talk at that moment. She had just encountered a ghost, or her imagination had conjured something, for heaven's sake. But nor was it safe for her to drive. Her neighbour's concerned expression enveloped her, convincing her to take her latter option. Reluctantly she got out of the car to be greeted by a wide smile and an outstretched hand.

'I'm Molly.'

No wonder Jack was attracted to this lovely vision. Abigail studied Molly as she reluctantly followed her into their home. Thick blonde curls wound their way down her back, stopping at a very toned backside tucked into cropped pants. Effortlessly Molly moved aside small sacks of mulch as she went up the path, kicking away gardening gloves and a Delia Owens bestseller from the front step. Abigail pegged her as being in her forties, so a fair bit younger than Jack.

'I was taking a break, catching up on a book, when I saw you,' Molly explained. 'Come on in and I'll put the kettle on. Would you like a glass of water too?'

'Yes, thank you.' Abigail was suddenly embarrassed, certain that Molly must think she's a fruit loop. She hoped Jack hadn't told her about the knee incident.

'How's your knee?' Molly passed her a pretty teacup covered with pink peonies. A matching teapot and sugar bowl were waiting. 'Milk?'

'Just a drop. My knee is fine, although I'm sure the sprint down a staircase and along the slippery pavement like a madwoman didn't help.'

'Well, you certainly looked like you'd seen a ghost.'

Abigail shot her an alarmed glance, but Molly was busy putting the milk back in the fridge and missed it.

Molly didn't pry further. 'Now, my remedy for shock is cake.'

Abigail knew that Kate, bless her, would certainly have pounced on her, never giving up until she had all the gory details. Abigail wasn't in the least hungry but took a bite of her cake to cover the silence. 'Oh, this is delicious.'

Molly's face lit with a wondrous smile as if unaccustomed to praise. 'It's a new recipe. Lemon yoghurt cake.' She nodded between nibbles. 'Oh yes, it's a keeper. You'll have to take some home with you, otherwise I'll end up eating the whole thing.'

Molly seemed happy to expand on why that would be

the case. 'Our daughter, Rose, is away for the term at one of those Year 9 campuses that schools insist fourteen-year-olds need these days. Anyway, there are only a couple of contact opportunities and, although this cake is seriously good, Rose will have to go without.'

'You must miss her,' Abigail said, thinking of her boys.

'Like crazy! Much more than she misses us.' A sad shadow drifted across Molly's face. 'Sorry. I'm waiting on a text from her now, to hear if she's coming home on her next break. Apparently, there are more interesting things on offer than visiting her parents. I'd show you a happy snap, but all the photos are still packed. We've only been here a short time ourselves and ...' Molly hesitated, patting her pockets. 'Gosh, I must have left my phone outside.'

Abigail turned and took a quick look around the room over the lip of her teacup. It was an open, airy space that joined the modern kitchen with a large family room. She hadn't noticed the sea of unpacked boxes strewn across the floor.

Molly witnessed her taking it all in and smiled broadly. 'You get the idea that I'm more of an outdoor person than a housekeeper, except for cooking and collecting china. Sorry it's messy.'

'Not at all,' Abigail replied, waving away Molly's excuses.

Molly took a sip of tea before continuing. 'Jack said you've bought both sixty-four and sixty-six. You've got your work cut out for you, not that I've seen inside either property so I shouldn't have said that. Is renovating something that excites you?'

Abigail immediately warmed to Molly. Her new neighbour seemed to be cheekily upfront, a quality that Abigail increasingly valued in friends. 'Yes. It does excite me. I'm still undecided about sixty-six, but I will be moving into what the agents called the cottage. I live only a few streets away so it's easy to pop by anytime to check on how the builders are coming along.'

'It's good you've sold your house already, so you can move when you're ready,' Molly offered.

'No, I haven't sold it yet.' Abigail noticed Molly's slightly surprised expression. Her mind raced with something to say, but Molly had moved on.

'Well, don't worry about your slack neighbours here. We are on a mission to get this place in tip-top shape as soon as possible. It helps that Jack is in the landscape business, although he's more on the architectural side. I love plants and gardening.'

'Where did you move from, Molly?'

'A little farther down the coast, but we always knew we wanted to live closer to the city. Rose was awarded a partial scholarship at her school and it's so much easier for commuting from here. It's not easy having a husband who's away all the time, although it does have its advantages too.' Molly gave Abigail a wink before continuing, 'I finally dug in my heels and insisted we move, and luckily we found this house. Once I pull it into shape, I'll get back to looking for a J.O.B., before I go stir crazy.'

Abigail smiled. 'I'm sure it will be fabulous.' She could see similarities between Molly and Jack – their love of the outdoors, even their way of talking. A match made in heaven, seemingly. Heaven! The word jolted her back to why she had run away from Binalong in the first place.

'Thank you, Molly, for the tea and company. It was very sweet of you.' Abigail stood to leave.

Molly walked her to the door, just as a black and white cat materialised from behind one of the boxes. 'There you are. I bet you found a patch of sun to have a sleep in. This is Rose's cat, Smokey. She's feeling a bit displaced, aren't you, Smokey?' Molly picked up the cat, stroking her lovingly.

Cartoon images of the cat-shy Nigella meeting Smokey came and went in Abigail's mind, and she grimaced at the possible consequences. 'Bye, Molly, and if you see me next door, please come on over and I'll show you around. Any suggestions are most welcome.'

'I will. I'll keep an eye out for any feathers too.' She smiled absently.

Abigail stopped. 'What do you mean?'

'Oh, you know. I said you looked so white, like you'd seen a ghost. Spirits leave trails, like a feather or a butterfly or a coin.'

Abigail felt her stomach drop, as if plummeting on a rollercoaster. She was deciding whether to ask more just as Molly's misplaced phone pinged with a text, distracting them both. Abigail mouthed goodbye and headed to her car. She shook as she flicked the lock.

# CHAPTER TWELVE

'WELL, I would have knocked that attic door down by now. Aren't you curious?' Steph asked as she looked through the menu. The friends were catching up for lunch at one of the street cafés near to Ferryman Road. Huge trees spread their protective branches across the narrow, cobbled road and long timber tables, making the café's front terrace dappled but cool.

It was on the tip of Abigail's tongue to share with Steph what she had encountered, or thought she had encountered. But it was too raw and unknown, so she kept the strange 'Liam experience' to herself. The serious truth was, Abigail just couldn't face going back to Binalong. She didn't possess a solid checklist of what to expect. By association she hadn't ventured into the cottage either, but she did know she would have to overcome her increasing hesitation. And soon.

'Let's do it after lunch. You've got the keys, haven't you, and I've got a toolkit in the car for my installations.'

Steph's voice was low as if she was plotting a bank robbery.

Abigail shrugged, knowing that once Steph set her mind to something, any opposition would be flicked aside like a speck of dust. She couldn't quite remember where she'd left her own screwdriver.

An hour later and they were at the base of the stairs in the cottage. Abigail felt a little guilty at asking her friend to do her dirty work, but she asked just the same.

'Steph, the plans are next door, in the upstairs bedroom. I ... um ... left in a bit of a hurry the other day and forgot about them. Would you mind grabbing them for me?' They swapped the keys for the toolbox.

Moments later her friend was back, rolled plans tucked under her arm, seemingly undisturbed.

'All okay?' Abigail probed.

'Sure. Gosh, you're going to get fit running up and down all the stairs.' Steph paused, catching her breath. 'Let's go.'

The mystery door sat in front of them. Steph frowned. 'I don't know why someone walled off this section. It has been used as an attic, so why not keep it as one large space? Mind you, it seems like only thin plaster so it won't be hard to take out.' She knocked on the wall to prove the point.

Abigail jiggled the door handle, turning it both ways. Both women jumped back as the door popped open a few centimetres.

'Whoa, that was locked the other day; I know it was.' Steph frowned. 'Do you think someone has broken in?'

Abigail quickly glanced around, although she had no

idea what she was looking for. 'I doubt it. I'm sure it must have been the agent. They said the door to the upstairs room could have been locked when it was an Airbnb. So maybe they came in and left it unlocked.'

Steph puffed out a breath. 'They can't come in, Abby. You know that. You're the owner.'

'Well, I don't know. Old buildings do odd things, like creak and move, so maybe it was just stuck last time. Let's take a look.'

Abigail swung open the door, feeling along the side wall for a light switch. The dusty yellow globe swept a dull glow around the walls. The room ran the width of the attic but only had a depth of about four metres.

'It's as musty as old gym socks, but not damp, which is a relief,' Abigail said.

'There's the third chimney.' Steph pointed to a brick fireplace sitting off-centre on the back wall.

Its condition proved it hadn't been used for a long time. Most of the tile surround was cracked beyond repair, and debris and ash speckled the worn hearth and floor. Abigail found the silence eerie, but she had to admit it seemed like everything was veiled in a spiderweb of 'strange' to her lately.

'It's like an attic within an attic. Maybe they closed it in to contain any animals or birds that come down chimneys. I had a friend who went away on holiday and came home to a disaster zone in their lounge room. Apparently, a bird had flown down and pooped everywhere and torn their curtains in its panic,' Abby said.

Steph stepped behind a battered old desk, abandoned

to one side of the small room. 'Ooh, and what do we have here?'

Abigail stopped short as she came around the desk, surprised to see two parcels stacked against the wall. They were tightly bound in dusty, opaque bubble wrap.

'They could be from when Binalong was active as a gallery. The two buildings were owned by the same person.' Abigail frowned. 'Or nothing to do with it, more likely. Surely you'd store artworks in the gallery. Damn, I thought there might have been something valuable in here, or at least relevant to the history of the building.'

'Well, they might be. Will we do an unveiling?' Steph was already slicing through the tape and peeling back the plastic, eager for the mystery to be solved. The first package held four small unappealing landscapes on stretched canvas.

'You're the art historian, but I don't know that these are going to shatter any auction house records. What a shame.' Steph sighed.

Abigail reached for the other parcel as Steph leant in to read the signature on the landscapes. She shivered. 'They're all by an artist called F. Lisi. Gosh, it's suddenly got cold in here. Abby?'

Abigail stood, holding aloft an unwrapped canvas. Shaking from the cold and shock, she put it back on the ground, then snatched up the final piece. She ripped apart the bubble wrap, gasping for breath.

Steph stared at the two canvases. 'Is that who I think it is?'

Spikey tendrils wrapped themselves around Abigail's

heart. It wasn't only that the portraits were of Luca, it was that it had been a long, long time since her late husband had looked at her with the love and longing displayed in the two artworks. Seeds of doubt cracked open in Abigail's mind.

She couldn't help it. She slumped to the floor and sobbed as her friend gently removed the painting from her grasp and placed it against the wall. The light in the room dimmed.

'What!?' Abigail whipped her face up to the overhead globe.

Steph wrapped Abigail in her arms. 'It's okay. Let's go. It's too cold in here anyway. I can come back for these later – or whatever.' Gently she ushered Abigail out of the claustrophobic room and pushed the door closed. With Abigail under one arm and the plans under the other, Steph led the way downstairs. As they escaped onto the sidewalk and into the sunlight, Abigail took a deep breath and gave Steph a shaky smile.

'Sorry about that. It was just such a shock. Who painted those, and what on earth are they doing hidden in that room?' Abigail didn't wait for an answer before rambling on. 'Maybe Luca had them commissioned from this Lisi artist, as a present for me or something, but he died before he could give them to me.' Something else niggled on the outskirts of her thoughts, like an evasive mosquito.

'Sure, that sounds feasible.' Steph's tone suggested she didn't believe it was even a remote possibility. 'You could Google the artist and try to track him, or her, down.'

They stood together, rubbing their arms yet knowing they were no longer cold.

'Abby?' Steph looked sideways at her friend.

'Mmm?' Abigail blew her nose in the offered tissue.

'Why did you yell at the light?'

'Did I?' Abigail looked confused.

'Yes. You did. You seemed really angry at someone or something.'

Abigail didn't remember doing any such thing, but if Steph said it had happened, then she believed her. Her heart still thrashed inside her chest, hot and cold flushes seeping along her body. Maybe she should come clean about her disturbing visits to Binalong to try and see everything through someone else's eyes. To get some clarity. Or maybe not.

'It was just seeing Luca's portrait like that. It was so weird, wasn't it?' Abigail heard the weak excuse in her reply. 'Let's go have an early drink somewhere.'

'Oh, I would love to, but I fly out tonight. Remember I'm off to pitch for that spa design project in Bali? Sorry, but I really need to go and pack and get to the airport. Are you going to be okay?'

'I had forgotten. Of course, you go. I'm fine. Look,' she said, holding out trembling hands. 'Cool as a cucumber.'

ABIGAIL HAD NEVER LIKED surprises in any form, preferring to have her own plan for the twists and turns in life. Audrey had realised that after booking out Luna Park for Abigail's surprise tenth birthday – Abigail had been so embarrassed she had insisted her friends take her place on all the rides. Luca had constantly organised events, with and without her, on a moment's notice with no regard for her plans or wishes. And now, there appeared a locked then unlocked room with paintings of him inside. Surprise!

As she headed home, Abigail thought about their startling discovery and how she apparently had reacted to the dimming light. Her patience had run out. This business with Binalong – not wanting to venture there in case she passed out, seeing people who weren't there – had to stop. She slammed the front door behind her, poured herself a large glass of water and paced while her computer started. Her anxiety had transformed into a little capsule of anger.

She let a 'Hello, I'm just checking you are okay. Take care' call from Steph go to messages.

A quick Google search for 'F. Lisi artist' brought no results. She decided to come back to it, but in the meantime shot off an email to the Arpels company solicitors asking them to do a more detailed search. She didn't have to give a reason but offered that it was in relation to the purchase of Binalong, and there was no hurry.

Her customary way around feeling unsettled was either to meditate or plough on determinedly. She ploughed on as though an invisible hand was against her back, pushing her forward. Abigail unrolled the now squashed plans for No. 64 and drew a red squiggly line through the flimsy internal wall, writing a giant *Remove!* directive in the margin for the builder. The chimney was marked *Rejuvenate but not for use*. Once a bathroom had been installed, the open plan would be perfect as a visitor's retreat – or more particularly space for her sons. The downstairs area didn't require any structural changes, just new kitchen appliances and glass doors that would allow the kitchen to spill onto an updated outdoor courtyard. She double-checked all her previous notations, changed a couple, then re-signed each page. Her architect had recommended Brad's building company as being familiar with many of the area's Victorian terraces, so they wouldn't be major alterations to his team.

Initially she had toyed with knocking through the common wall between the two terraces, combining the upstairs of both buildings into one huge loft-style space, with dividers only for the bedrooms and bathrooms. The buildings weren't heritage listed but it would have created multiple council applications, so she had shelved the idea.

Had she known somehow, deep inside, that she needed to keep the properties separate? Had her mindset to let go of past attachments already shifted without her realising?

# CHAPTER THIRTEEN

SATURDAY MORNING BLOOMED clear and perfect for a trip to South Melbourne market. Abigail arrived early to find a car space, quickly bought armfuls of waxy green shrubbery and popular white Alstromeria before the florists sold out, then dropped them off in the car. They would survive while she trawled the tempting range of delicatessens.

But first she needed a strong coffee and a warm croissant. Her sleep the previous night had been almost non-existent, tossing and turning then waking even before Nigella. The dog had been the winner with a brisk walk around the block before Abigail left for the market. She promised herself it would be a Binalong-free day; her mind couldn't cope with all the scurrying thoughts and concerns that threatened every moment she revisited what had happened since purchasing the property. She needed to distance herself from it all, at least for one morning.

'Hi, Abigail.'

The hot coffee caught in her throat as Jack propped on one of the trendy café's little stools at the adjacent table. He seemed all legs and arms as he juggled his own cup, a bunch of fresh silverbeet and a couple of crusty baguettes.

'Good morning,' she said, trying not to laugh. 'Here, would you like to put those on this bench next to me? You look a little crowded.'

'Thanks. In fact I'll join you for a coffee, if that's okay. If you're not expecting someone.'

*That lopsided grin really was so enticing.* 'Of course. Is Molly with you?'

'No, she's on a mission to buy plants. It seems your visit has inspired her.'

Abigail grinned. 'I can't imagine why. It's good that you're at home for the weekend though to help with the garden. Molly mentioned you were away a lot.'

He looked perplexed as he reached for his coffee. Abigail felt for Molly; her husband didn't seem to appreciate how lonely it could be when a partner is often absent, particularly with Rose living away as well.

As she took a bite of her croissant, she noticed raised red scratches on the back of Jack's hand. His eyes followed her concerned gaze.

'I could say they're from heavy-duty pruning duties, but unfortunately Rose's cat has taken a dislike to me. It seems the house move has upset my acceptance rating. Bloody thing.'

'Smokey?'

'You do know how she got that name, don't you?' Jack nodded seriously. When Abigail shook her head, he continued. 'Rose and Molly saw the old neighbour kick her. I know, it's awful. So, Rose stole the cat just before they moved. Hence *Smokey and the Bandit* – bandits, plural.'

Abigail laughed. 'No!'

'Yes! Molly had to explain who *Smokey and the Bandit* was to Rose, naturally, but the cat's old name was Mouse so it's an improvement.'

'Well, a bit of aloe vera on the cuts will help. Oh, sorry, I'm telling that to a man who handles plants all the time.'

Jack waved away her apology. 'Thanks for the concern. I haven't had much sympathy.'

Abigail let the comment go, finishing her coffee.

'Well, I'm having another caffeine hit,' Jack said. He looked directly into Abigail's eyes, offered another grin and asked, 'What about you?'

She hadn't been sure if Jack had meant Molly was looking at plants within the market or somewhere else, so she figured her neighbour might wander past. Abigail thought of all the shopping still to do and the flowers in her car. 'Sure. A strong soy latte, please.'

Jack stood at the busy counter waiting to be served. She watched as he patiently let a young woman push in front of him. Catching her looking at him, he shrugged, then wiggled his eyebrows towards the cake display. Abigail shook her head, pointing at the crumbs on her plate.

Jack propped back on his stool. 'They don't cater to tall people with these seats, do they, just slim bodies like yours.'

Abigail glanced away, surprised.

The café bustled as the dense coffee aroma settled around them. It was going to take a while for their second round to arrive, and Abigail realised she should have asked for a takeaway cup.

'Don't you just love the market,' Jack said. He sat forward, elbows on his knees and hands loose between his legs. The front of his shirt flared open. 'The Italian deli over there has the best veal meatballs – big spicy balls in thick tomato sauce and mozzarella drizzled through. Oh, I'll have to get some – *you'll* have to get some.'

'Are you a good cook?' Abigail enquired.

'Heavens, no. A roast or a BBQ are my go-tos. But I've eaten enough of those meatballs over a short space of time to be on first name terms with the mama who makes them.' He paused mid thought. 'I guess I do value good food. You know, fresh and exciting. I'd rather go without than eat a soggy bacon and egg breakfast.'

Abigail nodded. 'Or a yummy avocado and feta on toast covered in that sickly brown drizzle. I don't even know what it is. Mind you, it's a bit of a first world country's problem to have, isn't it? I feel guilty even thinking such a thing.'

'True!' Jack agreed, slapping his palm against his knee.

'Apart from greens and bread, what are you here for?' Abigail asked.

'I think I'm done. I don't even know why I bought the silverbeet, but Molly will find a use for it; she's a great cook.' Jack nodded fondly. 'What about you? Are you cooking up a storm for guests?'

Abigail wilted at the thought. She couldn't remember the last occasion she had catered for a crowd. Jack was looking at her, waiting for a reply.

'I'm a bit like you. I love coming to the market and getting swallowed up in all the aromas and the hustle. I used to come with my husband all the time.' Abigail registered a quick enquiring flicker in Jack's eyes. 'He, Luca, died. Anyway, I love the butchers' calls and the way the fishmongers toss around the ice. I see items but have no idea what they're used for, but then I'll spy a parent sharing a slice of peppery cheese with a toddler. It's so, so ...' She waved her hands around searching for the word.

'Sensory,' Jack offered.

'Exactly.' Abigail smiled. *Exactly*.

She drained her cup and stood to go; Jack collected his purchases and they stood awkwardly.

'Great to catch up,' he said.

'Yes. See you later. I told Molly to come over if I'm in the building and I'll show you around.'

Jack turned away, raising the baguettes in the air as a farewell salute. Abigail watched him weave effortlessly through the crowd, a warm feeling of friendship spreading through her. She also recognised a sliver of regret.

After another hour of wandering the stalls, she felt happily weighed down with bags of fresh produce, plus a small container of spicy meatballs from the mama on the corner.

ABIGAIL'S PROMISE TO have a 'live in the moment kind of day' was fine until that evening. It came to a grinding halt as she inhaled the delicious bouquet of herbs and spices wafting from the meatballs. The Italian-ness of it was something she couldn't ignore, but Jack was right, they were amazing. Nigella hovered under her feet, her quivering nose in the air.

Luca was as present to her in the kitchen as if he was standing over her shoulder, gathering the steam from the meatballs in a show of picking out the flavours. Perhaps mentioning him to Jack had triggered the memories. Abigail was transported back to all the different bars and restaurants they had visited, trying out new foods and ideas, all in preparation for Grappa. It was to be a chic village-style bar, providing a wide range of spirits and wines accompanied by Italian tasting dishes.

Luca hadn't been a chef or even a cook – he just liked the thought of running his own trattoria. He would describe how he planned to welcome groups of diners into his domain, to regale them with colourful stories of vineyards and the good life. If Grappa had eventuated, he would have been in his element. His maternal Italian side would have been overblown and loud, his patience short with all those around him, including herself. Unfortunately, his father's Australian heritage had always been downplayed despite Abigail's urging to appreciate it. She knew that, somewhere in his boxed-up belongings, there would be a journal outlining various panini and lemon potato croquette recipes, but none were of Luca's own making. He had been very persuasive when asking for various chefs' ideas and elated when they have given in to him.

But it seemed, even a couple of years later, every happy

memory was balanced out by a troubling one. It was as if they were each on opposite ends of a see-saw. Certainly, towards the end of his life, Luca had become focused on things other than her. Abigail had known, with every heart-breaking night alone, that his attention was being drawn elsewhere. Having his portrait painted was obviously one such distraction but she had no idea how that had come about, or when.

Suddenly remembering her email to the solicitors, Abigail poured herself a glass of Chianti and turned on her computer. Bingo!

*Abigail: Initial searches didn't bring up much for F. Lisi artist. No social media sites and only one reference for Francesca Lisi, artist. Could this be her? Past positions have included curator and arts management roles, mostly in regional galleries (we can obtain more information on exactly where if needed). The most recent was listed as Gallery Manager, Binalong Gallery, South Melbourne. Regards, Josh Mapleton.*

Within five minutes, after snapping off the oven and tossing Nigella a biscuit, Abigail was parked once more in Ferryman Road. Wasting no time, she headed straight into No. 64 and raced up the stairs. She strode into the smaller attic room, her body cutting through the air like a hot knife through butter. Icy fingers pinched at her as she quickly folded the bubble-wrap back around the two portraits and tucked one under each arm. She ignored the chill, quickly thumping her way back down the stairs to her car. Tempting as it was to place them carefully on the back seat,

Abigail flung the paintings into the boot for the short drive home.

———

LUCA'S dark eyes challenged her as she sat facing him. She nibbled through the meatballs and gulped her wine, surprised she could stomach anything after reading the email. Abigail tried to analyse Luca's expression, to read his thoughts whilst he had sat there facing the artist. It was like chiselling away the thin layers of all she had loved and doubted about her husband, to reach his core. She held a hope that somewhere along the way she might discover what lay beneath, the *why* and *how* these portraits had been created.

His hair was slightly tousled in one portrait, a curl dropping over his forehead as it tended to do. It was slicked back in the other, as though someone had casually run their fingers through the thickness. In both paintings there was a glimpse of denim-blue around his tanned neck – an upturned collar portrayed in heavily textured acrylic. They were similar but not identical, a perfect pair. Perhaps they had been painted from photographs. This woman had taken a clandestine photo of him at some stage and then painted the portraits without his knowledge. In the same thought wave, Abigail knew she was kidding herself. His piercing expression, slightly softened around the edges from emotion, was beautifully reserved for the woman in front of him. As it had been for her at one time.

'I don't know what all this means, Luca, but let me tell

you I'm going to find out.' Deep gulps of suspicion worked their way to the surface as tears misted Abigail's dead husband. Because deep down Abigail knew that she now recognised the name Francesca Lisi – she had met the glamorous gallery manager on several occasions when she and Luca had visited Binalong. Josh's email confirmed it. She had thought they'd returned to scope out the space, but perhaps there had been another reason.

Her chair toppled backward as she jumped up, turning to her computer again. She stabbed at the keys:

*Thanks, Josh. Please go ahead and see if you can find anything else on Francesca Lisi. Regards, Abigail.*

A thought wormed its way into Abigail's mounting fears as she pressed send on the email: had Francesca lived next door at No. 64? Is that how the paintings came to be stored there?

# CHAPTER FOURTEEN

MOLLY SEARCHED Abigail's face as she held open the front door. 'Come in, Abigail. Would you like a cuppa?'

Abigail sensed Molly could read her mind or had managed to tune in to her nervousness, but she was pleased her neighbour was home.

'I hope I'm not interrupting.'

Molly turned, placing a hand gently on Abigail's arm. 'I'm due for one. I think I've finally cracked the back of unpacking. What do you think?' She moved into the kitchen and gathered her cups and plates together on the bench.

The room now looked ordered and welcoming. A couple of scrunched mint-coloured wool throws were casually draped across chairs with the small splashes of donkey brown and terracotta on cushions successfully cutting back any threat of girliness. But it was the array of scattered items that caught Abigail's attention: little pebbles, uneven stacks of books, bowls of silver and copper trinkets appeared amongst the furniture, across windowsills and small tables. They made the room eclectic and personal. A large old tapestry cushion sat plum in the middle of the room, with Smokey asleep on top in a beam of sunlight.

'It looks gorgeous. I thought you said you weren't a decorator.'

Molly laughed. 'Well, it helps that I've washed the floorboards. A couple of rugs and furniture and voila! I figure I can bring my garden inside with some more plants and by incorporating every shade of green under the sun. I still have to add a few bits 'n' bobs and our artwork, but it's coming together.'

A small gathering of photos in simple frames sat on a round table next to a thriving potted Fiddle Leaf Fig. Even at a distance, Abigail could see the laughing girl in the frames must be Rose. She was a mini-Molly with the same halo of curls.

'I'm not sure about our paintings though. I think they'll be a bit overbearing for in here.'

'Well, art is my background, mainly on the history side, but I paint too. If I can help, just let me know. I'm happy to hold them up against the wall while you decide if they fit in,' Abigail offered.

Molly rotated the teapot. 'Really? You'll have to tell me more about that. Rose loves painting and going to galleries. She is pretty good too, if I do say so myself, and that's not just a mother speaking. Not that I'm allowed to voice my opinion – you know how teenagers are.' Molly shook her head, her eyes housing a tinge of sadness. 'It's a glorious morning, let's sit on the front deck.'

Abigail followed Molly outside to a rattan setting that was nestled amongst tubs of all sizes. Lush green bushes flourished in each. Work in the front yard hadn't progressed since her last visit, so Abigail presumed Jack must be away again.

'I see the artists' co-op is staking a claim,' Molly said. 'You'll have artists waving placards and paintbrushes before you know it. A lady called Sandy gave me a leaflet and asked if I objected to the development.'

'Oh dear, are they doing a letter drop?' Abigail winced. 'And it's not a development. It was the end of their lease so they were hardly evicted. I do feel a bit mean, but the renovations will be starting soon. It will be noisy which is not ideal for their classes anyway.'

Molly glanced at her, obviously waiting for the reason for her visit. Abigail's stomach clenched as they both sipped their tea in silence.

'So,' Abigail began. 'I'm not sure how to ask this or exactly what I'm looking for or expecting to hear. And if you have absolutely no idea what I'm talking about, then it doesn't matter. Really it doesn't.'

Molly's laugh stopped her. 'Heavens, Abigail. Out with it, or it will be cocktail hour before you say what's on your mind.'

Abigail took a deep breath. 'The other day, when you mentioned feathers and coins being signs, what did you mean exactly?'

Molly flopped forward. 'I'm so relieved. I thought you

were going to say you wanted to erect a brick wall between our properties or something. Um, oh yes, I remember. When I said you looked like you'd seen a ghost?'

Abigail nodded, trying to appear nonchalant.

Molly paused for a few seconds before answering. 'They, whoever "they" are, and I'm not sure how I know this exactly, but they say that if, out of nowhere, you find a coin or feather directly in your path, you should pick it up. That it's a sign a good spirit is nearby.' Molly stopped and waved as her attention was diverted toward Ferryman Road.

When Abigail squinted across the fence, she saw the old lady in black shuffling by. She gave Molly and Abigail a tentative smile.

'I have no idea who that lady is. She walks by here a lot lately but never seems to have any shopping, or even a handbag, with her,' Molly said before picking up her thread. 'Where was I? Oh, yes. It's also the same if a butterfly hovers around you. That can be the soul of someone who has passed.'

'I don't know if I believe that though.' Abigail's voice was heavy with uncertainty.

Molly shifted. 'I think you should believe whatever you want to. Personally, I think that if you've lost someone, then having some kind of tangible sign would be a comfort. We all know that just because someone isn't physically here you don't stop missing or loving them. But I believe you have to be open to it. I mean, I think it's very powerful when you meditate and open yourself to feelings. Who's to say that messages aren't around us all the time, but we just don't know what to look for.'

Abigail's eyes focused on the shimmering space where the old lady had passed. 'Mmm. Well, I meditate but nothing has ever presented itself.'

'Has something happened, Abigail?' Molly asked carefully.

'Oh, no. Well, I'm not sure but I'm prepared to say no. It's just a weird feeling I get when I go into one of the rooms in Binalong, and a couple of other crazy things that I am most likely imagining.' She tossed her head as if to bat away any possibilities.

Molly peered into her tea for a moment, then spoke softly. 'Well, let me tell you, if you ever get the opportunity to be open to anything, grab it. I had an incredible experience once.' She paused. 'I'll tell you about it if you like.'

At that moment, the breeze died down and any leaves holding tentatively onto branches floated to the ground. A whisper of woody scent circled then left, leaving the women in a cocoon of silence as if the outside world had gone on holiday. Abigail sensed the swing and shifted nervously in her seat.

Molly took a deep breath, fiddled with the cushion's tassel and gazed at the treetops. 'I had a ... a happening, I guess you'd say. It was wonderful. Like a dream, but when I woke up, I knew something amazing had passed. I was dreaming that I was being chased down a mountain. It was shaped like a cone and I was running around and around, which is silly but that happens in dreams, doesn't it. I was super scared and nearly out of breath. Then when I reached the final turn and burst out the bottom, someone grabbed me and pulled me into his arms. When I looked up, it was into my late grandfather's face. His expression was one of pure tenderness and joy.'

Her voice dropped to a whisper. 'I knew he was holding me, but I couldn't feel him. It was like ... like a shadow but so powerful. Like nothing I had ever felt before or since.'

Molly's eyes flicked across to her visitor as if judging whether she should go on, but Abigail's rapt attention must have left her in no doubt. 'I'm not a religious person at all, Abigail, but you know when you read about feeling over-whelmed with love? Well, it was like that. But not earthly or romantic love. It was, gosh it's hard to explain, but it was inside and outside my body. Calming and comforting.' She gave a little shrug. 'And then I woke up and I felt so incred-ibly calm and happy.'

Time seemed to stand still as the women sat with their own silent thoughts. Abigail glanced across to Molly, and noticed tiny glistening tears. She waited for her to continue.

Molly offered a small smile. 'I have tried to hang onto that feeling, but it kind of diluted over time. I've never forgotten it though.'

'Was it a dream then?'

Molly shook her head. 'I truly believe it was a visit. The way I reacted and the emotions I couldn't control were too potent and strange for me to have imagined that such a thing was even possible. To be honest, I don't care if anybody else believes me because I know it happened. It's mine.'

'Why do you think he visited you?' Abigail asked, now not doubting a word Molly had shared.

'It was soon after our mum had died and I was having a few problems at the time. I took it as meaning that everything was okay. That I was being released and should be happy. I don't know why my grandfather was the one rather than Mum, except that I was very close to him when I was a little girl. I mean, I know you can read something into anything, can't you, but I kind of feel privileged for having seen him again. It's always just tucked away inside me.' Molly's open palm gravitated to cover her heart.

Abigail nodded. 'Yes, we all wish for life beyond death, I guess.' She leant over, placing her hand on Molly's knee.

Molly sniffed. 'Sorry. I'm not upset, it was just such a special thing to happen to me, and I fear I'll never come across it again. I wish everyone could experience it. It's hard to explain, particularly when some people would think I'm mad if I mentioned it. Which is why I don't, except I get the feeling my little story may help you in some way.' She searched Abigail's face. 'Jack has his own story too, although his encounter was different and he doesn't allow himself to linger on it as I do. We often joke that we'll be picked up by a UFO if we're not careful.'

Abigail eased back into the deep cushions. 'That's a coincidence, isn't it? I mean that you married someone with the same experiences. Unless you met at a séance or something.'

Molly clapped her hands, shaking her head. She looked, wide-eyed, at Abigail. 'Jack isn't my husband. He's my brother!'

'What?' It certainly had become an afternoon of surprises. Mentally, Abigail recounted meeting Jack and their later discussions but couldn't pinpoint why she had decided he was, or wasn't, Molly's husband. It certainly explained why she'd thought they were so similar.

'But you said your husband was away a lot. And Jack lives here, doesn't he?'

Molly could hardly speak for laughing. 'My husband is away a lot, and yes, Jack might be moving back to Melbourne for his work. He lives in Sydney but is staying here with us until he sees how long the project is for, then he'll find his own place to live, I guess. I think he's here more to keep me company, which is nice. He's quite a few years older than me and plays the big brother and uncle role too well sometimes. We don't have any other family.'

It was obvious how close the siblings were.

'Oh, I feel a bit of a goose,' Abigail said, wondering why Jack hadn't mentioned his relationship with Molly. But really, why would he?

Molly continued, 'It's great having him here to help with the property, so when Tom comes home our time together isn't taken up with too many home duties. Mind you, Tom constantly tells me I have no trouble adding to his list anyway.'

'So is Tom a fly-in/fly-out worker with the mines or something?' Abigail asked.

'Yes, but on the Human Resources side of things. All of the company's management team has to do the two weeks on, one week off thing. The weeks he's not here are better when I have Rose at home and I can try to do more things with her. That doesn't always go to plan though. It's not forever and the pay is great while he can manage the commuting.'

Molly grinned. 'So that's us in a nutshell. Ha, I can't believe you thought I was married to Jack. He's not married, but he'll get a laugh out of that.'

'Please don't tell him. I'm sure he thinks I'm a bit of a ditz already. I've had a lot on my plate, and I'm obviously not thinking straight. My vibes must be out of kilter.'

Molly had the grace not to go back to earlier questions about spirit signs, and Abigail needed time to think over what Molly had said. She stood to leave.

'Thank you for the tea and for sharing your story, Molly. Gosh, I owe you quite a few cups.'

'Any time. Take care, Abigail. See you soon.'

Abigail chuckled to herself as she clicked the front gate closed. She had always considered herself to be a perceptive person, and certainly in her profession she had been known for her eye for historical detail. But when it came to personal stakes, she was obviously way off. She shook her head. She could be such an idiot sometimes. One thing she did know for sure was that she had enjoyed Molly's company and was looking forward to being her neighbour.

The staccato beeping of a car horn interrupted her thoughts. She stopped as Jack parked his car, unsure whether to wave and keep going or wander over. Kate would have called it a *Seinfeld* moment: that 'should I go or should I stay' situation.

He waved as he opened the car boot and took out a black golf bag.

'The golf bag is an interesting accessory for your who-invited-the-boss look.' Abigail raised her eyebrows, taking in how well his body carried his stylish French navy suit, snug white shirt and soft lemon tie.

Jack's warm eyes reached out to her as he loosened his tie. Abigail didn't object, particularly as he wasn't Molly's husband anymore.

'I had meetings in the city all morning, hence the boss part of your comment. I played in a corporate golf day last week – appallingly, I might admit – so thought I'd bring the clubs home and get in a bit of practice tomorrow morning.'

He relaxed back against the car as though he had all the time in the world to stand and chat with her. Abigail liked that.

'I've just had a lovely catch-up with Molly,' Abigail said.

Jack nodded at his clubs, apparently not wanting to be distracted. 'Do you play?'

'Yes, but I'm a bit rusty. I was playing every week at one stage but, well, you know how it is. It's a great game though.' She let her excuse sit between them, unexplained.

'Why don't you come with me tomorrow then? I was just going to get some buckets of balls, but I can book us in for a quick nine holes if you're interested.'

'I don't know. What's your handicap?'

'Not playing enough.' He chuckled, his eyes dancing at his comment. 'Sorry, old joke.'

'That sounds like a challenge to me,' Abigail replied. 'One that I will accept.'

They exchanged mobile numbers just in case something cropped up, and Abigail gave him her address. Jack swung his bag over his shoulder and headed in to Molly's house while Abigail continued home to clean her clubs and locate her golf clothes.

# CHAPTER FIFTEEN

MOLLY HAD DIVULGED that Jack wasn't married, but did he have a partner? Abigail was mulling over the idea and whether she should care or not. Surely not, if he had asked her to go with him today. It was Steph she was looking out for; after all, she had enough on her own plate. She needed to stop her mind ping-ponging between issues. It never used to be a problem, her analytical brain over-riding interruptions, phone calls, even mealtimes on many occasions. Now, details about the sale of her house, her conversation with Molly and what it could mean, and the mystery of Francesca Lisi all floated around the edges.

But Jack seemed to be taking up an increasing amount of space in her thoughts where there wasn't much available room. Who knew where he was in his life though. And it was only golf, right?

'I HOPE WE GET A GAME IN,' Jack said, glancing out the car window towards an increasingly grey sky. 'The radar doesn't look too promising, but you just never know. Have you got a rain jacket?'

Abigail nodded. Their clubs were tucked into the back of Jack's 4WD and they were on their way to a course only a half hour away. She knew the club had reciprocals with Royal Sydney, so she presumed Jack must be a member up there. She was about to point out that Adam was a member at the same Sydney club, but the conversation had veered off onto other topics. Probably for the best. Adam was very competitive and could rub people the wrong way.

'So tell me about Abigail,' he said.

When Abigail filled Jack in on what an art historian's roles were, he had shaken his head. 'I'm sorry, I don't want to sound rude, but that just doesn't fit you. It sounds somewhat serious.'

Abigail laughed. 'It can be, but I tended to steer towards the more interesting, arty side. I haven't worked in that arena for quite a while now.' She didn't explain that a couple of life dramas had got in the way.

'What would you like to do then?'

Abigail stole a look at him, surprised but pleased to hear such a genuine tone to his question. 'Well, I have to start pinpointing what I want Binalong's use to be.' She tugged at her bottom lip. 'But do you know what? I'd like to paint again. There, I've said it out loud.'

Jack threw her a wink as he parked the car. 'Okay, first we'll master the golf course, then the art studio. Damn, it does look like rain, though.'

Abigail had only been to this particular course a couple of times. Luca hadn't played golf and her interest had slipped over the years, but she had to admit the traditional clubhouse and beautifully curated course would convince anyone to get back into their game if they could afford the huge fees. It was stunning, the colour of the greens and fairways vibrant in the unsettled light.

Jack suddenly stopped on the way to the Pro Shop to sign them in. 'I'm sorry, Abigail. I don't know your surname.'

'Croucher. What's yours?'

'Mattingley.'

She gave him a thumbs up as they grinned at each other.

Abigail took the opportunity to check out Jack while he took care of the club's formalities and discussed the weather with the pro. She imagined he would be a good listener when receiving a client's brief, yet firm in his response and opinion, poised and self-assured in any situation. She found him very attractive, but quickly turned her gaze to the course as he wandered back out to her.

'There's a storm closing in, unfortunately. How about we hit a few balls and see what happens.'

Abigail nodded, turned her cell phone on silent and collected her bag.

Once teed up, Jack's attention was fully focused on his swing. Abigail pretended to gauge the practice fairway as she watched him out of the corner of her eye. She was rewarded with a slow, measured backswing then whack, a powerful hit, flexible hip swivel and smooth follow-through. Nervously she addressed her ball, swearing under her breath when she cut her first drive short and sliced it. Jack kept his head down and methodically hit ball after ball.

Large raindrops plopped around them, followed by the rumble of distant thunder. A moment later the siren sounded, summoning all players off the course.

Jack shot his driver back in his bag. 'Looks like that's the end of our game. Do you want to stay at the clubhouse for coffee or head down the road?'

'Let's head off,' Abigail replied, surprising herself at her quick decision. Perhaps, circumstances permitting, she needed to ask him a couple of questions and preferred a more informal setting than the club.

They were soon huddled over steaming cups of coffee in a cosy café. The rain had intensified with rolling thunder and occasional flashes of lightning. But inside the café the air was thick with the aroma of ground coffee beans and the chatter from full tables – it appeared they weren't the only ones caught out by the downpour.

'So much for the radar,' Jack noted. 'I think I'll change apps.'

'I bet you are very competitive on the golf course,' Abigail ventured as she looked across their small table. She liked the way his lips puckered as his cup came to meet them. She could feel the warmth of his knees against her own.

'Why do you say that?' Jack asked, pretending to be offended. 'Mind you, you're right. I figure that if you're going to do something, whatever it is, then you give it your all. I reckon you'd be the same. Art historians are a cut-throat lot, I imagine.'

Abigail knew he was teasing her but admitted, 'I'm an historian, not someone caught up in whims and uncertainty.' As the words swirled around her, she realised how false they were. Maybe that was her life once, but hopefully not anymore.

'Why not?' Jack asked.

'Why not what?'

'Whims and uncertainty. Why not get caught up in their web every so often?'

He grinned as he took a bite of his ham and cheese toastie, followed with a nod of delight. 'This is good. You must know all the haunts.'

'We, my husband and I, did a lot of research into the dining scene at one time. Luca wanted to open a restaurant-slash-bar. He wasn't a chef himself so we used to trawl around and see who had good coffee, what menu selections were on offer and where, who the best chefs were. It became all-consuming. I did like getting ideas for the décor though.'

'You're an artist, right? Couldn't you have whipped up something?'

Abigail's heart warmed at Jack's presumption of her painting ability. 'Whipping up something isn't as easy as it sounds, and Luca's plans changed as to what our venue was to look like.' She paused. 'And then he died.'

Jack's handsome face creased with concern. 'I'm sorry, Abigail, I was being offhand.'

Abigail hesitated, wondering if this was her moment,

then decided it was. 'Actually, Jack, I was going to ask you something.'

He looked at her expectantly, his brown eyes intense yet a little wary.

'Molly and I were talking. She told me about her dream, you know about her, your grandfather and ...'

Thankfully Jack nodded and leaned forward. If his expression had brought down shutters she would have changed the subject, but he seemed to be happy for her to go on. In fact, she seemed to have his full attention.

'She said that you'd had an ... um ... encounter that was similar but different from hers. I understand if you don't want to tell me about it, but I thought if Molly had mentioned it, then you wouldn't mind sharing what happened. I only ask because something happened to me that I don't understand. I went through denial at first, then I was scared but curious and now, because I'm not addressing it, I'm wondering if I just imagined it.' Abigail shrugged, unsure of what to say next, but Jack's hand was warm and reassuring as he reached across the table and squeezed her fingers.

'Whoa, slow down. Whatever you've experienced has obviously unsettled you so, no, I don't mind telling you. However, you might think I'm the one with the vivid imag- ination.'

Abigail waited. Jack's eyes reflected the rain-splattered window as he looked beyond it into the past.

'I had a close mate who used to fly Tiger Moths for a hobby. One day he was out flying and the engine sputtered, then died. Long story short but sad, he bravely steered that box into the bay rather than have it hit a crowded beach. He died instantly.'

It was Abigail's turn to cup her hand onto Jack's as he continued.

'Matt's funeral service was held in the hangar of the flying club. He was seen as a bit of a hero as well as being a really decent guy, so the large space was full to the brim with mourners. You may know that it's tradition for planes to fly in formation over funeral gatherings, then for one to thread away to represent the pilot who died. It's incredibly moving. Well, I was sitting towards the back of the hangar and as that single plane headed off, I looked up and there was a large black butterfly fluttering just a few inches from me. It circled me and our other friend who was sitting beside me for a good minute, rested on my shoulder for a second, then flew away.' His fingers fluttered by his ear, as though he could still sense the butterfly's gentle vibration.

Abigail's eyes were filled with tears. 'How beautiful,' she murmured. It hadn't escaped her that Jack's speech had slowed during the telling of his story, his voice becoming husky.

'It was.' Jack nodded. 'I wouldn't have thought anything of it, but a woman behind us said something like "Look, there's Matt still flying around." It's hard to describe, but in the same moment I felt this amazing feeling of peace. Which is odd when I was at a friend's funeral, but that's what I felt. The woman's comment made me think about it all, and of course Molly had her theory.'

Abigail cleared her throat before gently asking her

question. 'Jack, do you think it was your friend saying goodbye?'

He didn't answer immediately, although Abigail guessed it might have been a question he had asked himself many times.

'What happened, definitely happened. I know that. I guess it's what you read into it and what you want to do with that. Maybe it's the same for what you're grappling with.'

Abigail started, suddenly unsure about sharing her stories about the butterfly and feather at the auction, the coin in Binalong's hallway, not to mention seeing Liam. Liam, not Luca. It was all too silly to try to verbalise.

'I'm a two-cup girl. My treat this time if you'd like another.' She smiled at Jack, stalling.

'Yes, I'd like one, but I'll ...' he replied, reaching for his wallet.

Abigail quickly went to the counter. She could feel his eyes on her as she placed the order. Hopefully he wasn't wondering what kind of cosmic weirdo he was having coffee with, but he had admitted to his own connection. Jack had graciously answered her question and didn't deserve to be cut out; she owed him something and suddenly felt comfortable telling him about Luca and Liam.

Jack was silent, expectant, as Abigail sat back at their table. 'I can't believe how open you and Molly have been about your experiences. And accepting. I'm really trying to work through it all, but here it comes.' Abigail straightened her back. For some reason she felt the need to appear more *Sixty Minutes* reporter than the psychic Alison Dubois.

'Okay. Luca died a couple of years back. It was a car accident. He was out with his best friend, Liam. Well, Liam was my friend too – a bit of a wild Irishman, but a dear friend nonetheless. I thought. Liam was driving that night; "fast and erratic" the police said. He lost control and slammed into a construction site fence. Luca didn't have his seatbelt on, and the impact was forceful enough to kill them both instantly. I don't even know what they were doing in that area.'

She took a shuddering breath and stared out at the heavy rain. 'That was the trouble when Luca was suddenly gone. The police record is there as to the how but so many questions remained as to the why. In my mind, anyway.'

Abigail didn't remember finishing her coffee but an empty cup sat in front of her.

Jack nodded. 'I guess that's why you'd go looking for signs.'

'But you saw a sign. You saw a butterfly and felt ...' She frowned.

'But I didn't go looking for it. Molly is the one who pulled it all together.'

An involuntary shiver crept over Abigail's body. Did Jack think she was one of those gloomy people who spent their lives holding onto the past? Embarrassed, she excused herself to go to the bathroom.

Jack's innocent comments, albeit gently shared, had pierced her confidence. She quickly pulled herself together and returned to their table. She summoned a smile and suggested they head home. Jack gave her a surprised look but downed his coffee and they raced through the easing rain.

Their conversation was general and noncommittal on the way home. Abigail filled the space by chatting about her time in London. She touched briefly on her marriage to Martin but Jack showed more interest in her sons. She felt guilty at suddenly shutting down the topic she had initiated in the café, but why had Jack said anything if he didn't believe it?

When they arrived at Abigail's house, Jack turned off the ignition but didn't open the door. He half-turned towards Abigail, seeking out contact with her eyes.

'You know, Abigail. You can smooth the rough edges of bad or sad memories so that over time they become bearable.'

She held his concerned gaze, knowing he was trying to help. 'But is that being true to yourself, or the past?'

He shrugged. 'I don't know. I guess we all approach such things differently.'

Jack carried her golf bag to her front door. As soon as it opened, Nigella bounded out and leapt onto his chest.

'Nigella, down! Sorry, Jack,' she exclaimed. She grabbed the dog's collar and dragged her down the hallway.

'No problem.' He shrugged, stepping over the threshold. 'Where do you want these?'

'Pardon?' Abigail called from the living area as she ushered Nigella through the back door. She was relieved by the way the dog had innocently lightened the mood between them.

'Your clubs ...' Jack had followed her but had stopped short. Abigail turned to see him staring at the portraits of Luca propped on the sideboard. She still hadn't managed to find somewhere to store them, or in reality to satisfy herself she wanted to keep them.

'I've left your bag near the front door,' he continued, turning back up the hallway, as if caught with his hand in the cookie jar.

Abigail quickly followed him, embarrassed. Surely he would now be convinced she was gripped by the memory of her dead husband.

'Jack, thank you for the game we didn't have. And the chat.'

He reached across, dropping a gentle kiss on her forehead. 'We'll try again another time.' He turned and left.

# CHAPTER SIXTEEN

'HI, MUM,' Abigail had intended to call Audrey for days, but time had just slipped by and now her mother was onto her. Abigail glanced at her watch; she was due to meet her builder so would need to keep the conversation brief.

'Now, Abigail,' Audrey began.

Abigail sighed and tossed the lighting catalogue aside.

'I was at Adam's office yesterday and that nice young assistant of his showed me the properties you've bought on Giggle Earth.'

Her mother was extremely switched on in so many areas, but technology wasn't one of them. Abigail could picture her batting her eyes with a 'just not knowing about anything look' as the poor fellow had been sucked in to help her.

'I'm a little concerned. That building on the corner doesn't look, well, stable.'

'Of course it's stable, Mum. It passed all the building

inspections under the sun, and you know I had Arpels check the contracts. I'm about to start the renovations, but really so much has already been done over the years to open up the rooms that it's not too onerous at all. I could move into the cottage now.'

'It doesn't look very big though,' Audrey insisted.

'I don't need big. Heavens, I have two Victorian terraces side by side. That's pretty sizeable and more than enough room for me plus the boys when they visit. And you of course.' Thundering silence at the Sydney end of the call proclaimed Audrey's unwavering opinion.

'I'm getting pretty excited, so please just trust me, okay?' How many times had she asked her mother to do that over her lifetime?

'I just don't understand why you didn't buy it with Luca if it meant so much. You know you could have afforded to make any offer to the owner, even if it wasn't on the market. And now you can buy another lovely home. The penthouse in Marjorie Clayton's South Yarra complex is for sale. Why not take a look?'

'No. I don't want an apartment. I need a yard for Nigella, and me too.'

'Well, Adam does say you are always so set in your decisions.'

Abigail tapped her pen impatiently on the table. 'I'm about to put my house on the market. I'll send you a copy of the flier when I have them. Or ask that nice assistant to bring it up on the screen when you next visit Adam.' Abigail couldn't keep the bite out of her tone.

'Now another thing ...'

Why was there always an ulterior motive with Audrey? Abigail had been waiting for the other shoe to drop, as the saying goes. She waited.

'I've been working on a charity event to fund a disability housing project. You remember I told you about it.'

Abigail vaguely remembered Audrey mentioning it but her mother's philanthropy was never-ending; it was difficult not to get caught up in every project.

'It's in a couple of weeks. Arpels is the major sponsor, so I think you need to attend. Also, the good news is that Martin and Christine will be in Australia around that time so I've asked them to support the night as well. Christine can offer some kind of celebrity cooking prize in the auction.'

This must be the visit the boys had mentioned. Abigail wasn't surprised her mother knew of her ex-husband's visit as Audrey kept in regular contact. Being the father of her precious grandsons, Martin could do no wrong. Audrey apparently hadn't factored in that it would be a trifle difficult for Christine to offer her personal services for an auction prize when she lived in London. She did love a celebrity though. The ongoing silence announced Audrey was waiting for a commitment from her daughter.

'Count me in, I guess.' Abigail hoped the evening would allow her to quiz Martin on James's sudden involvement in Christine's career, if nothing else.

'As a single?' Audrey pushed.

'Yes, a single,' Abigail replied, grimacing. She could

picture her mother drawing her lips into a thin, unhappy line.

'No problem. The event will be a sell-out so we'll find someone with deep pockets to sit next to you.'

Abigail could just imagine her mother putting her name on the seating plan with a large question mark next to her – she hoped it didn't also say 'find a husband for Abigail'.

'I'll send you the invitation so you have all the details for your diary.'

'Okay. Talk with you soon.'

Nigella nosed Abigail's arm, yearning for a scratch. 'Ah, Nigella, she's like a hurricane, isn't she?'

---

BRAD WAS WAITING PATIENTLY outside Binalong when Abigail pulled into Ferryman Road.

'Sorry I'm late, Brad. My mother called just as I was about to leave.'

Brad nodded knowingly. 'I used to have a mother-in-law like that. Always ringing about something or other, butting her nose in.'

Abigail chuckled at their shared dismay, then turned her attention to their meeting. Excitement buzzed through her body.

'I would like to do the cottage first, because that's going to be my home and it won't take too long, then Binalong. Oh, and I meant to confirm that taking out the attic wall would be okay. It looks only temporary anyway.'

'No problem.' Brad nodded, squinting at the building's exterior. 'This will look good once we sandblast it back a bit. Good decision on keeping a building's character, I always say. Both your places here have good bones. Have you got a gardener for the courtyards? I know it's down the track a bit but Period Pansies can ...'

'I'm sorted, thanks.' Was she really? Was she planning on growing a green thumb or was it more that there was a happy gardener and well-built landscape architect next door? If she hadn't scared him off with her theories on the afterlife, that was.

'We can work on several areas such as the bathrooms across both buildings at the same time. It's more cost effective,' Brad said.

Abigail appreciated his plan, even though the expense wasn't an issue. Her priority was that the finished properties would be as perfect as possible. It would be the next chapter in her life.

They wandered into No. 64 Ferryman Road. Brad took notes as Abigail led him through the rooms. She trailed a finger along the cool surface of the walls, still absorbing that this was where her future would be.

'You know,' Abigail began, hooking her fingers into air quotes. 'I read somewhere that a house should "radiate a natural ease". Do you think that's how my home will end up?'

Brad frowned, then squinted at the ceiling. 'Yeah, sure. Well, we'll do all we can. I mean, I guess it depends on the decorating doesn't it, and "the vibe".' Brad imitated the finger quotes.

They grinned at each other at his reference from *The Castle*, an iconic Australian movie.

As they moved next door to Binalong, Brad pointed at the brickwork. 'Are you going to keep the paper decorations?'

Abigail winced to see that the artists had added another co-op poster to the wall, along with a petition. Thankfully the only signature was Patricia's.

She shook her head and shrugged, relieved to see that Brad found it amusing.

Abigail took a deep breath as they moved inside. 'Now, I've made a decision about the paintwork since we last spoke. I've decided to paint a couple of walls myself.' She laughed at the look of horror on the builder's face. 'Don't panic! I have painted many mural-type pieces. What I mean is that I won't need your guys to do the full number of coats on those areas. Just one coat should do it for me.'

'Okay. Well, we can go through that again later if you're still keen.'

'Oh, I'll be keen, don't you worry. So, good to go?'

'What about the upper floor?' Brad asked as he headed for the stairs.

Abigail faltered. 'Oh, let's go through that another time. Here's a spare set of keys but I'll need the whole place re-keyed for security when we're finished.'

Brad nodded. 'No problem.'

Abigail wondered how many times she would hear that phrase before the job was complete. She thought fondly of her dad – he had always maintained that as soon as someone said 'no problem' or 'she'll be right', it was time to double-check the details.

---

THE REAL ESTATE agents welcomed Abigail with open arms. It seemed to elevate you in their eyes when you bought a couple of high price properties – with another to sell – whether in workout gear or not. Abigail had chosen Miss Pearl Lustre's company, which had sold her the two Ferryman Road properties. She figured she now had a history with them, the agents knew the area and the company seemed to have a long list of potential buyers. 'Nothing's done until it's done,' Adam had always warned during business dealings, but Abigail was happy with her choice. Before she could say 'stilettos' they had pencilled in a date for the photographer and the auction. Abigail was keen to sell before the auction, despite the agent's firm opposition to the suggestion. She couldn't bear the thought of an auction day and all the stress it brought – strangers traipsing through her home, the hand-wringing moment waiting for bids, the last-minute decision-making as to whether to part with her home and a chunk of her life. She much preferred to be on the purchasing side.

After the formalities, Abigail almost skipped to the closest café. She always felt energised when plans started to take shape. When she and Luca had first scouted the area for their house, her love of history had immersed her in how the area had evolved. Emerald Hill, as South Melbourne had originally been called since its 1840s settlement, had always boasted many terraces and English-style squares. Its multicultural flavour derived from a strong migrant background. More recent property booms had seen the restoration of many original terrace homes, yet the area had maintained its friendly village feel. Abigail's efforts would always hold true to key architectural features, but she was eager to push the boundaries as well.

Her coffee arrived just as she finished texting Steph and Kate on the latest developments. Thumbs up and messages of 'let's catch up over dinner' quickly pinged back to her phone.

Magazine tear sheets, colour samples, descriptions, inspiring thoughts and wishes spilled out of Abigail's journal as she eased off the thick rubber band holding it all together. She started to reject pieces of paper and cross out some of the ideas now that she had reviewed them with Brad. She was grateful for the opportunity to discuss the changes with Steph; her friend would pull her back on track if needed. A shadow fell across her page.

Before she raised her eyes, Abigail knew who it was.

'There are too many decisions in life, aren't there?' the woman muttered, eerily mirroring her thoughts.

'Yes, I guess there are,' Abigail replied, although she noted the woman didn't seem concerned about her answer.

Her wrinkled face was upturned, her focus diverted from Abigail for a moment. She squinted at a leaf as it sailed and fluttered to the ground. Abigail noted that Molly had been right in that the woman didn't carry a handbag, or any shopping. Wisps of hair floated around her head like ashen fairy floss. Had she even noted the woman's hair before? Abigail couldn't recall.

Once the dying leaf stilled, the woman peered some inches above Abigail's head and continued as if Abigail hadn't spoken, 'But you know ...' She paused, piercing eyes flicking onto Abigail's face so quickly that Abigail shifted uncomfortably under their keenness. '... it is very important to resolve some issues before proceeding with others. To clear the mind, the conscience and all the questions that abound. Because if you don't, those worries and suspicions and opinions – yes, opinions – will sit like hard balls of concrete in your heart.'

Abigail frowned, unsure of what to do.

'But I think you know that,' the woman added before turning and shuffling back toward Ferryman Road.

---

I WONDERED *when Abby would start with the renovations and by the sound of the discussion downstairs, it seemed that Brad would be around a fair bit from now on. Interesting. Interesting because I have no idea how that will affect me, except that it will limit the opportunities for me to be with Abigail, to do what I am here to do.*

*I had assumed that I would come, tell her what I desperately needed to, then leave. That will be very tough on me, and I guess the reason why I haven't worried too much about the wasted days between our reunions. My earth life saw me eager to move on to the next big thing, whether it was a business deal or a sparkling party. But now, I want* time to stand still. It's something I can't control, and it will be so difficult for me to finally say goodbye to her. But then, perhaps we should get it over earlier than later, before I change my mind.

Can I change my mind? No, I was warned that I couldn't. Another thing I can't control.

The old woman is my answer, I realise that now. Her presence in my little world is constant, my exposure to her spirit somehow stronger and stronger; more so when she wanders the street below or nears Abby. The silly old crone is from my world, I know. She is my Fetch, my initial contact after the accident. She sends me messages to hurry up, sharp words that whisper around the walls. Will she always be my keeper? Maybe.

The thought that she would urge Abigail back to me had no sooner left my mind than I saw her toddle up the street, trailing Abigail's path. What I wouldn't give to break the ties to this building and follow her, to check what she is saying to my friend. I hope she doesn't frighten or upset her. Just politely nudge her in my direction is all I ask, and I'll do the rest.

My Irish impatience is fighting to get out. It would be easier if I was a Puck, a shape-shifter of some sort. I could remould to a dog and sit by Abigail's side, or become a tree and offer her shade from her troubles. And she'd never know. How do I even know such a thing is possible when I am still unsure how to communicate with her?

I sense she found Francesca's paintings. Naturally they hurt and puzzled her. I know Abby well enough to presume she's doing her research to find out more about the elusive F.

Lisi. *That can't be good. I want to talk to her before she goes any further on that quest. I need to soften the blow.*

*Solemn echoes of the past constantly drift around me. As I pull some from my memory, I realise they only serve to upset, not comfort. I let them go to settle elsewhere, like flakes in a shaken snowdome.*

# CHAPTER SEVENTEEN

THE EMAIL from Josh Mapleton jumped off the screen at Abigail as if it was highlighted in neon yellow. He had tracked 'F. Lisi (artist)' to a tagged photo from an art auction. There had been no references to recent artworks by her.

Abigail immediately flicked to the attachment, and found the physical proof she had wanted. It was a face she recognised, despite the stunning woman's glossy black hair having been cut to a stylish bob. Francesca had worn it full and wavy when she had managed Binalong – when Abigail and Luca had met her on one of their gallery visits, and then again when they had been invited to an exhibition. Abigail remembered asking Luca how the gallery had acquired their email address, and Luca had just shrugged. She also recalled finding them close together during the evening, 'discussing artworks', Luca had said. She had been hurt that he hadn't taken the time to discuss them with her. Then there was the time they had bumped into the woman at a local restaurant. Francesca had given her a warm hug, but even then Abigail had felt their surprise meeting had seemed forced. She slammed the computer lid closed.

Sometimes, Abigail had casually asked Luca about his whereabouts, his inability to answer his phone on occasion, but he had swatted her concerns away and smothered her in kisses. She hadn't pushed it, hadn't demanded an explanation, and certainly hadn't made any connection to this beautiful, personable woman. She had been blind.

She probed her memory, trying to find a reason why she hadn't been more suspicious when Francesca kept popping up. Abigail had seen her walking past the front of the house on several occasions but had presumed she was heading home from the gallery. What had she been doing there, hanging around the edges of their life?

The large windows reflected Abigail swaying with sadness, a glass of wine in her hand and heaviness in her heart. How stupid she had been. Nigella sensed her owner's unease and slumped at Abigail's feet, sharing the grey view of melancholy and misty rain.

Abigail turned, drawn to the portraits as if caught in their magnetic field. What had Luca been up to the night of the accident? How could he have left her alone with all these questions? Tears ran down her cheeks like little stinging rivers. She peered into her late husband's face, searching for answers and trying to ignore the mischievous glint in his eyes as he looked back. She had to accept that his lover had painted the portraits. She grabbed the canvases and ran up the hallway to the garage and quickly threw them back into the car boot. The corner of one of the frames dented as they tumbled face down onto the floor. Luca's smouldering eyes were blinded. Anger coursed through Abigail's stomach and chest like a volcano about to explode.

Flicking open the computer lid again, Abigail studied Francesca's photo.

'You weren't even a good artist,' Abigail enlightened her rival before firmly pressing the delete button. She knew it was a petty statement, but cleansing somehow. She was taking action; she was cancelling the woman out of her life and it had only taken the push of a button.

But in the back of her mind Abigail knew that wasn't true; cutting off a branch doesn't uproot the tree.

Nigella took herself off to her peaceful dog bed as Abigail jumped up and continued to stride around the table, then up and down the hallway, flopping into the lounge only to jump up and set off again. Her head spun with dates and questions but few answers.

Had her friends known? They would have welcomed the opportunity to rat out Luca, but then maybe this was the reason they hadn't accepted him. Apart from the money angle. Perhaps they just wanted to protect her. Surely Steph would have broached the sensitive subject with her at some point. Abigail reached for her phone to call Steph and ask her straight out what she had known. She set it back down on the table. Abigail had had assurances from Liam that Luca wasn't having an affair – had it been an affair or just a friendship that she had been excluded from?

Liam. Liam was her answer.

I FEEL *every one of the sparks flying from Abigail's body as she draws closer. It's dark and drizzling outside but her approach shines like a beacon. A woman on a mission, so I can only assume this is to be our showdown. I had wanted, like a self-righteous Holy Joe, to be the principal person in the conversation, the one explaining in my own way. But I am now concerned that Abigail will be calling the shots. Even at a distance I can tune in to her waves of determination, hear her heavy footsteps as they pound along the glistening pavement. Thank the heavens she has left her dog behind; I don't need any additional reactions to try to gauge.*

*Unaware that I have quickly readied the front door for her, she fumbles the key in the lock, storms inside, and starts up the stairs into my hushed and dusty world. Midway she stops, panting, possibly unsure. Understandable when you think of what she is, or isn't, expecting to find in this room. I'd like her to be somewhat calmer, though, for our encounter to go well. She shivers, perhaps with cold or anticipation, most likely from fear of the unknown. I flick on the downstairs light in welcome, but it makes her jump and clutch at her dripping coat.*

*Then slowly she continues to climb, and stumbles back into my 'life'.*

ABIGAIL HALTED IN THE DOORWAY, as if the decision to take one step over the threshold meant no return; that the frame would collapse and trap her inside forever. Somewhere in her agitated mind, she registered the rain beating against the window, knocking to come in. Perfect for a meeting with a ghost.

Determined to finish what she had come to do, she shrugged off her wet coat, letting it pool on the floor. Any hesitation lay with it as she moved further into the room. She let out the deep breath she didn't realise she had been holding. It caught for several long seconds before leaving her pursed lips. The minty fragrance was strong, beckoning her.

'You're here. I know you are.' Her jaw tensed. Her eyes darted around the walls as her body swayed in anticipation.

Suddenly she felt cornered, but knew she had to continue no matter what it took. 'Come on. Prove to me you're here. That's what you want, isn't it? Or are you trying to make me think I'm going mad, to make me sell up Binalong and ...'

'"Your feet will bring you where your heart is". Do you remember me quoting that Irish saying, Abby?'

Abigail started, unprepared for Liam to address her directly. But then what had she been expecting – sign language? Some secret spectral mindreading? She had no idea what she was even doing there, standing like a soggy idiot in a building she now feared she should have left behind years ago. Had she lost all sense of reason?

She could feel her heart beating strong and clear as she squared her shoulders and stood a few inches taller. She would decide later if it was the stupid or the courageous box she had ticked, but now she just had to get on with it.

'I am in no mood for Irish sayings, no matter who said them. Or is saying them.' Abigail took another step, challenging the darkness.

'Shh. Abby, please.'

Tears of frustration flooded Abigail's eyes as she frantically searched for a tissue. A shimmering weight pressed around her body. Sniffing, she ran her fingertips under her eyes and when they refocused, the light burned brightly. Liam stood in front of her. Her old – dead – friend, Liam.

'Oh. It *is* you,' she whispered.

He didn't reach for her but kept his hands clasped in front of him. The gap between them yawned with questions and possibilities.

'You're certainly not going mad. You're more beautiful than ever, but I need to talk to you. That's why I'm here.'

A pleading tone seeped through the lilting voice she remembered so well. She shook her head, wishing she had done a computer search on #afterlife #life_after_death #ghosts #otherworld. If she was honest with herself, she had planned to do just that but had been too scared of what she might discover. So here she was, with no research to lean on.

Liam and Abigail stood facing each other, a vignette forming under the light. All else in the room dissolved into the still, silent background. The scent of the discarded wet raincoat mingled with Liam's signature Tic Tacs, forming an eerie mix of mustiness and mint.

Abigail calmed and wondered if Liam could cast some kind of spell over her. She needed answers.

'And I need to talk to you. Was it you who left the

feather out front, and the ... the coin here? And, were you the butterfly on the day of the auction?'

Liam nodded. 'Ah, the butterfly wasn't me exactly, but I sent it.'

'Well, aren't you clever,' Abigail snapped. If there had been a spell, it was a weak one. 'And how was I supposed to know that; in fact, how am I supposed to know anything about this? How do I know you're real?'

Abigail reached out her hand, snatching it back quickly before it reached him. 'Well, you're not, are you.'

'Why are you so angry at me, Abby?'

His question was like running into a brick wall. Why was she angry? Shouldn't she be excited, full of wonder and expectation?

'Because I don't understand what's going on. I suspect I've been lied to, by Luca and by you, and I'm tired of it. Prove it, Liam. Have you seen Luca?'

Her eyes widened, a sudden thought creeping forward. Quietly, her voice catching on the words, she asked, 'Would you know it was my dad if you saw him over there, wherever it was you were heading before returning here? Can you bring them both back to me?' Abigail hadn't even been aware that she had been wondering such a thing until the questions were out of her mouth.

A tremor of anticipation rippled through her. How wonderful that would be, to hug her dad just one more time.

'Oh, if only I could fulfil your wish, Abby, to turn your beseeching look into a smile. You surely know I would if I could but it doesn't work like that.'

Liam paused, looking at his feet as he continued: 'Trust me, I do wish I was "real", as you say. Please accept that I'm here; not in a true body like yours, but in spirit. Would you like to sit down?'

'No, I don't want to damn well sit down. I want to know what is happening.'

Abigail edged to the wall and slid to the floor anyway, tucking her knees against her chest.

The light flickered and the air grew chill as Liam edged away. He propped against the window sill.

His eyes – such sad eyes that no longer sparkled, Abigail thought – roamed her face, seeming to search deep into her soul.

'Jesus Mary and Joseph, it's good to see you,' he said.

Abigail tapped her feet as she tried to summon random words from Molly and Jack's encounters, but she had yet to feel any great love or unforgettable sensation as they had. Her fingers plucked nervously at the buttons on her cardigan. Suddenly she was lost for words. Liam waited.

'Do you know people say that when a spirit steps forward from the afterlife, their energy is strong and loving?' Abigail demanded.

'No, I didn't know that, but I only feel love for you ...'

'Well I'm not feeling it, let me tell you.' Strained silence whispered around them as the words she had flung at him melted away.

The portraits of Luca hovered back into Abigail's mind, a reminder of why she had raced back to Binalong.

'So, Liam, seeing as we're both here, I have a question.'

Her voice dripped with sarcasm as she continued, but he didn't seem to care.

'I presume ghosts or spirits or whatever have memories, so you will remember I asked you about Luca. Where he was disappearing to, if he was having an affair?'

She held up her hand to halt his interruption.

'Who is Francesca, Liam? The beautiful dark-haired, apparently artistic Francesca?' Abigail hugged her knees, willing them to stop shaking from her simmering fear. It was clear who Francesca was, but she needed to hear Liam's answer.

'Abby, can I start at the beginning? So much has been left in tatters. I have so much to tell you and I'm scared ...'

'You're scared! Put your otherworldly feet in my shoes for a moment.'

'Of course. I know.' Liam held both palms up towards her as though warding off any further verbal assault. Then, in a quick turnaround, he looked at the floor and placed his hands casually in his pockets as if he didn't have a care in the world. It took Abigail back to when they were all together, all mates. Not young, not old, but all with a shared history and substance, she liked to believe. If the fireplace had suddenly sprung to life, offering warm flames, it would have been a cosy touch.

Liam had been the well-heeled, sexy Irishman with the quick wit and magnetic appeal. He had been successful at investing money, charming a crowd and gathering many and varied friends. His generosity was valued by those close to him, and by the many he had helped out during financially tough patches. They had had a lot of fun together. The fact that Abigail suspected he cared deeply for her on a romantic level had been pushed aside by her love for Luca.

She presumed Luca had pressured Liam to finance Grappa. But that wasn't what she had come to find out. She opened her mouth to speak, but Liam gave a small smile and said, 'I grew to be happy as a threesome, if you know what I mean. We were complete and I didn't want to lose that.'

Abigail saw an aching loneliness in his smile. 'But there were four, Liam. Francesca was there too.'

Liam shook his head. 'Not for me. She didn't hold a candle to you, Abby.'

Abby looked away and waited.

'Okay. We met Francesca, do you remember? Here, in Binalong. She was the manager.'

'I want to know what she was to Luca. She was nothing to me.' Abigail's voice faltered.

'I'll get to that.'

Abigail started with surprise. A searing arrow threatened to laser her heart into jagged pieces. Her throat constricted, forcing her to breathe shallowly. So, there had been a connection between F. Lisi Artist and Luca. Of course there was. She steadied herself; she had to know exactly what had transpired with Luca.

'How do I know you're going to tell me the truth?' accused Abigail, one half of her brain telling her how absurd it was that she was even conversing with a dead man. 'Why didn't Luca come back instead? Didn't he want to see me?'

'Abby ...'

'I mean, why didn't he visit me? In the middle of the night when I missed him most. Why didn't he lie beside me, whisper to me that everything would be all right, or at least share what had happened? I was left with so many questions.'

She choked back the words, gasping at what she was accepting. She started to stand up. 'What am I doing? I think I'm talking to a friend who died. A friend who lied to me while he was supposed to be looking out for me, but obviously loyalty to his mate was stronger.' As the lights dimmed she stumbled on, 'I put you in a box, Liam, with a white ribbon on it, and blew you away. You're from my past, not my present, and certainly not in my future.'

'Abigail,' Liam said firmly, a tone of desperation edging his words. 'Remember your friends' stories of wonderful, positive encounters with those who have passed, remember my signs to you? Don't you realise the old lady is here to keep an eye on me, and also to try to get us together? She's from where I am, or rather where I was heading to when I was given the option to come back and explain things to you.'

Abigail frowned, suddenly afraid. She had spoken with that woman several times, had seen her walking the streets like any other person. But then she seemed to have appeared out of nowhere. Had Nigella sensed something amiss?

She went back over Liam's words, her eyes narrowing with suspicion. 'How do you know about my conversations with Molly and Jack? Have you both been spying on me?'

Liam shook his head. 'No, you told me, remember? I'm stuck inside this building waiting for you, but sometimes I just seem to know things about you. Some things, not everything. It's like an emotion inside you that you're holding on to, that radiates, that I can read. I don't truly know how.'

Abigail paused, reluctant to let go of any explanation about Luca. She slumped down and heard Liam sigh with relief.

The rain had eased, and the room seemed to settle as if they were back on safe ground. The light brightened in response as Liam said, 'You asked the question so, I'm sorry, Abby, but Luca and Francesca did connect. They met at the gallery, then, um, for some time they did have an affair.' Liam had his face lowered as he spoke, but as he uttered the last confession his eyes searched Abigail's anguished face.

'I don't want to hurt you,' Liam pleaded.

'I feel like such a fool. The paintings ...' she whispered, pointing weakly toward next door, to the building that was to be her home.

Liam nodded. 'I sensed when you discovered them. She stayed next door on occasion as the cottage was owned by the same fellow who owned the gallery business and Binalong. I never saw the paintings but after Luca, well, after Luca and I died, I guess she moved on. I don't know what happened to her, Abby, I swear. She isn't my concern or my focus.'

'So all those times I thought he was away on business, he was really with her. Shit, having his portrait painted?' Abigail felt cold, not from the room's sudden uneasy atmosphere but from the escape of all the sincere hope she had held tucked inside. She shrugged. 'No. He was evidently doing more than just having his portrait painted. You all must have had a laugh. Silly Abby, still holding out for a long, happy life with Luca. Every time we visited Binalong it was so Luca could see her, wasn't it, not to plan our future.'

Without warning there was a scraping noise from the ground floor, a banging on the door and a call up the stairs. 'Hello? Hello? Just letting you know your front door is open. Is anyone there?'

As Liam flicked his eyes to the doorway, the overhead light downstairs went dead. Abigail jumped to her feet then looked behind her for Liam. He had gone. Dust was resettling on the floor, a shimmer of light pulsing then fading, a sudden stab of cold air. It had all happened so quickly. The room was as grey as a field mouse.

'Hello?' echoed from below.

Abigail bent for her coat, her body feeling heavy and sluggish.

As she headed for the stairs, Liam's voiced trailed after her. 'Abby. I'm not finished. Please come back soon.'

Whoever had been neighbourly and called up the stairs had gone by the time Abigail reached the front door. There was a pull to return to Liam, but exhaustion overtook her.

Abigail slipped her coat on and sank her hands deep into the pockets. She dragged her feet for home. For a moment she paused, and turned to seek out the rain-misted window. Could Liam really be behind it, and would Binalong always be a building of sad-eyed ghosts to her?

She watched the gleaming sidewalk slowly slide

beneath her, little spurts of water exploding around her feet. Unable to lift her head or her spirits, she only sensed when a couple sidestepped her onto the grass as they passed. The air smelt fresh as if the rain was determined to clean away everyone's sorrow, everyone's worries. She wished it luck.

As she reached her gate, Abigail looked to the heavens. As droplets silently dampened her face, she whispered, 'enough'. But she was uncertain to whom she was speaking as the darkness protected her against the outside world.

---

I WATCH *Abby trail away from me. When she turns and gazes back toward the building, I try to send some kind of connection, an invisible touch, but she doesn't appear to feel anything. It is puzzlement on her rain-kissed face, not longing. She doesn't return.*

*At least she acknowledged me, said my name. I know that she'll be back as soon as she can. Because you never plough a field by turning it over in your mind. She needs to know things, and once that happens or my time is up I will lose her again. The door will click closed on that small whisper of air that we share, but this time it will be forever. It will be a tiny sound to her, no doubt, but a deep tunnel into the unknown for me.*

# CHAPTER EIGHTEEN

AFTER A NIGHT of stabbing dreams and restless sleep, Abby lay in bed, gazing at the ceiling. She felt strangely displaced. She questioned if the whole incident with Liam had indeed been just another dream but her soggy shoes tossed against the wall told her otherwise. She admitted that Liam hadn't divulged anything she didn't already know or suspect, but was she prepared for what else he had to tell her? She wanted to confront him again as soon as possible, but the builders had taken up residence in Binalong to store their gear and to work on both buildings, so he was out of bounds during the day.

She threw herself like a woman possessed into preparing her house for the agent's photoshoot. It already had a pre-sale clean but Abigail went over all of the surfaces again, steely in her determination not to be dragged down by what Liam had confirmed. Luca's smile had covered a lie, but Liam had now brought her husband's behaviour into hard, sharp relief. She tugged at the few weeds in the front and back garden and scrubbed the water feature to within an inch of it disintegrating.

Nigella sensed the anger and distress her owner was trying to shake, pushing her nose under Abigail's elbow whenever she could get close. Apologising, Abigail shooed her away, unprepared for any show of sympathy.

Visions of Luca's portraits lying quietly in her dark car meshed with silly head conversations: Is that a body in your boot, ma'am? No officer, that's just my husband. He is dead, but has been for some time. And now he is deader than ever. Is that a word officer – deader?

She couldn't phone Steph or Kate to discuss it. What would she say? Oh, guess what. I've been chatting to Liam's ghost and he's had the most amazing things to say. No, not about heaven; he doesn't seem to know much about that. But he knows everything about Luca. And Francesca. Luca *and* Francesca.

The fact that Francesca had lived in the cottage, even briefly, was a momentary hiccup in her plans. Abigail was glad to be moving on from the house that she and Luca had called their home. She would make the new properties her own in every way, although she admitted a good sage cleanse might be on the agenda to rid them of their past. *Note to self: Google South Melbourne Eradicators of Bad Energy.* She doubted there would be any.

By the time the sales team arrived, the house was glistening like a diamond. Old habits seemed to die hard as Abigail hovered to brief the photographer on what shots she thought would be best. When they made it clear she wasn't needed, she leashed Nigella and headed out for a brisk walk, avoiding Ferryman Road.

Her last encounter with the spirit had both terrified and fascinated her. It certainly hadn't been the warm experience that both Molly and Jack had enjoyed, but it was still unforgettable. She would take their advice and open her mind to whatever was in front of her. As much as she didn't want to confront Liam after dark it seemed the only option, and in the meantime she would fill her daylight hours and her racing mind with moving on with her life.

She kept a sharp eye out for the old woman, unsure of how she would react if they crossed paths. The woman hadn't done anything wrong; in fact, she had been very pleasant and helpful on all occasions. But that wasn't the point. She was like an uninvited guest.

Abigail could smell the warmth on the breeze as it swirled, collecting leaves and petals on its journey. As it slowed, releasing its cache around Abigail's feet, a wave of loneliness settled over her. She reached up and wrenched the elastic band from her ponytail, shaking her hair loose. The heaviness in her heart remained. Fidgeting, she roughly tied her hair back up. Unbidden tears prickled her eyes, then spilled over onto her cheeks.

Nigella lifted her head and barked, her tail wagging like a metronome. She tugged on the leash toward a 4WD that had pulled over toward her. Abigail took a deep, wavering breath as she recognised Jack's car. The passenger window rolled down.

'Hi, Abigail, Nigella. How's ... Oh, are you okay?' In a flash Jack was out of the car and at Abigail's side.

She dipped her head and squeezed her eyes shut. Biting her bottom lip, she tried to regain some composure.

As Jack gently lifted strands of loose hair and tucked them behind her ear, he dipped slightly to study her face. He placed the palm of one hand against her back and took the leash from her limp hand.

'Sit, Nigella,' Abigail heard him whisper firmly. She sniffed, easing herself into his closeness. They stood for a minute, still and silent.

Abigail looked up into his handsome face, his customary lopsided grin replaced with a worried frown. He had dropped his hand back to his side, perhaps unsure of where he stood with her after their last time together. The gap between their bodies now seemed cavernous, the silence waiting to be filled. She wondered if he would be ready to gather her up again if needed.

'Oh, Jack. I'm sorry. I ...' Abigail sighed. She tried to smile, to make light of the feeling of a loss she was suffering to her core. The loss of what, exactly, she still couldn't put her finger on. Was it wasted years? She just knew that something tugged at her heart. The fact that he had stopped to check on her was welcome, that he had held her, wonderful.

'Do you want me to take you home? Nigella will fit in the back of the car. Or a cup of tea with Molly? I don't have any Turkish Delight on me.' He held his palms to the sky in mock exasperation.

A small smile escaped Abigail's lips, amused at his attempts to cheer her up. 'Do you mind if we take a walk? Unless I'm holding you up.'

'A walk is good. I was just on my way for a run around the lake, so luckily you didn't catch me after that sweaty episode.' He clicked the car's remote lock.

They strolled, Jack holding onto Nigella's leash. The dog tested him several times, but he gently tugged her to heel. 'I miss having a dog but it wouldn't be fair to a pet when I'm travelling so much. I'll have to get Molly to swap Smokey.'

Abigail knew he was trying to put her at ease, to pull her past whatever had caused her to cry in the street. Walking made it easier to put into words all the emotions that were flicking around in her stomach.

'The photographers are at the house getting shots for its sale.'

He nodded beside her, and she wondered if he was presuming that was why she was upset.

'That's not the problem though. I'm actually looking forward to starting something new. It's time to take my life into a new space,' she said emphatically.

'Right. Well, that's a good thing.'

She liked that he didn't pry, that he left it to her to explain what was going on, or not.

'What, or who, upset you then?' he asked in the next moment.

Abigail gave a little laugh, accepting that his questioning was okay with her too. It showed he cared.

She waited for a few heartbeats. 'Have you been married?' When she sensed a slight change in his pace, she hurried on. 'Gosh, I always seem to be ambushing you with questions, don't I? I'm sorry. The reason I ask is that, um,

I've just found out something about my husband. You remember I mentioned he died. Well, it seems that our marriage wasn't what I thought it was. I don't really want to go into the details, but imagine another woman in the mix. It has come as a humiliating confirmation of what I guess I already knew.'

'Heavens, you have had a few things to deal with lately, haven't you,' he replied.

Abigail caught a shimmer of concern in his tone. She hoped he wasn't avoiding her question, but it felt good to be sharing her thoughts with him. She waited.

They had veered into one of the area's small community parks, where a bench beckoned them to take a moment. Sparrows dipped and wove around the trimmed hedges, tiny daisies sprinkled the grass like confetti. A teenage couple, hand in hand, lingered along the path, probably hoping for some privacy. As Jack and Abigail sank onto the seat, they glanced at each other and wandered away.

He still seemed distracted so Abigail quietly took in his athletic body, the way it settled nicely into running shorts and a loose T-shirt. She could imagine him sweaty and breathless after the run and, even in her current agitated state, found the idea very inviting.

'Yes. I was married,' Jack replied, his full attention now back in the park with Abigail. 'Molly and I had a pretty average upbringing. You know, no money and even less love thrown around while our parents tried to find more income. They both worked long hours but any extra dollars went to the local pub takings. Then our brother, Sam – he was the middle child between Molly and me – got sick from some bacterial infection and he died.'

Jack chuffed out a sigh. 'It all happened so quickly and Mum and Dad went off the rails a bit. Understandable, I guess, but it was a rocky time for all of us. When I was about to finish school Molly and I went to live with our grandparents, and Grandpa applied for me to go on an exchange when I graduated. In hindsight I reckon he just wanted to get me away from the bad crowd I was starting to hang with. I wanted to stay to look out for Molly who was only young, but a scholarship came through and I went, fully funded, to England.'

He looked sideways at Abigail and grimaced. 'Sorry, tell me to stop if this is boring, but it does get to your question in a roundabout way.'

'No, please keep going,' Abigail said.

'I'm named after my grandpa. Jackson. My name's actually Jackson. Anyway, my exchange program was to work at a school down south near Redding. I'd never seen anything like the huge grounds the school sat in, or the little village nearby; it even had a deer park and seemed so gentle compared to my life back in Australia. I used to travel up to London whenever I could and had the best time.'

Abigail nodded. She had no problem imagining what he had got up to in London. Her boys had been the same at that age.

He caught it. 'I got up to a lot of mischief but pub crawls weren't part of it. I wasn't going to make the same mistake as my father. At the school, I was rostered to help with their sports training programs and I went on all the camps. It was great fun. I also had to help with the maintenance and that's where I learnt about gardens. Old Fred kept me on the straight and narrow whether it was snowing or during a ten-hour work day.' Jack smiled, his obvious affection for the old man still evident. 'He included me in his life which was quite a novelty to me. I mean, I knew I had my grandparents' love but they were so far away, back in Australia.'

Another similarity with Abigail's distance from Scott and James.

'As it happened, old Fred had a granddaughter called Britt who I grew, um, close to. I went back after my visa expired, we dated for a while and got married. We moved out here and I worked in a garden business while I studied landscape architecture, but Britt could never settle, particularly with the Australian heat. It wasn't all her fault, I admit – I had an inbuilt fear of not being successful, of having no money, so I studied and worked way beyond what my marriage could support.'

Abigail nodded. 'It was the norm in our household for Dad to be working late at the office most nights. It couldn't have been easy for Mum but they seemed to weather the separation.'

Abigail's privileged upbringing didn't seem relevant to their discussion after Jack had shared details about his family's hardships. Liam too had had stories about his family's troubles in Ireland, and she knew it had always been his mantra that 'This little leprechaun wasn't going to live in poverty'. Every day he had driven himself to achieve financial success. A little like Jack, but a far cry from her life.

Luca had always glossed over details of his youth which had been spent between Italy and Australia, before he finally stayed in Australia. Abigail's knowledge of his early days, and friendship groups, was patchy. He always shrugged off memories of that time, saying they played no part in the man he had become.

Jack shrugged. 'It was pretty brutal in the end with a lot of arguments and long silences. Britt found someone else who gave her ... whatever. She went back to England, married again and lives in Sweden, I heard.' He sighed then added, 'It broke my heart, as first loves often do. I guess I learnt to tread too carefully as I haven't married again, but I've had a few wonderful long-term relationships.

I bet you have, Abigail thought.

They both watched as a dad and his young boys passed with their football. The afternoon shadows grew longer, the day cooling. Nigella pulled on the lead to follow the family's playful labradoodle but was firmly called back by Jack.

'No children?' Abigail asked.

'No, luckily. Well maybe not luckily in that I would have liked to have had kids but, you know, no relationship was stable enough. I've put the past to rest in that regard.'

Abigail didn't push him but sensed what he was about to share.

'I would hate to think I couldn't afford them, or give them enough time, or both.' He laughed. 'Anyway, I have the effervescent Rose.'

They sat in comfortable silence for a moment. 'You always worry how divorce will affect your kids. But I know my boys had a childhood full of love and the care and attention of two parents. Martin, my first husband, and I never ever had huge arguments in front of them or used the boys as pawns during the separation. They were young men by the time I had to return to Australia for Mum. There was always a little ache in my chest that I'd done the wrong thing, that I wasn't hands-on enough. Twenty/twenty hind-sight, I guess.'

'What do the boys say?' Jack asked.

'They always assured me all was and is perfectly fine. I presumed they'd try living in Australia for a while but it didn't happen, so I visit them as often as I can. Martin's wife seems to, um, include them in her life.' Abigail squinted across the park, not welcoming any unanswered questions of her own into her thoughts. There simply wasn't enough room in there.

'It's nice that you and Molly are so close. Adam and I have a competitive relationship but we get on, I guess. Dad died some time ago but Mum has continued to keep Sydney on its toes.'

'You were close to your dad?'

Abigail caught a sliver of regret in the tone of Jack's question, as though he would have loved to have had a better relationship with his father. But she had to reply honestly. 'I would have loved for him to have known my boys. I miss him every day.'

They sat in easy silence, each with their own memories. 'Luca didn't have children.' A row of ants scurried along the pathway at their feet, parting as a solitary ant approached from the opposite direction. Abigail watched the line re-form. 'I wonder if he ever actually loved me.'

Her hand flicked her words away. 'Sorry. I'm just a sad sack today. I didn't mean to actually say that aloud.' She was embarrassed that the words had escaped her thoughts as to why Luca had felt the need to have another person in his life when he had her. Particularly when she was sitting with Jack.

Jack turned to Abigail, searching her face. 'But you don't have to have been married to be cheated on, deceived or left behind. I think any relationship, no matter how long it has been going or whether it's between siblings, lovers or friends, deserves complete honesty.'

Abigail scraped at a splinter on the seat. 'I just feel like it's all happening again. He left me when he died and I grew stronger. But now I know about his affair with someone I'd met. I feel … oh, I don't know.'

'You feel deceived and left in the dark. I get it,' Jack said.

Abigail heard Jack's own loss revisited and reflected in those words. She couldn't believe she had shared so much with him.

'Thank you, Jack. I'm glad you stopped for me. I guess I'd better get back to the house,' she said, slowly rising.

He glanced at his watch. 'Sorry, that was all a bit deep and meaningful on my part. I have to get back too. I have a late flight to Sydney.'

They wandered back to Jack's car, glancing into the various homes they passed and commenting on the gardens. They each pointed out features they were drawn to and Jack appraised the layouts and plants. It was a pleasant diversion but she wondered if he was still thinking about their conversation, as she was.

'Well, I'll definitely need your input when I do my landscaping,' Abigail said. 'Particularly irrigation systems.'

Jack returned her smile. 'I might know a lot about landscaping but that doesn't amount to a hill of beans, or mulch, if you're not comfortable in that space. Whatever it is you're creating has got to come from your own heart.'

'That is so true.' Abigail nodded.

'I admire you. You're selling your place and moving on in your own way. Good for you.'

'That's nice of you to say so,' Abigail replied.

Jack kissed her cheek. 'Are you okay?'

'Of course,' Abigail said with a confidence she didn't feel. She waved goodbye, putting on as cheery a face as possible, then headed home to her very clean, and silent, house.

---

AS ABIGAIL PREPARED Nigella's dinner, she thought about Jack's history and his comments about family.

Adam had often called out Abigail for being too emotionally invested in issues. She knew he saw her reactions and goals as being weak and impulsive, the opposite to the ruthlessness he often bared. Usually she was content with this softer side of her character but such emotional upheaval took its toll. Her energy had been screwed tightly into a ball and tossed away, leaving her totally drained. After Luca had died, she had spent her days curled on the couch or asleep into the late morning. Nigella hadn't left her side, only nudging her awake when her dinnertime had passed. Then, surprisingly, Adam had arrived on her doorstep one day, under their mother's instructions, to take her back to the Arpels enclave in Sydney. Audrey had broken Abigail's lethargy by dragging her daughter out for long walks along Sydney's coastal tracks with rousing calls to 'Breathe in the salt air, Abby. It doesn't do anybody any good to wallow.'

That's what she needed to do again, to welcome the outside world back into her own. Otherwise Luca would continue to control her, even from the grave.

When her mobile pinged with a message, she presumed it would be Kate confirming their lunch date for the following weekend, or Steph announcing her return from Bali. Instead, Abigail was surprised to see Jack's contact number and quickly read his text.

*To prove you're not the only one with local dining knowledge (!) how about we try the new restaurant in Cardigan Place. This Saturday night? I'll pick you up at 7. Jack.*

Abigail smiled. She had told herself she needed to revisit Liam, but it would have to wait. Jack was proving to be a very warm and perceptive man and she wanted to focus on him.

# CHAPTER NINETEEN

'NOW I CAN'T EAT TOO much because I'm going out for dinner,' Abigail teased. 'Although that little salted caramel macaron does look delicious.' It reminded her of the sweet tooth Jack seemed to indulge.

She had changed her lunch date with Kate to a morning coffee catch-up. They met at Swimmers, one of the old bayside bathing pavilions that had been converted to quaint tearooms. The café had lowered its plastic walls to keep out the stiff onshore breeze but still allow views of the sparkling water. Although it was still too cool for swimming, Port Phillip Bay always came up trumps with skimming yachts, kite surfers and a beautiful expanse of beach. The friends were now ensconced at a tiny table, ready for updates on each other's busy days.

'Whoa,' Kate exclaimed at the mention of a dinner date. 'I expected lots of news about the renovations, not about your love life. Do tell!'

Abigail laughed, rather pleased to discuss Jack with

someone other than his sister. 'I wouldn't go so far as to say it's my love life, but he's nice. He's my new neighbour-to-be. Actually no, that's not right either. He is staying with his sister Molly, next to my new house. He lives in Sydney.'

'Where in Sydney?'

Abigail paused. 'I don't know. I haven't asked him.'

'Got a photo?'

Abigail laughed. 'Of course I don't have a photo.'

'Well, who does he work for? I'll google him or go on LinkedIn. I have to vet all new romantic possibilities, you know.'

'No, you don't, you stalker. And he's not a romantic possibility. We just connected. That's all. And trust me, he's seen me at my worst possible moments – abusing him for flooding my yard, having a fall and wrenching my knee like an old lady ...'

Kate held up her hand. 'No! Once you reach a mature age you need to say you fell over, not had a fall. Old people have falls.'

Abigail continued ticking off her embarrassing moments '... rabbiting on about ghosts ...'

'What ghosts? That's the second time recently you've mentioned something about being haunted. Is this Luca?'

'No, not Luca.' Abigail could honestly reply, albeit a little sadly, that it wasn't Luca. Wouldn't she just love to confront her late husband on several issues he had lied about. But she wasn't ready to talk to Kate about her encounters with Liam; her friend was way too practical to accept anything remotely otherworldly. But then, Abigail had to admit that had also been the case with her until recently.

One thing Abigail did know was that mentioning Jack had opened Pandora's box, so Kate's attention could easily be diverted away from ghost stories.

'His name is Jack. He's a landscape architect and is in Melbourne working on some business park development. Something to do with integrating green space with employee needs, both around the acreage and across the rooftops of the office buildings – to quote.'

Kate put on her bored face while motioning for her friend to get to his more interesting points.

'His younger sister, Molly, lives next door, as I said. She's married to Tom who is away a lot, you know fly in/fly out, so I haven't met him yet. And they have a teenage daughter called Rose whom I haven't met either, but I get the impression she's a bit of a handful. They're very nice and have been so helpful. I'm lucky to have such friendly neighbours.'

'Oh, I don't know. Have they met Nigella yet?'

'Kate, Nigella is a gorgeous dog. A little scatty some-times but Jack has met her and it's mutual admiration.'

'Well, I expect a full texted report tomorrow. Not too early, just in case you two need to sleep in,' Kate said with a wicked glint in her eye.

'There will be none of that,' Abigail scoffed. 'Not at my age.' She felt a little kick in her heart as she voiced one of her fears. She had met very few single or available men and certainly hadn't opened up to any the way she had to Jack. That had to mean something, didn't it?

'I'll pretend you didn't say that. You know, Freddie has often said we both look pretty good for seniors, and how nice he thinks you are so you haven't lost it, but he's mine. Anyway, how are the building works coming along? I do hope you will be including one of your beautiful murals somewhere.'

'Yes, I will be. Well, I'm pretty sure I will be. The For Sale board goes up on my house any day and I'll move into number sixty-four as soon as I can. The renovations won't take long, Brad assures me.'

'You can't keep calling it number sixty-four. That sounds like a robot. It needs a proper estate name.'

'You're right, but what? I'd been so caught up in Binalong that I didn't even think of a name for my new home.'

'You know I say this with love in my heart.' Kate gave her a steady, girlfriend-type look as she placed her palm on her chest and continued, 'Grappa is no longer. It was Luca's bar, not your future now. If you rent the property out, the building stays as Binalong; if you open a business yourself, then that's another name you'll have to conjure up. Binalong is just bricks and mortar. But your new home definitely needs a name too. How about The Mews or Abigail's Acreage or ...'

Kate held up her hands as Abigail grimaced. 'What's that for? You should be excited about what's ahead for you. A whole new start. And a man who, hopefully, won't prune your ideas, if you'll excuse the horticultural pun.'

Abigail laughed. 'More like a friend who will give me space to grow.'

'Now I'm going to groan,' Kate said. 'But let's face it,

Luca wasn't the most generous person at giving you free rein, was he.' It was a statement, not a question.

'He was always the life of the party though,' Abigail replied weakly.

'So long as he was the centre of it, dear friend.' Kate reached across and patted Abigail's hand. 'You became a shadow of your former confident self. I always felt you were trying to match him with enthusiasm when it wasn't always your "thing". And I am confident I can say that to you now that enough time has passed. It's not as though he can come back, is it.'

Abigail felt chilly fingers run down her body.

Misreading the reason for Abigail's silence, Kate ploughed on. 'You have your own strengths and talents and I just don't think he appreciated that. But enough said. Sorry, Abby. Was that mean? You can have some of my pecan slice if you like, to make up for my inane comment.'

Abigail declined the peace offering. 'I guess it's all so clear in hindsight. I mean, I know what you're saying, but I loved him and was entirely caught up in our plans. They were ours, definitely.'

It had been Luca's overwhelming confidence that had attracted Abigail. She had loved his bravado, his swagger, his ability to talk to anyone, his open laugh and robust love-making. She had chosen to see his charm rather than his control. As she had with Martin.

If it was true that girls marry men similar to their father, then something had gone wrong with her choices. She would always remember her father's charm as well as his inclusiveness of everyone he met. Sometimes it flew in the opposite direction to how Audrey seemed to view acquaintances. He would say, 'Abby, it is often those you meet fleetingly who leave the greatest impact. Always look beyond the head table.' She had liked that.

Abigail continued. 'I was just kept in the dark about some things – well, many things. I didn't know he was so focused on money for a start. Did you know he tried to get crowd funding for Grappa?'

'Yes,' Kate said, not making eye contact with Abigail.

'He didn't ask you guys, did he?'

When Kate gave a little nod, Abigail gasped. She couldn't believe she had missed another red flag about her husband's activities.

'But we didn't. Couldn't, really, and it doesn't matter one little bit now. Don't look so mortified.'

'But ...'

Kate held up her hand. 'I just know that my friend Abby is the kindest person I've ever met, and my best friend. I would have discussed it with you if we had thought about being involved, or if Luca had persevered.'

'I hope so,' Abigail said. She was grateful for the escalating buzz of customers' voices and the clattering of dishes that dulled their conversation to those sitting nearby.

Kate nodded. 'I'm not going to add my two bobs' worth into what you're doing with your purchases, but it's not through lack of interest. I'm good at history, not the future, so I will leave such creative endeavours in your and Steph's capable hands. I just can't wait to see how it all steams ahead. What fun.'

Abigail sat for a moment, warmed by Kate's honest,

supportive words. Again, she wondered how many others had protected her from Luca.

'And you know that I am free to meet Mr Jack Whatever as soon as possible. Oh, here's Maisie,' Kate cried.

'Surprise, Abby,' called the girl with the Cameron Diaz smile. Abigail jumped out of her seat as Kate and Freddie's daughter held out her arms for a heartfelt embrace. Abigail hadn't seen her goddaughter in months. She quickly pulled across an extra chair to squeeze her onto their table.

The threesome spent another hour together, with Maisie telling Abigail about her wedding plans and Abigail sharing news of her sons in London, although she suspected Maisie knew more about their activities than she did. Abigail was wired with caffeine and laughter by the time she hugged them both goodbye, ignoring the cheeky wink Kate had given her.

ABIGAIL HAD BEEN ready for over an hour, nervously filling in time until the front doorbell rang. She was excited about the evening ahead but unsure of exactly what to expect. She wasn't aware of the restaurant's vibe so she'd chosen a tailored olive-green Cèline pantsuit featuring a low-buttoning jacket, heels and clutch which were stylish, but not too dressy. She had straightened her hair to curve around her face and, as usual, had kept her makeup understated. She was surprised by her desire to make a good impression.

While she waited for Jack, Abigail fiddled with the

delicate long chain she was wearing, the gold end-tassel the only evidence of its 1920s origins. Abigail's main obsession had always been Art Deco jewellery; her wedding ring, now relegated to a jewellery box upstairs, had been an Art Deco-style band of faceted diamonds and sapphires. She had an enviable collection, but for Abigail and fellow historian Kate, the appeal of that era had always been that it represented more freedom for women after the war; the opportunity to let loose in fashion. Audrey had never understood this preference and had many of her jewellery pieces remade in the ostentatious styles of the 80s. Abigail had kept her opinions to herself but had been disappointed to see her father's gifts handled with such a lack of sentiment by her mother.

There was only one item she had asked Audrey to keep aside for her – a pair of elongated onyx and platinum earrings. Her mother had been surprised as they were nowhere near the value of her other pieces. But they had been a wedding anniversary gift from Allan, made even more special to Abigail because her father had asked her to accompany him to the jeweller to help choose his present. Luckily they would be too low-key for Georgia so Abigail presumed they were still in Audrey's safe.

Nigella announced Jack's arrival with a friendly bark from the backyard, just as the doorbell rang. When Abigail swung open the front door she was confronted by a wall of foliage. Closer inspection showed it to be a stunning white camellia in a large grey-washed pot.

Jack popped his head around the glossy greenery. 'It's a camellia,' he announced, emerging into the downlight.

Abigail laughed. 'I do recognise camellias. It's beautiful.'

She ran her eye over Jack as he squatted and carefully shuffled the pot into the corner. He looked so handsome in a pair of deep navy trousers and loose taupe-coloured shirt. Simple and classic. Not a speck of dirt had made it onto his clothes, but she did notice a grey smudge on his cheek. She resisted the urge to reach out and brush it away.

Jack ripped off his gardening gloves and continued without taking a breath. 'I said to Molly, "Abby doesn't need a large plant. She's moving soon and it will only be another thing to have to load." Then she says to me, "Well you'll just have to help her, won't you, brother."'

He rubbed his hands together and sent Abigail a huge beaming smile, then leant in to kiss her cheek.

She caught the scent of his cologne, a sexy mix of citrus and cinnamon. 'Did you want to wash your hands?' She pointed to the powder room.

Abigail turned and smiled as Jack returned, hoping her eyes carried the warmth she was feeling. 'Thanks again.'

'No problem, and you look great, Abby. Are you ready to go? I'm starving.'

'So am I,' she replied, noting he called her Abby.

Jack held the door as she went through. 'Good. I like a girl with an appetite.'

Her dad would have been pleased with both the action and the observation.

Spirit Thai was lively, even though it was early by Melbourne's dining standards. Abigail hoped it didn't have a double-seating policy as many restaurants seemed to; she wanted to linger over good food with a handsome man. The restaurant had received positive reviews in the gourmet magazines, so it was the latest place to dine. The brick façade had survived the old building's upgrade with modern glass windows spilling the restaurant's light and atmosphere onto the sidewalk. The restaurant interior was neutral and sparse, except for a solitary large abstract painting. Abigail gazed at its composition whilst waiting for their table, realising that if you lost focus, the kaleidoscope of silver, green and gold colours morphed into a large leaf made up of hundreds of small leaves. She loved it.

Their square table sat alongside the front window. Abigail pondered their reflection as Jack ordered a beer and glass of champagne from the prompt waiter. Did they look like a couple on a date or good friends catching up? Did it matter? After all, she did consider Jack to be a friend and the fact that he liked to eat out was a definite bonus. She had already decided to keep the conversation light with no reference to past loves or current visiting spirits. It would be her opportunity to find out a little more about Jackson Mattingley.

'I hope I didn't spook you out with all that strange talk about butterflies at funerals,' he said, raising his beer.

Both siblings had a way of coming straight to the point, and it seemed that Jack could read her mind yet say what he wanted to anyway. Abigail held his gaze over the lip of her glass. Her champagne tasted cold and dry, just as she liked it, and she settled in for a fun evening. But on her terms.

'Not at all. I'm so glad you chose this place, Jack. I love

Asian food, or is it Asian fusion? I never know. What are you thinking of trying?'

A slow smirk crept across Jack's face as he turned his attention to the menu, as if to say, 'Okay, you won that round but the subject isn't closed.'

They shared a small plate of Thai street food pork skewers, minced chicken and tamarind dumplings with pomelo salad, and chatted about their travels.

'I've not been to Vietnam or Cambodia, I'm ashamed to say, but my friends say they're amazing,' Abigail said.

'Absolutely, but it's been a very long time since I was in Southeast Asia,' Jack admitted. 'I travelled with a close mate, and I don't remember much about it. Too much sun and Bin Tan, or was that Bali? But I have visited many Asian and Indonesian cities, both as a reckless young lout and more recently for work.'

He stopped as if embarrassed by his passion for adventure and travel, gave a laugh and raised his beer in a toast. 'Here's to Old Fred who set me on my way in the first place, may he rest in peace. Now there is someone I'd like to visit me back on planet Earth.' Jack glanced at Abigail for her reaction.

'Are you making fun of me?' she probed.

'No, of course not. I guess ...' He paused as if searching for the right words. 'I guess what I'm saying is that I think you should go with the flow and accept what is being put in front of you. Although I am still somewhat sceptical about the whole visiting spirit thing, I am a great believer in the universe looking after you.'

'It sounds like you've tried walking in my shoes for a

moment.' Abigail couldn't help but feel touched that he had revisited their conversation and her confession.

Jack nodded. 'I have. And I'm grateful that your story reminded me of my own experience and how I felt. God, I sound like Molly.'

As their bottle of Riesling arrived and was poured, Abigail tried to analyse the new friend sitting opposite her. Here was a man who could discuss wine, gardens and different parts of the world with charisma and knowledge, yet never let go of his past. He seemed proud of his troubled childhood in that he had grown beyond it. He had enjoyed an alternative life thanks to his grandfather and an old gardener, when others had let him down. He had stayed dedicated to his remaining family. He was a mixture of so many endearing qualities. Abigail's imagination lingered on Jack's unsettled youth, the hint of his wild side lighting a spark in the base of her stomach.

She wondered if that was where Rose inherited her apparent spirit. 'I'm looking forward to meeting Tom and Rose.'

Jack raised his eyebrows. 'Hopefully Rose does come home to spend time with them during the holidays. I'm not letting out any family secrets, but Molly is a bit worried about who Rose is spending a lot of her time with. On a couple of occasions she hasn't been at a girl-friend's house as she had told the school's boarding house.'

'Would she speak with you if she has a problem?'

'I'm sure she would if she was in serious trouble, but who knows. I hope so. The last time I dared to ask if everything was okay she said she could just use a little under-standing in her life. I'm not too sure what that means.'

'Ouch,' Abigail said, wincing. She was certain that Jack would be there for his niece in an instant.

'I reckon you would have been good at sitting down with your young boys, trying to get to the bottom of their troubles,' Jack said.

'Being nosy you mean?' Abigail replied, but the warmth in Jack's eyes told her he wasn't being flippant. 'I'm sure that's what they thought I was doing. I'll always be there for them that's for sure.'

They both turned their attention back to their meals.

'This crab curry is amazing. What were these again?' Jack asked.

Abigail glanced at his bowl. 'Betel leaves. I did a Thai cooking class once,' she explained. 'It was part of a restaurant in Bangkok called the Blue Elephant.'

Abigail omitted the part about her parents spoiling her and Kate with the trip for her birthday, plus accommodation at a private hotel called The Eugenia while they were there. The scent of lavender on linen still took her back to that divine stay, one that she would appreciate forever.

She pressed on, 'It was a half-day cooking class and started with a trip to the local morning market to buy all the fresh herbs, spices and vegetables needed, including your betel leaves. My family came over a few days later and we went to dinner at the Blue Elephant restaurant. It's in this gorgeous Colonial-style building with traditional Thai décor. But I'm saying all this because I ate the Massaman lamb and it came in a pot just like this.' Abigail pointed at

her half-eaten curry. 'And this is just as mouth-watering let
me tell you.'

Jack took a deep breath of the lingering aroma, closing
his eyes with delight. Abigail ran her eyes over his handsome face.

'Here, you must try some.' Abigail pushed the steaming
pot a few inches across the table. Jack forked a piece of
lamb and lifted it to his waiting mouth, but not before a
little of the chocolate brown sauce splattered on the white
tablecloth. Abigail quickly moved a small rice bowl over the
top of the stain as Jack winked his approval.

The hours quickly passed, the conversation and
laughter coming easily between them. Abigail noticed that
Jack steered the conversation away from the personal.
Perhaps he didn't want to go over old ground more than he
already had – she sensed it hadn't come easily to him. She
soon realised how entertaining he was, his stories regularly
punctuated by wide descriptive hand gestures and deep
throaty laughter.

The restaurant started to clear of diners while waiters
hovered, keen to finish the evening service. Jack settled the
bill then moved to hold the door open for Abigail. She
paused in front of the leaf artwork.

'I love that painting, don't you? The more you take the
time to look at it, the more you see.'

Jack smiled, looking deep into her eyes. 'Isn't that the
way with so many of life's treasures,' he replied.

Abigail gave an involuntary shiver as the cool night
breeze whistled along the village street, but the warmth of
his comment had radiated down to her heart. Jack put his

arm around her, cupped her shoulder and gently pulled her closer as they walked to his car. Abigail leant into his snug, firm body, savouring the contact. Neither was anxious to fill the time with words.

The sensor lamp flicked on as they approached Abigail's front door, as if telling the world they had arrived and that Abigail's heart was keeping pace with the speed of light. It had been a long time since she had been taken home after a date and she had no idea what to do.

She turned to Jack and looked into his dancing eyes. 'So, what's on for tomorrow? I mean ... what are you doing?'

Jack grinned as he put his arms firmly around her. His lips brushed her own as he murmured, 'I have to go into the office first thing for a meeting. I missed my flight down and the scheduled meeting yesterday, so tomorrow it is.'

'Even though it's Sunday?'

He nodded. 'Even though it's Sunday.'

Searching her face, Jack lowered his lips onto hers once again and gently kissed her. He eased her to him. Abigail was unable to resist linking her hands behind his neck and returning the kiss. She felt his mouth curl into a smile and opened her eyes to find him openly studying her.

With one easy touch he moved his thumb slowly across her lips. 'I hope you play golf as well as you kiss,' he murmured.

Somewhere in the background Nigella was giving short, sharp barks, alerting the neighbours to activity in her front yard.

'What a lovely night. A great restaurant and even better company.'

She held her hands against his chest, felt his speeding heart, and dropped them to innocently search for her key. 'It was. Thank you, Jack.' She paused before adding, 'I'll have to cook you that curry from a time when my life was so much simpler. Gosh, where did that come from?'

'I look forward to that and I'll see you soon,' he said, the accompanying grin promising so much more.

# CHAPTER TWENTY

WORKERS' trucks continued to occupy several of the parking spaces in Ferryman Road. Abigail winced whenever she saw them and made a note to drop a letter of apology into all of her neighbours' letterboxes. Some houses had their own narrow driveways but most residents had to park on the street with a permit. Abigail and Brad had accessed the council's Tradespersons Permits for the duration of the renovation, but she still felt guilty if her neighbours couldn't park near their own homes.

She pulled into a spot a few hundred metres away and walked back, stopping in her tracks at Molly and Tom's front fence. Someone had been busy. In no time their front garden had been nearly transformed from messy and overgrown. The courtyard had been planted out with pretty layers of emerald-green and silver shrubs that fell away gently to a smattering of cottage plants. The crushed stone path was still being perfected but the meandering outline was there, promising to link it all together.

Additional large pots of flowering shrubs had been added to Molly's high-tea nook at the end of their deck. She felt a little envious of how the siblings' green thumbs had transformed the garden into a warm, welcoming entrance to the home.

Along Abigail's boundary were at least twenty smaller neutral pots, each holding hints of spring bulbs on the rise. They were lined up as if waiting to be adopted.

She tore her eyes away and rushed to her meeting with Steph. 'Well, look at you. Don't you look relaxed and Bali-fied,' Abigail said.

'I have to admit it was one of my more relaxing work ventures,' Steph said, bringing her hands together in thanks. 'I have the contract to do the interiors for the spa and also the resort's upgrades early next year. So, I'm cele-brating!'

The friends hugged, Abigail searching Steph's face as she pulled back. 'Don't let me hold you up if you need to get back to it. My little endeavour here is nowhere near as grand or exciting as an international resort.'

'Don't be silly, I can't wait to see your progress. I don't suppose your hunky neighbour is due to visit, is he?' Steph started up the path to No. 64's door.

It had been on the tip of Abigail's tongue to share news of their dinner together and of Jack's landscaping expertise, but the moment passed. With guilt about her hesitation still hovering, she turned the key and entered her space, her future.

'Kate said I should give my new home a name. Any suggestions?' she asked, ushering Steph inside.

'Oh, I agree. But that should come last, don't you think, after it has its new character and Abby stamp.' She glanced sideways at Abigail. 'I don't suppose Portraits from the Past is in the running?'

Abigail's response was a hearty laugh and a wagging finger.

'Don't even go there, Steph. Lord knows I've been trying to avoid it. I have done a bit of digging though, and it turns out F. Lisi is Francesca Lisi who used to manage Binalong. Do you remember her from when we used to go to exhibitions? Long, dark hair, very attractive.'

'Oh?' Steph suddenly stopped inspecting the carpet swatch Brad had left. Not making eye contact with Abigail, she wandered down the hallway, flicking through the colours.

'What is it?' Abigail followed closely on her friend's heels. She felt out of the loop and slightly annoyed that everyone seemed to know something about Luca. Hopefully she was mistaken this time.

'Nothing,' Steph mumbled, but she had to continue when she saw Abigail resolutely glued to the spot with hands on hips. 'It might not have been her, but I do remember seeing Luca and a woman. I thought she did look familiar at the time but I couldn't place her, though now you mention it ... maybe. They were standing on a corner in Prahran.' She shrugged, trying to downplay her confession.

'And yet you remember seeing them. Why didn't you ever mention it?'

'Abby. It was nothing. How often do you catch up with a friend, male or female? I didn't recognise her from Binalong, only that I thought she looked familiar. They were just chatting and by the time I'd decided to go and say hi the lights had changed and they'd moved on. Luca didn't see me. Anyway, I'm not sure. It was so long ago.'

The excitement of touring Abigail's properties had been squashed, a slight tension hanging over the two women like a thin veil of duplicity. Brad suddenly materialised and Abigail wondered if he had overheard their conversation. They rapidly ticked off choices on light fittings, doorknobs and fireplace surrounds.

'This is much better,' Steph said as they reached the upper level. The mini attic's wall, behind which they had found Luca's portraits, had been taken out, with the open space now ready for the addition of the visitors' amenities. Just that one change had brightened Abigail's mood when she had seen it, as if another link in a rusty chain had been dismantled.

The friends kept any conversation focused on Brad and the renovations.

As they headed next door to Binalong, Steph looked sideways at Abigail, saying, 'Abby, Jane said she left a message for you, to catch up for dinner, but hasn't heard back. You're not still mad at them, are you, after Don Carmelo's?'

Abigail had seen the message, ignored it then had forgotten about it. 'No. I've just got so much on at the moment, you know? Keeping the house looking amazing, staying on top of the renovations as well as everything else.' They both knew she referred to the mystery of the paintings. 'And I'm due to head to Sydney soon too, for some fundraiser Audrey has organised. When I'm back from that we'll do it, yes?'

'Okay. But don't isolate yourself, Abby. That's not good for you or your friendships.'

Abigail turned the conversation back to Binalong, mentioning the mural she had planned for the front room.

'It will still depend on an idea which had been smouldering at the back of my mind, but I think it might all come together,' she said.

Steph clapped her hands in approval. 'I swear you don't need my input at all.'

Abigail hoped her reaction was genuine and not an effort to be agreeable after their terse conversation about Luca.

Brad shuffled in behind them with the plans, obviously keen to show off the progress.

'Hasn't this staircase come up well?' he said.

Steph inspected the builder's test on the railing woodwork. 'It will be beautiful,' she said to the beaming builder.

Abigail started to chatter to cover her nervousness as they headed up the stairs. 'Because of the mural downstairs I've asked Brad just to do an undercoat on the walls.'

'Damn,' Brad exclaimed as they reached the landing. 'There's that breeze again. We can't locate it.'

'Don't worry about it,' Abigail said, flicking her eyes around.

Brad gave her a questioning look. 'No, we have to find out if there's a vent or a hole somewhere. I'll have the chimneys rechecked, so something might come to light then.'

They wandered single file to the front room, Abigail bringing up the rear.

'No problems with this front room?' she asked casually. She could pick up the peppermint scent again and feel a slight breeze, but not the cold air that accompanied Liam. The others didn't seem to register the scent.

'No problem at all. There's a bit of work to be done on all the windows but no water damage anywhere. It's better than I expected.'

'This room is delightful, Abby.' Steph held out her arms as if she was on the prow of the Titanic. 'Any new ideas for its use?'

Abigail had been toying with an idea, one that was taking form and making her so excited with its potential. How she was going to get rid of its ghostly lodger, she had no clue about though.

'Nothing concrete. Okay, I think that's it for the moment.' She scurried from the room, very aware of Liam's presence in the far corner. She could never say how she knew he was there, only that he was. Which was odd when she hadn't been aware of his presence on auction day – perhaps she was becoming more attuned to the unknown as Molly and Jack had. It unnerved yet excited her all at the same time, as if she didn't want to know an answer to something, but would die if she didn't find out. Which was probably not a good comparison when liaising with a ghost, but at no stage had she felt unsafe in Liam's presence.

As they stepped out onto the footpath, Steph nearly collided with a passer-by. 'Oh, I'm sorry,' she apologised, reaching to steady the old woman.

'I'm fine, dear,' the woman said as she quickly slid out of reach. She looked directly at Abigail. 'My time hasn't run out *just yet.*'

Abigail didn't miss the emphasis on the last two words, as she ushered Brad and Steph away from the entrance.

'You two go on ahead. I won't be a minute,' Abigail said once the woman had strolled away.

Abigail ran up the stairs and along to the front room. She felt surprisingly determined and calm; pleased to finally be taking steps to uncover what Liam was about. She stood in the doorway, confident as she addressed the empty, misty room. She knew he was there.

'I'll be back this evening. After the builders have left. And I expect a lot of answers.'

Her words echoed behind her as she dashed back down the stairs.

---

OKAY, *I'm ready, more than ready. If nothing good comes from her return, and how can it, at least I'll be with her again. I'll have my chance to say I'm sorry.*

*I know she can't be mine, but it still tears my heart to pieces to see her with the fellow down the street. Her eyes light up when she approaches his house. Even her wretched dog seems to like him. A love between Abigail and me isn't to be, not on Earth and certainly not now.*

*Abby once loved me; as a friend, I know, but even that thin thread meant so much. It's hard to be in love with your best mate's wife, particularly when you know he is deceiving* her. It wasn't hard to work that one out. Luca always had a sense of ownership of people, whether it was his relatives or his friends, his lovers or his wife.

Initially, I feared he had been attracted to Abby for her money, even though she is the last person to flaunt her wealth. But then when I saw them being married, I put that suspicion aside; they seemed so much in love.

'Oh, Liam,' Abby had laughed. 'Luca has gone over the top again. He wants a big wedding in Italy, for heaven's sake! He wants the whole exhibition of strolling along cobblestone streets through a village to the church, then a reception at a castle or something.'

'What do you want, Abby?' I had asked.

'Just to be married,' she had sighed. 'You know, to have all our friends and family at a big party. We could fly his family out to Sydney from Italy and put them all up in the club, no problem. I want my boys by my side, not to be lost in some European extravaganza.'

Of course, Luca had won and we had all headed off to Conti di San Bonifacio. I tingle even now at the memory of her dancing in my arms, though her fine wedding gown was for my friend. The bud lights, strung through grapevines across the villa's terrace had reflected in her eyes and the little diamantes in her hair. She was radiant, but I did notice how much more relaxed she was at their party back in Sydney after their European honeymoon.

Then the money issue raised its ugly head again. I had been put to the task of finding funding for the restaurant, and I had pulled out all stops with my banking contacts. But no one wanted to take the gamble unless Abby would guarantee it. Luca had thrown his hands in the air, furious that he had to rely on his wife. I remember it like it was yesterday. I had offered a small amount, but it wasn't sufficient for him and our friendship stumbled. Luca had approached his extended family in Italy, but no money had been forthcoming.

Abby had been embarrassed when she had discovered Luca had tried to crowd-fund the restaurant online. All in all, Luca Croucher wasn't a good risk. I knew that Adam and Arpels had done some sniffing around to see what he was up to – they may have warned Abby about giving him large amounts of money, I'm not sure. He was a bit of a chancer, but I presume the decision was still hers.

When that decision hadn't gone his way, the trouble in their love nest apparently got worse. Enter Francesca Lisi.

# CHAPTER TWENTY-ONE

IT WAS time to confront Liam again. Abigail strode towards Ferryman Road, hoping the walk back home later would release some of the nervous energy she knew was coming. It was twilight, a beautiful time in Melbourne when office workers were still scurrying home and lights were flicking on in welcome behind drawn curtains. A soothing breeze whistled behind her, seeming to urge her on.

She was unsure why she felt so buoyant. Yes, she was thrilled with Brad's progress, but she couldn't ignore the warm glow that lingered after her date with Jack. Also, her meeting with Liam would allow her to tick boxes, to have closure on the many questions she had had for so long. The fact that those answers would be coming from a ghost, a dead friend if she wanted to be brutally honest, didn't matter. She now believed in what and who she had encountered in that room in Binalong; she just had to hold herself together one more time.

Abigail giggled as she found herself sneaking past Molly's house, as if she was a child out beyond a curfew. She realised Rose must be home soon for the holidays and made a mental note to meet her. The artists' poster had disappeared from the brickwork. Perhaps Brad had taken it down after all, or Patricia had had a change of heart. She reached for Binalong's key.

Scrambling but coming up empty handed, Abigail realised the key was still on the kitchen bench. Perhaps she wasn't as calm as she thought she was. The front door clicked open. Smiling, Abigail slipped inside, gently closing out the world. The overhead light popped on, washing her in a mellow glow, then faded as she took a deep breath and found the first step. Despite there being no other lights on she could see her way; the steps were lit as if glow worms nestled underneath, each one turning off as she passed. It now seemed perfectly natural that things would materialise in her path. The old building held its breath.

At the top of the stairs, Abigail turned towards the room where she pictured Liam waiting for her. She gasped as the room's light spilled into the silent hallway and over a trail of beautiful white feathers. It was as though a hundred angels had recently passed by. But her meeting was with a ghost. Abigail scooped up a feather, holding it gently in her hand and slowly approached the doorway.

Liam was sitting in the box seat of her new window. He leapt to his feet and approached Abigail, his footsteps silent against the floor.

'That's all very theatrical, Liam,' she joked nervously,

tilting her head towards the hallway. She bit her tongue at the blanch of disappointment that crossed his face.

She tried again. 'I hope the builders aren't a nuisance for you,' but blushed when she heard the words, feeling ridiculous that something could obstruct a spirit. Could it?

Liam shrugged, presumably not caring either way.

'I think your friend, the old lady, is getting impatient. So I guess we should get on with it.' Abigail flicked at the feather, not knowing how to continue.

Liam motioned for her to sit down where he had been, and he edged away.

A chilly tingle seeped through her body as she slid onto the seat. It was distracting, like when your body goes numb after being in the one position too long. She tucked her hands under her knees as a buffer, hoping the seat hadn't permanently absorbed Liam's 'hum'. It would be hard to explain: That vibration? Yes, that's from when the ghost of a late friend took up residence in this room. Nothing to worry about.

Abigail stared at Liam and waited for his lead.

'It's good you've met the neighbours,' he ventured, not bothering to disguise his brittle smile. 'What's his name?'

Abigail jumped to her feet, picking up on the slight accusation in his tone. 'Listen. I am here because you have interrupted my life. I didn't ask that you visit, that you come back or whatever you call it. I don't understand any of this and let me tell you, I'm scared by it. So don't check on my life or what I'm doing, okay?'

She glanced aside, her impatience beginning to falter

under Liam's stare. The overhead light flickered and returned, the air chilled and Abigail thought she saw a few of the feathers drift across the doorway from their resting place along the hall. She had to remain firm because Liam held the answers. She returned to the seat and Liam leant against the wall close to her.

The night was still and quiet as they regarded each other. Abigail asked her first question. 'Why didn't Luca come to see me? Why is it you?'

Liam slowly shook his head. 'I'm sorry, Abby. As I said earlier, I don't have all the answers because I don't know how it all works. I just know that after I died, my essence or my mind, I guess, insisted I had to return to clear up what had happened that night. To share with you all that happened. It was unfinished business. I didn't know if I would be in a bodily form or an aura or what exactly. I didn't really have the opportunity to think about it, and truth be told I've only really thought about the aura thing since I've been here, waiting. I don't remember seeing Luca after the accident, you have to believe me.'

Abigail started to rise again, but Liam put up his hand, willing her to stay. 'Sit down, Abby. This isn't easy for me either. I don't have any concept of time or what happened after the accident, so I probably have just as many questions for you. In many ways I feel lucky to have this opportunity.' He sighed. 'Maybe you should too.'

'You mean, there was no hovering over your body, watching your funeral from the ceiling?' she asked, not totally convinced by Liam's words. Stills from the TV series *Medium* and stories about near-death experiences flashed through her mind. Liam shook his head.

'What about when a butterfly swoops; didn't you say that was your soul or something?'

'That was a sensation I felt and created for you, not actually me. It was wonderful because I could watch you from the window here and see your reaction. Which wasn't as enthusiastic as I'd hoped.'

'Well, I had no idea that was happening. Anyway, it's not all about you, Liam. As I said, I've heard other people say it has happened to them too ...'

'How was my funeral, by the way?' Liam interrupted.

The question cut through Abigail. His lilting voice took her back to when he was alive, how he was always the life of the party, the one to tease and provoke. He could diffuse a tense moment with a wink and a toast of 'Here's to a long life and a merry one'. But sitting here with him, bizarre as it was, Abigail caught a potent undercurrent of sadness. She glanced at his throat, where a small pulse used to beat, but it was still.

'Abby?'

'Yes? Oh, it never occurred to me that we wouldn't know about our own funeral, but I presumed it was all over by then anyway.' Her long-held beliefs spun off into a million directions like grey confetti thrown to the wind.

She could feel his eyes searching her face, imploring her to give in, to accept him. All at once it was important to Abigail that Liam knew how loved he had been. His funeral had been emotional and somewhat intriguing, and he deserved to hear that.

'You certainly know how to go out with style, Liam. It seemed that word of your passing had spread and you had a great turnout of relations, friends and work colleagues. And ex-girlfriends. Don't look so surprised, what did you expect?'

Liam looked down at his shoes, trying to hide the smirk that crept across his face. Abigail couldn't help but grin with him.

'They – the girlfriends, that is – were in black from head to foot, all dressed to the nines like out of a Godfather movie. They were beautiful, all clicking down the aisles in their stilettos. I'm told they eyed each other off through the whole service, which was at a city cathedral no less, so everyone could fit in.'

Liam nodded, apparently impressed.

'Your service was a week after Luca's funeral because a few of your relatives from Ireland wanted to attend. I can't remember all the details as I wasn't quite together, as you can imagine. It was a blur. But let me tell you, when those bagpipes started "Danny Boy" as everyone was filing out, there was not a dry eye nor a heart that wasn't breaking.' Abigail took a deep breath, tears threatening to spill as she relived that dreadful time.

'Ah yes, beautiful.' Liam recited the last couple of heart-wrenching lines. 'For you shall bend and tell me that you love me. And I will sleep in peace until you come to me.'

Such powerful words. The world stilled for them both at that moment. Abigail could no longer hold her hot tears, and they spilled down her cheeks. The light in Liam dulled and smeared as if he was about to disappear completely. Abigail fought the impulse to reach out to him.

'Did you cry for me, Abby?' he whispered without looking directly at her.

She could hear the desperation in his question. 'I did. I cried for you, I cried for Luca, I cried for what you did to him, I cried for me. So many tears that I couldn't bring myself to go to your wake. Was that enough crying for you?'

Liam slid down the wall, his silent landing somehow deafening. Apart from a slight blue haze every so often, anyone entering the room would think he was 'of this earth'. Particularly as tears streamed down his face.

Abigail thought she heard a soft 'I'm sorry', but couldn't be sure.

'And Luca's funeral?' he mumbled faintly.

Abigail waved his question aside, unable to go back to that agonising place. 'I can't bear to think about Luca's funeral, and I certainly can't talk about it. Little did I know what would continue to unfold about Luca's life as mine unravelled. What happened, Liam? Please, please tell me. Was it all just a giant sham?' Abigail's shoulders shook, each of her hands clutching the other in support.

Liam took long shuddering breaths, pulling himself back under control. 'I remember that I kept saying "I have to go back, I have to go back. I have to explain." There was a huge bright light, just like people say there is. I somehow knew, I just knew, Abby, that I had to make the choice then – to go to the afterlife or return and make things right. I was desperate.'

He raised his stricken gaze to search Abigail's face.

'Although I'll never be able to make things right, will I? As my granny used to say, "May you be in heaven half an hour before the devil knows you're dead."'

Abigail gave in to a small smile.

'Then a resolution, a conclusion or something, seemed to be made and I was here, in this room. The old woman came and told me I could stay only to clarify things to you. I have to stay in this building, but I can sense some things that happen elsewhere. Like when you entered the attic next door. She said it's too dangerous for me to go outside.' Liam glanced nervously at the window as if he expected a ghoul to burst through it at any second.

A shiver of fear ran down Abigail's spine as a trickle of sympathy went out to him.

'As I said, there doesn't seem to be any time relevance. I don't know why I couldn't return just after we'd died. Maybe I've been waiting here all that time without knowing it. This building was where we first met you, so maybe we had to wait until you returned here. Or until your heart was open enough to hear what I had to say. I do know that since we have spoken, I can feel myself draining away. It's as though our connecting thread is starting to spin and fray.'

'I can't believe this is happening. Am I going mad?'

'No.' Liam's voice was firm, but then faltered as if he was unsure if he should continue. 'Abigail, before I go on, I want you to know how much I loved you. I still do, but back then I loved you so much and it crushed me to see how Luca treated you.'

'He lied to me and you lied to me too. I loved Luca with

all my heart when I married him, and he loved me.' The words sounded thin, even to her own ears as she threw Liam a sharp glare.

'Abby ...'

'He loved me, Liam!' Even as the affirmation fell from her lips, Abigail wondered why she cared, why was she hanging on to the belief that Luca had loved her. She was positive that he had at one point, but then he had moved on. Had she been so mistaken in thinking she had too since his death?

Fear surged through her as she fought to stay or flee. She glanced to the door, making certain there was an escape path if needed. She stayed, and continued to wring her hands, the feather having dropped to the floor. Forgotten.

'Go on,' she whispered.

'We didn't go to the match that night as he told you,' Liam began softly. 'He met her in the city and then, I guess, went back to her house.'

Abigail frowned at him knowingly, daring him to go on with more of the details she wasn't aware of.

'Luca called me to collect him, saying he was too drunk to drive. He couldn't risk taking a cab and you seeing it pull up at your house. Initially I told him what an eejit he was, that he had to take responsibility; that he was making a mess of his marriage and I wasn't going to keep bailing him out.'

To Abigail, Liam's words hung around him like limp balloons.

'You helped cover for him more than once? That's not being my friend, Liam,' Abigail accused him.

Again, the light within Liam's body flared then dulled; she was sure now that he was somehow thinner in depth than when she first arrived but really didn't care. He didn't make eye contact with her, continuing his tale whilst staring at the floor.

'I took a cab to collect him. From Hawthorn ...'

'From Francesca's house, you mean.'

'He wasn't all that drunk when I arrived. Not really. I got stuck into him, telling him to stop acting the maggot, to stop hurting you. He never divulged anything personal about what happened behind closed doors with you, Abby. I swear. But I could see the rift, how you were hurting and that his ... his affair ... had to end.'

'He had been my world and then I lost him. And now I learn that that world wasn't as I knew it anyway. That is what hurts the most. The deceit.' Abigail didn't want to dance through this conversation anymore – dodging and prancing, looking behind and to the side. *Enough.*

Her breath shuddered in preparation for the answer to her question. 'And then?'

'And then. We hadn't gone far but we were both being real fools, and I guess I was driving too fast. Luca's car could really move and I wasn't used to it. He started waving his arms around, saying something but I missed what he had said. I turned towards him and just didn't see the red light until it was too late. I braked late and the car spun and ... well ... that's where it ended. Thank the lord I hit a fence and not another car.'

Liam sagged even lower, his vitality going. The overhead light flickered. 'I tried, Abby, I really did.'

Abigail held her face in her hands, sobbing. Any anger had gone. Regret and sorrow merged into one clotted mass until she was left with a thickness in her soul for both Liam and Luca. She started to feel sick to her stomach. The windowpane provided cold comfort as Abigail lay her cheek against it, and closed her eyes. The vision Liam had painted was all too clear. She slumped, suddenly tired and empty, but turned back to Liam as he spoke.

'He chose you. He agreed with me. About how he had treated you and said he would lift his game.'

The words bounced off her. Abigail wished she could grab them and hold them close, to analyse and accept them. But she couldn't. Too much time had passed and too many questions had been left for her to untangle. On her own. She would never be sure that Luca's final admission was what he truly felt. She knew that.

'Just like that? Lift his game? Not, "oh my God, I promise I will never see Francesca again" or "I have treated my wife so badly, will she ever forgive me". He didn't promise anything.'

'I'm so sorry.' Liam released a long, deep breath as though he had done what he had come for; that with every breath he was also exhaling another chink of his guilt. 'I needed to tell you that he was coming back to you.'

'Well he bloody well should have come back and said it to my face himself, shouldn't he!' Abigail's eyes flashed, her voice hardened. She knew Liam so well, how he was surely sitting opposite her, reading her reaction. His response confirmed it.

'You sensed something was amiss back then, Abby. If Luca hadn't died, would he have lost you anyway?'

It was an important question, but she couldn't ignore the strain of hope in his voice. Abigail kept it close to her chest as she eased back into the seat, her hiccupping breath slowing to uneasy acceptance. She could imagine the distant comforting noises of evening as the world continued to spin: Kate was preparing dinner; Audrey was studying a table plan; a bird was settling into its nest; a jogger was plodding on endlessly. Everything would go on with or without her, just like when Luca had died. She closed her eyes, waiting. This time though, Abigail was surprised that the knife of abandonment hadn't gone in nearly so deeply.

***

IT'S *an odd feeling having got past my admission, the reason for coming back. But then there are countless levels of oddness in this whole scenario, even for an Irishman.*

*Abigail has withdrawn from me, not answering my question. She gazes out the window, as if visualising the world spinning around us. Is she seeking Luca, knowing she can't follow? Why would she even want to?*

*Of course it has been a lot for her to take in, but in so many ways I am relieved. Relieved to voice the known fact that I accidentally killed my best friend; a disastrous action I would take back in a second. I was proud to tell Abby how I have always loved her, and relieved to tell her that Luca* planned to return after doin' a number on her. Not even I know how that would have gone.

She curls up tightly in the space and closes her eyes like a little girl. She seems exhausted and I think she may have fallen asleep. I let her be, alone with her simmering thoughts. A small smile suddenly appears, her shoulders relax and I know I have reached her.

Quietly and without moving she says, 'I know you were to blame for the accident and for Luca's terrible death, but thank you for trying to be there for him and for bringing him back to me. For just a moment.'

'Oh, Abby. What are we to do?' I breathe a shaky sigh of reassurance.

'We?' She pauses for a minute before uncurling from the seat. She walks straight past me to the door as I scramble to my feet. With one hand on the frame, she half-turns toward me and for a moment I think she will offer a smile of forgiveness.

Instead she says, 'Thank you, but you need to go, Liam', then walks down the stairs and out of Binalong.

The space, where she stood only seconds before, is now an aching emptiness. The air hovers, not knowing what to do with itself. It settles between her exit and my heavy heart.

Naively, I hadn't confronted having to let her go, so I rush to the window and press my face against the pane, like a child left behind from a picnic. My fingers spread-eagle against the cold surface. I wish I could call out to her, bring her back and have her with me for a while longer, but she can't hear me.

I watch as the dark shadows take her further from me

until she is out of sight. Her last words echo around the walls. "Thank you, but you need to go, Liam."

C.S. Lewis described it perfectly: *Her absence was like the sky – it covered everything.*

I am drained and unsure of what to do next, although I can sense the old woman is nearby.

# CHAPTER TWENTY-TWO

'I FELT IT, MOLLY,' Abigail uttered. Her cup of tea sat untouched by her side.

As though in a trance she had gone straight to bed after returning from Binalong and fallen into a deep sleep. She woke late, amazed that her mind had stilled itself long enough for any peace at all, but presumed it was from exhaustion. She certainly hadn't wanted to revisit her exit or the stunned expression on Liam's face. It was too much.

Molly had been the first person Abigail had needed to speak with. More than Kate or Steph, or even Jack. She supposed she needed a touchstone to Molly's own experience, and after all, Molly had graciously shared her own experience without really knowing Abigail. She was relieved when she had received a reply from Molly to her text:

*Yes, I'm home. Come for a cuppa. Jack has taken my very grumpy daughter shopping.*

Now, here she was again, sitting in Molly's welcoming

nook, surrounded by greenery, and cups of tea. Molly peeked at Abigail over the lip of her teacup, waiting as she rubbed her foot along Nigella's stomach.

Abigail squinted into the harsh daylight, ready to share all that had happened. 'I followed the feathers. I sat in a room with the ghost of an old friend and listened while he explained how my husband had died; how the car he had been driving had killed them both. How he had loved me while he was alive. And that Luca had too, despite all indications otherwise.'

Abigail gave a nervous laugh at how ridiculous it all sounded, but Molly smiled and urged her to keep going.

'After we had our little human-to-spirit chat, I felt it. I was on the window seat and all of a sudden ... it felt like a huge wave of emotion just washed over me. You know, how shrinks tell you to break an egg over your head and to visualise it putting a protective shield down over you? It was like that, just like you said. Overwhelming, unconditional love. And it was amazing. I soaked it in, not wanting to let it go. I mean, was it from Liam in front of me or from Luca or my dad much farther away? And how far is that anyway?' She flicked her eyes to Molly. 'I wouldn't even be saying this except that I know you understand.'

'Well, we're the special ones then.' Molly nodded. 'Not everyone gets to experience such a feeling. I'm sorry that yours came out of such a tragedy though, Abigail.'

'I think it came from my acceptance. I don't know and that part doesn't matter. I'm willing to give in to it.'

'You'll probably go over and over your reaction many times trying to work it out,' Molly said.

'Strangely it's okay. If all this had happened straight after Luca died, I might not be in such a good place, but it's okay.' Abigail paused, listening to the call of a magpie. 'You are right about us being lucky to have experienced it – I can't help wonder why though. I mean, there must be more important messages or cases or connections, or whatever. Why don't more spirits come back to clear things up, to announce who did a crime or where a body is buried? Or ... or to tell someone they love them?'

Molly shrugged. 'I guess it would bring Earth and the afterlife too close. My gran once told me that "Heaven exists so you can understand your life on Earth". I guess that applies no matter what heaven is to each person. And we still have to be open to receive the messages as I've said – who knows how many more encounters there would be if only we all took a calm moment.'

'To think and hopefully move on.' Abigail nodded. 'But at the moment, it's enough.'

The friends sat, comfortable in companionship and their own thoughts. Molly broke the silence gently.

'Now, speaking of moving on, you're certainly getting ahead in leaps and bounds next door. I hope you don't mind, but I did have to go in to the cottage the other day. One of the builders had cut his hand quite badly and needed a bandage. From what I could see your home is beautiful.'

'Oh, you should have looked around. I don't mind at all. In fact, do you want to take a look now?'

Just as she had spoken, Jack's car pulled into a vacant

spot and a curly-haired girl leapt out. She flew through the gate laden with shopping bags.

'Rose ...' Molly began.

'I need to text Louisa with photos of what Uncle Jack bought me,' Rose announced as she ran straight past them. Molly raised her eyebrows at Abigail as her daughter rushed inside the house, the front door yawning open behind her.

Then several things happened at once. Smokey darted through the front door, Nigella sprang up in surprise and took off in pursuit and Jack was too slow to close the front gate. Molly leapt to her feet, the tea sloshing into saucers as she knocked the table. She called out and ran after Smokey as Jack tried and missed to snag the Airedale's waving lead. The dog's wish for freedom seemed to be greater than any desire to catch a cat.

Abigail raced past Jack and out the gate, expecting to hear the screeching of car brakes at any moment. With her heart in her mouth, she knew that Nigella's total lack of road sense wouldn't save her if a car came down the road. The dog headed for the alleyway, slowing at the entrance to Binalong. Abigail pounced on her lead, pulling the dog to heel just as Molly returned with Smokey in her arms. The animals paid no attention to each other.

Brad was standing beside his truck, having witnessed the chase. As Jack joined the pursuit the builder called out, 'Jeez mate, you'll need to move quicker than that to catch these two.'

It broke the moment of potential disaster and they all gave a nervous laugh before returning to the house, relieved and out of breath. Rose stood on the veranda, arms crossed. 'Where did you go?' she demanded.

'Come on, Rose. Let's get the kettle on again. You've got to shut the door, my girl.'

'Okay, okay,' Rose replied, eyes rolling to the sky.

Abigail and Jack sank into the chairs. He tilted his head back towards his sullen niece as she followed Molly inside.

'She's not normally rude. There just seems to be an objection around every corner with her lately. I'm so relieved nobody was hurt.' He leant to rub Nigella, who was panting at his feet.

Abigail nodded. 'Disaster avoided. That was nice of you to take Rose shopping,' she offered.

'Oh, I enjoy it. It's become a bit of a school holiday tradition if we are both in the same city. I get to see a teenage girl in full shopping mode, and let me tell you it's an exhausting sight.'

His love for Rose, despite her apparent irritability, was evident in the warmth of his voice. Perhaps his affection was a reflection of what could have been if his marriage had survived and he had children of his own. Abigail was amused to feel a tinge of jealousy.

Molly returned with the tray of tea, Jack's coffee and another delicious-looking cake. 'I resisted adding a slosh of whiskey to the drinks after that escapade. Sorry, Abby,' she said. 'The cake is carrot with sour cream frosting. Tom's home tonight and it's his favourite, but he won't miss a couple of slices.'

Abigail smiled. 'These things happen. What are you going to do with all those pots along the fence, Molly?'

'I've got plans,' Molly announced in a dramatic tone. 'Not great plans, but it's a start. There used to be a wonderful little nursery around the corner apparently, but it closed when the owner moved. I thought I could start a business selling flowers and these pots to a couple of local outlets. It would be something I'd be passionate about building. I've started an herb garden in the backyard, so I'll have bunches of fresh herbs too. I don't use any pesticides, so that's a selling point. My only worry is that the market is too close, and they have a fantastic range there.' A shadow of doubt crossed her pretty face.

'I didn't know about this,' Jack said. 'I think it's a great idea. You could wholesale them further afield than around here, and the market isn't open every day, remember.'

Abigail could see the business cogs turning in Jack's mind as he mulled over his sister's idea.

'I've only just decided to give it a go,' Molly replied, but a quiet determination hovered beneath her words. 'Some of the potted-up plants are actually for you, Abigail, when you decide what you need.'

'Really? Wow, thank you. I was hoping I could call on you both for advice on my courtyards. The camellia is still alive, you'll be pleased to know.'

Silence nestled comfortably between them.

'I get the feeling I interrupted something earlier,' Jack prodded, glancing between the two women.

Molly glanced at Abigail and raised her eyebrows, indicating it wasn't her story to tell. Abigail took a deep breath before offering, 'Suffice to say that I have had a further glimpse of the afterlife, just like you both have had, and it was amazing. And still a little raw. I'll tell you about it another time though, Jack, is that okay?'

Jack nodded, giving Abigail a searching look but making it clear he wasn't taking offence.

'Would you like to come for dinner?' Molly asked Abigail. 'It's super casual but you are welcome, and you can meet Tom.'

Abigail glanced across at Jack, relieved to see a twinkle in his eye, so she gratefully accepted. She wanted a quiet afternoon with her thoughts first, so she gathered Nigella and wandered home.

———

FROM THE MOMENT she arrived at Molly's home, Abigail knew their dinner together would be relaxed and welcoming. The sound of laughter greeted her through the open front door; when no one heard her knock, she hesitantly let herself in.

Tom had his daughter in a rapturous hold, Rose squealing with obvious delight. Molly reclined on one of the sofas, calling instructions to Jack in the kitchen. He was the first to see Abigail appear in the doorway and waved her into the kitchen. He pecked her on the cheek, winked and took her offered bottle of wine.

'Would you like a glass of wine or would you prefer to start with something else?' he asked, tilting a tumbler of whiskey towards her.

'A whiskey would be nice.' Abigail felt a little kick in her stomach at seeing Jack again and at feeling so welcome in his world. She watched as he filled their glasses, moving with ease around the kitchen. His faded jeans fit him like a glove, his striped shirt with the sleeves rolled up to the elbow, was loose over his torso.

Molly jumped to her feet, gave Abigail a hug and led her over to introduce Tom and Rose. Rose was indeed a mini-Molly in appearance, whilst Tom was tall and broad like a cuddly bear.

Tom broke the ice with 'Well, I hope she keeps the noise down' while Rose gave a quick 'Hi, we met' before flopping onto a chair.

There was a moment's pause when Jack asked if anyone was in a hurry. 'It seems I forgot to turn on the oven,' he admitted.

'Oh, Jackson'. Molly sighed while Tom groaned good-naturedly, and everyone resumed what they were doing. Abigail asked Tom about his FOFO job and Rose became glued to her mobile phone, only looking up when directly addressed.

Finally, they all sat down to share large platters of roasted garlic vegetables, steamed broccolini combined with pine nuts and snow peas, and a carved rack of lamb glistening with Molly's marmalade glaze.

'Gee, Uncle Jack. You're out to impress,' Rose declared.

Molly and Tom glanced at Abigail, who spluttered with laughter. 'It smells sensational, doesn't it?'

'I'll have you know, Miss Rose, that I have already confessed to Abigail that my kitchen prowess extends to a BBQ or roast. That's it,' Jack said in a mock stern tone. 'I do admit though that this spread I have created is worthy of applause.' He held his arms wide in expectation.

'Just saying,' Rose declared, shrugging nonchalantly.

Abigail noticed a smile quivering behind Rose's lips but glanced away when caught out by the very observant teenager.

'Rose, can you put your phone away, please. Now,' Tom said firmly.

Rose sighed but dropped her phone under her chair.

Wine and easy conversation flowed. Rose entertained them with exaggerated school stories that had Tom threatening to get the headmistress out of bed for a strict talking to. Abigail loved his open sense of humour and could appreciate why Molly looked forward to having him home.

In the back of Abigail's mind was a reminder of the relaxed dinners she and Martin had shared with their young boys. They had been good times while they lasted. She had hoped they could be rekindled on the couple of times Luca had met her sons, but he never seemed to feel at ease. Mealtimes with her parents had been more of an endurance race for Abigail – Audrey had spent the time correcting her table manners, while asking Adam about his important day.

Abigail relaxed, warmed by Jack's body next to her. She smiled to herself as he fussed with her drink and asked about her plans for the décor of Binalong and her new home.

'I'll help with any of your painting projects, Abigail. A mural sounds really cool and I reckon I'd be good at that,' Rose offered boldly.

'Ah, school comes first,' Molly said.

'I'm just saying that I think I could help,' Rose huffed. 'Anyway, you haven't seen any of my art for ages.'

Abigail caught a quick, silent exchange between Molly and Tom. She looked to Jack but he was taking an intense interest in the wine label. Rose peered at her, waiting. Not wanting to upset any house rules, Abigail tested the waters. 'If it doesn't interfere with schoolwork or any jobs around here, I'm sure you have some great ideas, Rose.'

The moment passed and Rose mellowed a little, much to Abigail's relief.

A delicious pear tart followed for dessert. Jack tried to claim it as his culinary masterpiece, but everyone recognised Molly's touch, particularly with the little lavender sprigs that were dotted around its edge.

After Rose had drifted off to her room, they moved to the couches for coffee. The mellow voice of Katie Noonan's jazz settled around them like warm honey. Abigail leaned against Jack, her body curving easily into his side. She could feel the soft vibration of his voice humming through his shirt as he chatted to Tom. Unable to keep her eyes open any longer, she reluctantly thanked her friends for their hospitality.

'I'd stay and help clean up, but I'm really exhausted,' she apologised.

'I'd stay and help clean up,' Jack said with a smirk. 'But I should walk our guest home so she doesn't fall asleep under a bush somewhere.'

'Hang on, that means I have to clean up!' Tom said.

'And I had no part in making the mess. Well, except for eating my fair share.'

'Sorry, Tom. I should have driven here. But then I think I've had a bit too much wine for that too.'

The crisp air cleared Abigail's drowsiness instantly as she threw on her jacket and felt Jack's warm hand slip into her own. His hold was firm and assured. The sweet evening scents coiled gently around them. As they strolled close together, Abigail smiled, knowing there was no expectation to make conversation. The night sky was awash with a carpet of stars streaking above them. She loved all the mysteries that the universe and galaxies held, and had tried to capture them in a mural more than once. But she hadn't been able to match their wonder.

'It's beautiful, isn't it,' Jack said, stopping as he followed her gaze. 'I've never been interested in sailing, but I reckon the opportunity to be under that huge sky at sea would make me want to buy a boat.'

Abigail nodded. 'It's so vast and humbling, it makes you feel insignificant, like our world is just a dot. Someone described the night sky to me once as being a dark shield around our universe and that the stars are the light shining through pinpricks; like millions of holes in black velvet.'

The window in Liam's room came into her mind, followed by an image of Luca being somewhere on the other side of that cloth. She quickly pushed them away.

'But still all connected,' Jack replied as they resumed their slow walk.

Abigail paused. Was Jack trying to lead her into sharing her experience with Liam? She changed the subject, unsure whether it was the right time or place to discuss it. 'Molly said you've got a big project on in Melbourne. Do you think you'll live here for a while or move here?'

She sensed his frown. Had her comment sounded prying or had it just broken into their moment? She knew that 'needy' was the last thing she could be accused of being. 'Too self-sufficient' was a term more attributed to her by those who knew her well. But Jack had only known her for a short time; her comment had come out wrong and she tried to backtrack.

'I mean, Molly seems to really enjoy having you here for company and the novelty of flying back and forth to Sydney must wear off. Mind you, I have to do that flight a lot too. Oh, I never asked where you live in Sydney. You could be near my family.'

Her comment went unheeded as the front sensor light popped on as they reached Abigail's house. They both blinked. Abigail reached for her key, still mumbling into her bag.

Jack moved between her body and the front door. He eased her back against the wall, gently pressing his finger against her lips.

'Shh.' The light clicked off, and they stood motionless in the darkness.

Abigail's heart skipped as she felt Jack's breath close to her upturned face.

Gentle kisses interspersed his whispered words. 'Yes. I do have work here. Yes. I do like Melbourne. A lot. Yes. I will be finding somewhere down here. To live.'

He tasted of marmalade, pear and coffee; her senses tingled with anticipation.

Abigail felt him inch away as he added, 'Would that be okay?'

In the half-light Abigail contemplated his parted lips, then his brooding eyes. She hadn't missed the mischievous mocking in his tone. 'I guess,' she teased. She pushed uncertainty aside and asked, 'Would you like to come in?'

Jack hesitated. 'Yes, I most definitely would, but Abby, I am going to leave that pleasure for another time soon, if that's all right. I'm in Sydney for the next week while I finalise a few things, and then we will pleasantly pick up where we have left off. When we can take our time.' He pulled her to him, wrapping his arms around her. His kiss was firm, passionate and lingering.

Abigail caressed his back, swept up in his powerful embrace, and longed for more. His response had surprised and disappointed her, but she was determined not to read something into it that may not be there.

She smoothed his frown away with her thumb and smiled. 'Well, I'll look forward to that.'

# CHAPTER TWENTY-THREE

ABIGAIL RAN her hand down her body, reliving her final moments with Jack the previous evening. The ache she had felt as he held her had lingered throughout the night, a restless desire settling over her. Any woman would have sensed the shallow breathing and increasing urgency in his kisses as desire being kept in check. What a shame he had given in to it, although his sensual actions had made a promise of what was surely to come.

When her phone lit with Audrey's smiling ID, she couldn't face a conversation with her mother so early in the morning. She rolled over, frustrated by the interruption and listened to the ensuing voicemail. It reminded Abigail of Audrey's event early the following week; the fundraising dinner Abigail had forgotten about. Where had the days gone? She and Luca had both embraced formal occasions, dressing to the nines and dancing until the band's last hurrah, but she had lost interest over the last couple of years. This was another occasion she would happily forego.

She frowned, irritated that thoughts of Luca had weaseled their way into her much more pleasurable ones of Jack. Wait, hadn't Jack mentioned he would be in Sydney for a few days? Perhaps she should give him a call and see if they could catch up whilst both in the same city.

Nigella had taken up her usual morning position propped beside the bed, waiting for an outing. Abigail turned and scratched the dog's head. 'Well old girl, it's to Max and Pete's retreat for you while I'm away. And if Mr Mattingley phones, then I will suggest dinner in Sydney, otherwise I'll let things simmer a while longer. It's not as though I've got nothing to do, is it?'

Her phone pinged with a message:

*Arriving in Oz tomorrow. Christine has work commitments but we will see you at Audrey's shindig. Martin.*

Abigail shook her head in admiration for Audrey's planning abilities. Her mother had obviously pounced on Martin to attend her function as soon as she'd heard they'd be in Australia. Once again, something shifted in Abigail's heart, a pang of homesickness for Scott, James, and London. She longed to hug them, to join them for a beer and a good chat in a pub, and generally be a mum for a while. Waiting until after she'd settled into her new home to fly over was suddenly too far away. She would have to make do with a WhatsApp call to her boys from Sydney, and include Audrey in the video call. Her mother would enjoy that.

After showering and dressing, Abigail put Nigella on the lead and set off for Ferryman Road; she needed to shrug off her rollercoaster of emotions. It felt good, almost cleansing, to feel the chill in the air and the light sprinkling of rain against her cheeks. She plotted as she walked: *Set my business idea in motion before the entire year vaporises. Organise Christmas. I wonder if Jack spends Christmas with Molly. How can I still taste his delicious kiss on my lips?*

Molly and Tom were climbing into their car as she approached. 'We're off to the market. Do you need anything?' Molly called. Rose sat in the back seat chatting on her cell, but managed to flick Abigail a hesitant smile.

'No, but thank you. And thank you also for the lovely dinner last night. I had a great time.'

'May it be the first of many, eh?' Molly replied.

'I just wanted to say, I'm off to Sydney later in the week, but only for a few days,' Abigail said. She noticed Molly raise her eyebrows and wondered if she was linking her trip with Jack's. Feeling slightly ridiculous, Abigail ploughed on with an explanation. 'My mother has a fundraiser on and our family, um, well anyway, I'm going to support her.'

'Okay. We've got your cell number, haven't we?' Tom offered.

'Of course we do, Tom,' Molly said.

Rose's window wound down. 'Can we mind Nigella?'

'Oh, thank you, Rose but she's off to her holiday retreat. I'll bring her over to see you when I get back.' Abigail waved them away.

Abigail wandered through No. 64 with increasing excitement as she absorbed the work already completed. Tick, tick went her mental list. It was shaping up exactly as she had visualised, so she gave the builders her thumbs up as she passed. Abigail was certainly impressed with Brad and his team – they did amazingly precise work but weren't afraid to contact her for any clarifications and were ahead of schedule.

Plus there was the added bonus of living next to Molly and her family. She couldn't wish for better neighbours, despite her initial doubts when the supposed hippie had flooded her garden. The memory of her introduction to Jack, which they both laughed about now, brought a cheeky smile to her lips.

She wandered next door to Binalong. Nigella trotted happily beside her, neither growling nor gazing up the staircase, making Abigail realise that the old woman hadn't materialised on the street either. Could Liam have actually gone?

All the workmen were next door so the building was deserted. Abigail tied Nigella's lead loosely through the bottom banister then nervously climbed the stairs. No breeze gently pulled her up the last several steps, no lights flickered, no coin was to be seen, and despite how much she inhaled there was no hint of mint. The dense quiet sat on her shoulders like a sack of sad disappointment.

The room was empty; the smell of timber and fresh paint overwhelming. Abigail stood in the doorway, fat tears rolling down her cheeks. She searched the corners of the room but nothing seemed unusual. It was just four walls. The word 'empty' not only described how the space appeared in front of her, but also the state of her heart.

Abigail missed Liam already. She had more questions for him, but that didn't fully explain the pain in her chest, her overwhelming regret. But then she had firmly told him to leave – she needed to remember that.

'Liam?' she called into the still room, already knowing there would be no reply. 'I'm going away for a few days and ... um ... I was hoping you'd be here when I get back. I know I told you to leave, but can we meet just one more time?' Silence. 'Oh, Liam. I just need to know you are all right.'

Abigail waited. She turned on the light to give it the opportunity to dim, but it stayed bright. With a deep breath, Abigail turned toward the door.

For a moment she thought she felt the slightest chill, then a shimmer seemed to flash across the room. Perhaps it was a trick of the pale grey morning light. Abigail closed her eyes, breathed deeply and tried to quieten her mind and open her heart. She knew she would never regain that special feeling she had experienced whilst curled on the window seat that night, but she just wanted one more sign.

'Thank you, Liam. Thank you,' Abigail murmured into the still air, her words choking on all those she still had to share. She turned to the door and slowly left the room, stopping at the top of the stairs. Abigail glanced back to what she would always think of as Liam's room. Her breath shook with emotion as she gathered herself to go downstairs to the deserted gallery. Nigella gave a small whine from the bottom of the staircase. Abigail rubbed the bannister as if it was a magic lamp and scanned along the walkway one last time. A large butterfly was hovering in the doorway. Gracefully it curled its way in giant loops toward her, then hovered briefly on her shoulder.

It was mesmerising – black with little white and yellow

dots on its wing tips. Abigail smiled and whispered, 'You should be green, shouldn't you? Like a clover or a leprechaun?'

Impossible as it was, Abigail could have sworn the gentle tune of 'Danny Boy' strummed against her body. She crossed her palms across her chest, trying to hold it in.

As Abigail's sobs echoed throughout Binalong, the butterfly flitted away into the cool, minty air.

———

LIAM DIDN'T WANT *Abby to see his eyes, glistening with tears. He now knew that ghosts could cry, to feel true sorrow. His heart was quietly breaking but there was no one to hear it.*

# CHAPTER TWENTY-FOUR

AUDREY WAS IN HER ELEMENT. She had assembled Adam, Georgia, Scarlet, Abigail, Martin and Christine to her favourite restaurant in Bondi, and Abigail now watched her mother savour being the perfect hostess. Audrey was a regular patron of several of the old-style restaurants around Sydney, but she knew her chosen dining room overlooking sweeping surf was the perfect casual setting for English visitors. The water shimmered a sparkling cobalt as white-caps dropped like meringue from the crest of the waves.

Audrey had learned from her friend Isabel Wentworth that Christine was signed for a BBC series on Australian dining, so she had the waiters on alert.

All this she shared with Abigail as they made their way to lunch. Abigail was quite sure Christine knew all too well which establishments she needed to focus on for her series and only hoped the staff wasn't put out by Audrey's demands. Their group was seated when they arrived, a bottle of Pol Roger champagne and Adam's Negroni arriving soon after.

'To celebrate us all being together.' Audrey raised her glass for a toast.

Abigail quietly sent Scott and James a *Wish you were here* text and a photo of the brilliant blue Australian sky. They were the missing link. Abigail had moved past being nervous around Martin a long time ago. She no longer waited for him to correct or control her – she just needed to keep their relationship as amicable as possible for the boys, but at arm's length. A frothy get-together like this luncheon would be the perfect ice breaker before the fundraiser.

Abigail turned to Christine. 'You must be excited to visit so many of Australia's top restaurants. What do have on the agenda?'

'On the menu you mean?' Martin interrupted, laughing.

Abigail continued to look at Christine. 'No, I meant on the agenda. Your itinerary, the restaurants?'

Christine's eyes lit up making it clear the conversation excited her. Abigail admired her passion and her culinary knowledge.

'The BBC doesn't just want formal restaurants. I'll be visiting smaller establishments that are known for a particular style or dish, as well as casual restaurants around the Hunter Valley. Australian wines will be included, so the makers as well as the chefs will all be interviewed. I want to showcase the wide variety of scenery too, to anchor it in Australia. This trip is just for research, then we'll be back to finetune and film the best venues. It's a long process.'

'The boys tell me that your publishing career is about to take off as well,' Abigail ventured.

'Oh, I don't know about that,' Christine answered. 'I'm better in the kitchen surrounded by pots and pans and fresh produce than sitting writing about it. But a book would be a great spin off from the series.'

'If Scott and James are involved, I hope they can join the crew that comes out for more research or filming then.'

Christine glanced at Martin, who changed the subject to the state of the world's cricket.

As Adam stood to answer a business call, Georgia immediately turned to Abigail.

'So how are the renovations coming along?' she asked.

Having had very little interest from Georgia in any aspects of her life over the years, Abigail was struck silent for a moment. There had always been an unspoken rivalry between the two women as Georgia attempted to know everything about the Arpels wealth and use it to her advantage, and Abigail was wary of her sister-in-law for just that reason. What angle was Georgia taking now?

Before Abigail could reply, Georgia continued, 'I have a dear friend, Paris Cunningham, who lives near you. You wouldn't know her. She lives in the most divine house and was able to purchase it fully renovated.' She took a sip of her mineral water, challenging Abigail over the slice of lemon.

'Actually, Georgia, they are coming along extremely well. It has been such fun choosing all the fittings.'

'Don't you have a stylist?' Georgia's eyes popped with fake innocence. 'I'm sure Paris could find someone for you.'

'Yes. I do. My friend Steph is fabulous and of course there's Brad the builder.'

Georgia threw her a questioning stare, as if unsure whether Abigail was being serious. Suddenly Abigail saw the real reason for her sister-in-law's unusual focus. Georgia was holding her glass high, her right hand sporting a large solitaire diamond set in platinum; a ring Abigail recognised as one of Audrey's prized pieces of jewellery. From out of the corner of her eye Abigail saw Audrey frown slightly in Georgia's direction. Was she reprimanding her daughter-in-law for her indiscretion?

Abigail quickly redirected her attention to the view, determined not to fall into the trap and ask about the jewellery, but Georgia had already seen her reaction. Abigail longed to reach over and wipe the self-satisfied smirk off her immaculately made-up face.

It had been only a moment, but it spoke volumes to Abigail. Georgia was staking her claims on the family estate.

'Have you met your new neighbours, dear?' Audrey asked, delicately wrestling a crusted spear of asparagus.

'Oh yes, they're wonderful. I'm so lucky. Molly and Tom and their daughter, Rose. They haven't lived there for long either. Molly and her brother, Jack, said they'd help with the landscaping. He's from Sydney actually and ...'

'Oh,' Audrey interrupted. 'Speaking of landscaping and building, you all must bid at our fundraiser auction. We aim to raise $500,000 on the night for the Regroup Project.'

'What is it again?' Martin asked.

'Oh, it's such a good cause.' Audrey beamed. It was the

way she always began when explaining one of her undertakings. 'It's part of the ongoing support the foundation gives to housing for the disadvantaged. The Regroup Project is to build, um, like a mini village for those with disabilities who are in full-time care. So, six villas to house two young adults with their carers in each. Then there's a central complex with all the support facilities.'

'That's a lot more than $500,000,' Abigail said.

'As the major sponsor, Arpels has already donated the land. Adam is so marvellous with all the business side of things.

The golden-haired boy again. Abigail sighed.

'And we have managed to get everything else donated – the landscaping, the kitchen installations, custom furniture for the villas.' Audrey waved her arms with excitement. 'The $500,000 is targeted at the special needs equipment, but it would be marvellous to raise more.'

'I've heard that these young folk sometimes have to go to nursing homes because there isn't other accommodation for them. It's pretty outrageous, isn't it?' Abigail said. 'Let's raise a lot of money then. How many guests do you have?'

'Around three hundred hearty bidders.'

'As opposed to?' Martin asked.

'Five hundred guests who chat and drink and don't bid.' Audrey nodded seriously, as if it was a crime that she'd witnessed over her many years of being Sydney's fundraising queen.

THE FOLLOWING day was spent helping Audrey and her committee with last-minute details for the auction night, and of course driving her to hair and beauty appointments. Abigail had been tempted to call Jack a couple of times, but resisted and gave her time to her mother.

Although it was just the two of them at Audrey's apartment, there hadn't been a chance to raise the question of Georgia and the diamond. Abigail knew from experience that she needed her mother's undivided attention if she was to gain any concrete details. Otherwise, Audrey's focus could shift without a moment's notice and the opportunity would be lost. The only concession Audrey allowed in spending a quiet moment with her daughter was during her morning coffee ritual. Abigail smiled as she watched her mother make the milky coffee, sprinkle it with fine chocolate then let it cool in the cup, never a mug. She had made it the same way since her days as a young bride. Abigail would never dream of interrupting the flow with idle questions. She had decided to wait until after the event to find out how the ring had come into Georgia's possession. She supposed it wasn't really any of her business, but it would have been nice if her mother had told her.

Who got what from the family estate had never been of interest to Abigail as she was safe in the knowledge her father had structured the trust funds equally between herself and Adam. She suddenly wondered if, perhaps, she had been naïve and should check Georgia for any other unexpected items. Unfortunately, her sister-in-law was constantly on alert like a meerkat, and would never allow Abigail to know about anything she didn't want her to.

Abigail decided the idea was too tiresome, except for the emotional tug of the missing onyx earrings. A little probing might be needed to ensure Audrey wasn't being undermined though; after all, Scott and James were family too. But that conversation would need to wait for another time.

# CHAPTER TWENTY-FIVE

AUDREY WHIRLED like a hurricane between glamorous guests as they arrived at the Park Hyatt. Abigail was also pulled into various groups to be quizzed on what she was up to. She only had a brief opportunity to read through the Regroup Project material in the foyer of the ballroom before the announcement to be seated was made. It was an ambitious plan, but one that was sure to set a precedent. Once again, Abigail felt a rush of pride for the family's benevolent foundation her father had worked so hard to establish.

She spied Adam giving her a wave across the top of the milling crowd, pointing to their table. Of course, Audrey had appointed him to represent Arpels in welcoming the guests and urging them to dig deep into their moneyed pockets.

As Abigail quickly took her seat at the head table she was welcomed by Martin and Christine, two company directors and their wives, and Audrey. Georgia was already seated, her cell phone pressed against her ear. Audrey was effortless in her timeless style, wearing a straight midi satin skirt. A long strand of perfect Paspaley pearls glimmered against the deep plum shade of a matching voile shirt. Pearl and diamond earrings sat beneath her coiffed silver-grey hair.

Other sponsors' tables skirted the stage. The plush, dimly lit function room sparkled with magic from a million bud lights reflecting off silver and glassware. Each table was adorned with tall flutes cascading with green, burgundy and white flower arrangements, small white and gold gift boxes of chocolates nestling in each guest's place.

'You coordinate nicely with the floral décor, Mum,' Abigail whispered, leaning across Martin. Had she just imagined his hand brushing below her breast? She eased back. 'Did you have your outfit made especially?'

'I wouldn't want to clash, would I, dear.' Audrey smiled coyly.

Abigail had resurrected a favourite beaded dress in a light bronze tone. She loved the way it whooshed across the floor and sparkled as she moved, no matter how dull she was feeling on the inside.

A tight red sheath shimmered around a jazz singer's body as she crooned in front of the big band. Abigail tapped her feet to the sexy beat. She missed the sense of freedom that dancing always brought her, so told herself to buck up and enjoy the evening.

The room's chandeliers brightened as the formalities began. Sipping her wine, with half an ear on Adam's welcome, Abigail skimmed through the auction items. He called the other sponsors to the stage and introduced them. When Jackson Mattingley's name was announced, Abigail nearly dropped her glass. She swung around in her seat to view the stage. There he was. Jack was smiling broadly, his hair slicked back in a Gatsby style, his dinner suit fitting him like a second skin. He looked amazing.

'Are you okay, Abby?' Christine asked. 'You look like you've seen a ghost.'

'No. Not a ghost this time,' Abigail replied absently, shaking her head.

'Sorry?' Both Christine and Martin stared at her, puzzled.

Abigail couldn't take her eyes off Jack as Adam explained how Branch Manager Landscape Architects had donated all their time and costs to the project. Abigail was sure that if she was a cartoon right then, her heart would be kabooming in and out of her beaded dress like Jessica Rabbit's. It was so pleasantly unexpected for Jack to suddenly be in front of her, standing tall and very fetching. His eyes swept the crowd, acknowledging the other sponsors, then stopped dead on Abigail. She saw his slight frown, his lopsided grin paused with surprise. They nodded toward each other in amused greeting.

Abigail started to rise as Jack left the stage, but he couldn't make it through the groups of chatting guests and the staff trying to serve meals. He looked across at her and shrugged as his eyes flicked to each person at her table. Was he trying to see if she was with anyone or was he trying to work out what she was doing there? She had realised that he only knew her as Abigail Croucher, not Arpels.

She glanced across to his company's table. A woman was standing next to Jack's empty chair, clapping him as he approached; a tall, stunningly attractive woman, possibly of Indian background, in a long midnight velvet dress. Abigail's view was interrupted by a waiter and when she looked back, Jack was seated. She scanned his guests: stylish creative types who were all laughing and chatting happily. Jack had his back to her, listening attentively to the woman beside him who was leaning in close, her manicured hand resting on his sleeve.

Abigail wasn't even aware the auction had started until loud laughter erupted around her table. Cries of 'Oh no' and 'I'm not going' were the raucous responses to Adam buying a skydiving package for six people. Georgia's horrified expression made it clear she wouldn't be one of them. Abigail pretended to concentrate on the delicious salmon with steamed vegetables, but she was finding it hard to digest anything, knowing that Jack was only a few tables away. With a date. She decided to visit the ladies' room to tidy up during the next break in the auction program, then wander over to say hello.

The cream of Sydney society was at the event with every one seemingly determined to waylay Abigail to and from, and even within, the bathroom. By the time she managed to make it back inside the ballroom the band had started its next set. A fabulous brass section belted out an upbeat Michael Bublé tune as she stood on the sidelines of the dance floor, looking for a way through or around the couples. She ignored Adam, who was beckoning her to join him and Georgia, and started to inch her way to Jack's table when she saw him dancing not far from her brother. The woman in black's body swayed to the music as Jack held her. Abigail watched them; the firm clasp he had on her hand, the way her eyes never left his face. She felt a whisper of jealousy brush against her.

The overtures of a '70s disco hit caused a mass evacuation from the dance floor as Abigail threaded her way back to the table. She left her clutch on her chair and headed towards Jackson Mattingley. He was facing her, apparently waiting.

Now that she was there, Abigail wasn't sure what to do, how to address the situation, but Jack stepped in first, unaware.

'Abby, good lord. I didn't know you would be here. You're on the main sponsor's table, right?' He leant in and gave her cheek a light kiss.

'Hello, Jack. Yes, I'm on the Arpels table. I didn't know you'd be here either. I mean, I knew you were in Sydney but ... anyway. Here you are and here am I.'

She glanced at the woman behind Jack, whose back was turned to them as she reached for her water glass, her toned back shimmering within a low scooped cowl. With no further prompt from Abigail, Jack took her cue for an introduction and touched the woman on the shoulder.

'Let me introduce you,' Jack offered, his voice sounding a little uncertain as if he sensed something amiss but had no idea what it could be. 'Abigail, this is Nisha Varma. Nisha, this is Abigail Croucher. Abigail's a friend from Melbourne.'

All peripheral sounds and chatter peeled away from

Abigail like onion skins; the band sounded a million miles away. She faltered, caught out with a dozen questions swirling in her mind. Who was this beautiful woman? Was she a work colleague or Jack's Sydney girlfriend?

'Abby?' Jack prompted tentatively.

Abigail snatched her reaction back close. 'Pleased to meet you, Nisha.' Abigail extended her hand, which was warmly accepted.

'It's a wonderful evening, isn't it, Abigail. Jack has been so excited to be involved. Now, Jack, you have worn me out on the dance floor and I have to excuse myself for a moment.' With another dazzling smile she headed to the exit. Abigail glanced at Jack as he watched Nisha walk away.

'It's a wonderful contribution your company has made,' Abigail said. She could hear the formal tone weighing down her words but wasn't sure how to change it. Jack's association with Arpels, let alone being in the same room and so close to her, had blindsided her. She tried to lighten up. 'You rock a tux,' she attempted.

Jack laughed. 'Oh, I think someone is wanting you,' Jack said, nodding towards Martin, who seemed to be calling her back to their table.

Abigail gave Jack her best effort at a happy face. She needed time to think. 'Excuse me then.'

She was startled when Martin put his arm around her waist and whisked her away from the table. Christine was nowhere to be seen. Abigail could sense Jack watching her as Martin held her close, and a furtive glance in his direction confirmed it. As Martin jigged her across the dance floor she saw Jack approach Adam, the two men instantly deep in conversation.

'You look ravishing, Abby.' Martin's breath was hot against her cheek, his hands sweaty. 'I thought you might need rescuing,' he added, flicking his eyes in Jack's direction.

'I'm perfectly capable of looking after myself, Martin.'

Martin broke his embrace. 'Yes, we all know that, don't we, Abigail. An Arpels is always the boss,' he said gruffly, his words more than a little slurred. He turned back to the table, leaving her stranded.

A firm hand cupped Abigail's elbow as she tried to squeeze through the dancers.

'Abby.'

She stopped, then slowly turned to him.

'I didn't know you were an Arpels,' Jack said.

Abigail flicked her eyes to his. 'Does it matter?' she asked, a little too sharply.

'Of course it doesn't.' He frowned. 'Not to me anyway, except that we are working on the same project here in Sydney. Such an amazing coincidence, and I like coincidences.'

'I don't,' Abigail retorted. After Martin's unexpected behaviour, she felt impatience simmering not far from the surface. She just wanted to enjoy the evening, raise a lot of money and not have expectations thrown at her from everyone. Not even Jack.

She watched his lips tweak into the lopsided grin she had begun to expect, as he nodded knowingly.

'That's the historian in you, I'm afraid.'

When he didn't receive a reply, Jack took her arms with firm hands and peered down into her face. 'Are we arguing? I hope not, because I have no idea what it would be about.' A dark shadow had crossed his eyes.

She ignored it. It seemed she couldn't say a thing that didn't annoy someone.

Adam's voice boomed over the microphone, announcing the hefty amount raised for the evening. Ticket sales, donations and auction proceeds had totalled well over the committee's target. The guests rose to their feet with loud applause and the band did a drum roll of celebration. Jack and Abigail shifted uneasily next to each other. She needed space and time to go through everything that had happened, away from Martin in particular.

Jack, who seemed determined to continue their conversation, turned to face her but the appearance of Adam and Georgia cut him short.

Adam got straight to the point. 'Jack was just telling me that you know each other in Melbourne and you will be neighbours no less. What a coincidence.'

'Apparently,' Abigail replied.

'But didn't you tell us that one of your new neighbours lives in Sydney, in our home town?' Georgia pried.

At a hundred paces, Abigail could tell Georgia's question was a loaded one. And who could blame her – Jack exuded a huge magnetic charge of sophistication and fun. The fact that his company carried a large enough conscience to donate so generously to this cause was another huge tick as far as Abigail was concerned. She had to remember that, but doubted it was near the top of her sister-in-law's list of priorities.

'Well, let's just say I split my time,' Jack replied graciously, ignoring Georgia's coquettish gaze.

'I really should be getting Mum started on her farewells, otherwise we'll be here till dawn. She looks exhausted. Good night, everyone. Good night, Jack and thank you for your company's contribution.' Abigail gave the group a smile and left them to their conversation.

---

AUDREY CHATTED INCESSANTLY on the way home in the car, thrilled with how the evening had gone and the monies raised for the project. Abigail knew how tired she must be but presumed post-event adrenalin was fuelling her mother's ongoing energy. No doubt her follow-on routine would roll out tomorrow starting with a massage, then a post-mortem lunch with the committee, ending with a cocktail and early night.

'It's a great cause, Mum. You should be proud of yourself,' Abigail offered wearily. All she wanted to do was to climb into bed, but she was drawn back into Audrey's chatter.

'Your father and I always promised each other that, if we were to ever become rich, we would use our wealth to help others. I'm glad that I can carry on dear Allan's legacy.'

She slumped a little lower in her seat and stared out of the car window as the silent streets flashed by. "Rich' seems like such an old-fashioned word these days.' Her voice wavered, seemingly caught in her memories.

It was a rare moment of reflection and softness in Audrey prompting Abigail to glance across.

With a no-nonsense flick of her head to bring her back to the present, Audrey turned to address her daughter. 'Now, Abby, what's this I hear about you knowing that nice man from the landscaping company? They have been so generous. Did you know that they are going to undertake all the design and landscaping including the cost of the trees and plants, plus the installation? The villas will look so welcoming for the residents. I'm so excited. That Jack fellow told Vince, one of the carers, that his company will welcome any of the residents who would like to make suggestions. Maybe there should be a potting shed with wheelchair access.'

Audrey fumbled with her purse, no doubt needing to write herself a note about her idea, but another overlapped. Her eyes bored into Abigail. 'He could be important, Abigail, so make sure you are nice to him should you run into him again.'

'Yes, a coincidence, wasn't it.' Abigail sighed, ignoring the latter comment. 'It was a pretty emotional evening, actually.'

# CHAPTER TWENTY-SIX

'MOLLY, I'm overdue with my thanks for all your help and cups of tea. Why don't you, Tom and Rose come for dinner this week?'

It had been some time since Abigail had hosted a dinner party in her home, but on her return from Sydney it was the first call she made. After the hospitable meal she had enjoyed with Molly's family, she was eager to return the favour, even though Jack was interstate somewhere. They were her friends, with or without Jack in the equation.

A non-committal text from him the morning after the fundraiser had left her unsure of what their relationship was exactly:

*What a great night for a deserved cause. Hope you were pleased with the result. Jack.*

She had faltered when she had read it, as though her feet had slid from solid ground onto shifting pebbles. Had she put a wall up between them without realising it and this was an olive branch? It seemed rather stilted, but then it was easy to misread a text message.

She had been surprised by her jealousy at the fundraiser when she had seen someone else leaning in towards his body. But why wouldn't he have a date? He probably has a whole other life in Sydney after all, she had told herself. Georgia's flirting had pushed her buttons, Martin had continued to hover drunkenly around her, and Abigail had lost all her enthusiasm to continue to make small talk. She had gathered Audrey and left with only a quick farewell. She knew she had been rude.

It was only on her flight back to Melbourne that Abigail recalled Jack asking if she was staying in Sydney for a few days, as he was. She had said she was returning home the following morning but hadn't thought to ask him why or what he might have in mind. Now, she didn't want to imagine, or dream, what could have eventuated if she had only kept her impatience in check.

She replied to his text, again expressing thanks for his company's incredible involvement and a brief reference to catching up when he was next in Melbourne.

Despite her best efforts, Abigail couldn't get him out of her mind, and if she had been completely honest, she enjoyed thinking about him. She knew Audrey would be thrilled with that revelation. His gentle yet masculine and sexy manner, his cheeky grin, the way he looked deep into her eyes as though reading her every thought. The feeling of calm when he held her made her feel whole. When they were together, it seemed he had all the time in the world just for her.

ABIGAIL WAS ADDING a squirt of her favourite Tom Ford Eau de Parfum when the front doorbell rang, Nigella barked in response and her cell phone rang all at the same time. The real estate agent's number flashed on her screen. Surely this would be good news if the agent was ringing after hours, so she answered it as she skipped down the stairs and headed for the door.

'Hi, Michelle,' Abigail said. 'Can you hold on a minute, please?'

She swung open the door to be greeted by two smiling faces and one slightly sullen one; it seemed that Rose might have preferred to have stayed at home. Tom cradled a couple of bottles of wine while Molly offered her promised dessert.

'Come in, come in.' Abigail ushered her guests inside. 'The agent is on the phone, so just head down the hall. Okay?'

They both made signs of 'Oooh' and 'fingers crossed' as they tiptoed away. Rose had already found her way through the house and out the back door to pat Nigella.

By the time Abigail had finished the call, Tom had opened a bottle of red to breathe on her kitchen bench and Molly had placed an enticing chocolate concoction into the fridge. A little bouquet of gifted fresh basil sat next to the sink. Abigail heard her say, 'Nothing like making ourselves at home, Tom. I hope Abby doesn't mind.'

'Well, we'd all better get used to it,' Abigail interrupted, beaming from ear to ear. 'I'll be moving in next door to you guys soon. The house is sold, and with a short settlement.'

Hugs and a swift change to champagne to celebrate followed. As Tom quickly ducked out the back door to speak with Rose, Molly said, 'I hope you remembered to turn the oven on.' Her deliberate dig at her brother gave Abigail a little trip of disappointment that Jack wasn't joining them. She knew he would be thrilled for her.

'Yes, I did, but I'm a bit out of practice with last-minute preparations, so I'm organised and dinner is ready to go when we are. Is everything okay, with Rose, I mean?'

'Boy troubles, apparently,' Molly said, reaching for an olive. 'And so it begins, I guess, but I just wish she would share more with us. I live in fear of her getting involved with the wrong crowd and that we wouldn't have a clue until it was too late.'

She fell silent as Tom and Rose came back inside. Rose declared how hungry she was and promptly plopped into one of the seats at the table. Molly raised her eyebrows at Abigail in silent apology. The trio chatted easily around the kitchen bench while Abigail put the finishing touches to their dinner.

Mouth-watering aromas wafted through the air as Abigail placed a bowl of crispy potatoes plus a large baking dish of Greek lemon chicken on the table, with crumbled fetta and olives sitting in a separate dish. She tossed the green salad, found the servers, then returned to cut chunky slices of sourdough.

'Hey, Rose, come over here and help please,' Tom called. He organised the wine as, with a loud sigh, Rose shuffled to his side. 'I'm sure Abby would like you to take the bread to the table, and probably that dish of oil she has there.'

When they were all seated, Abigail raised her glass. 'Cheers and welcome,' she said, delighted to have her new friends at her table. With a jolt she realised it would be the last evening of entertaining in her house. She pushed the thought aside.

'Thank you for having us. This smells delicious. Look at those caramelised lemons,' Molly said. She nibbled at a chunk of browned chicken. 'Oh yes, and it tastes even more amazing. Is the chicken from the market?'

Abigail nodded. 'From the organic grower.'

'Is that supposed to make it taste better?' Rose mumbled.

'Rose, please. If you can't be civil then maybe you should sit outside,' Molly said quietly but firmly.

'I think it does,' Abigail said simply. She could remember times when she had to walk on eggshells around her boys during their teenage years but, again, didn't want to overstep Molly.

'Anyway, we'd have to sue Abby if she pumped us full of the extra hormones they put into chickens these days,' Tom joked.

The two women looked at each other then quickly at Rose, waiting for a reaction. Tom was unaware of his faux pas about teenagers and hormones, expecting a laugh but not receiving one. Rose had her nose buried in her salad, picking out any stray capsicum pieces she could see.

Molly broke into a fit of giggles, waving her hand in

front of her face as she mouthed, 'Sorry.' Abigail took a sip of water to cover her own rising laugh. Tom looked back and forth between them, uncertain what was going on.

Rose mellowed as the meal continued, asking about Nigella and again offering her talents when it came time to start the mural. Abigail assured her she would be the first to know.

As the evening light faded and the garden lights popped on, the courtyard offered a wall of twinkling magic, despite Nigella looking longingly through the window. Abigail hoped she could achieve as pretty a setting in her new home.

Molly's chocolate torte accompanied a strong brew of coffee for dessert. The conversation flowed around Molly's progress with her plants and Ferryman Road. When Tom referred to the fundraiser, Abigail paused.

'I had no idea Jack would be there or that his company is the one involved with the project. Thanks to them and a lot of generous donations, it was a huge success,' she said. She wasn't sure how much Jack had shared with them about her family background or her quick departure; she wasn't about to spoil the evening mulling over it either.

'I'm embarrassed that I haven't made it in to see what you've been up to next door, Abby, but Molly tells me you've made great headway. I'm looking forward to seeing what you've done,' Tom said.

'Well, if you are around tomorrow, I'll be there. Come on in. That is, if I can lift my body off this chair. That torte was divine Molly, and so rich.'

'Dad says it doesn't matter if you put on weight,' Rose stated.

'I think what he meant was ...' Molly began.

'It's a health thing, don't you think, Rose?' Tom offered, giving her all his attention. 'I mean, if you're healthy and fit, then a bit of chocolate is no biggie, right?'

'Whatever. Can I go and see Nigella, Abby?'

'I think it's probably time we went.' Molly rose from the table. She reached for the plates scattered across the dining table. 'Bring your plate to the kitchen please, Rose. Never waste a trip, I say.'

They said their goodbyes, with echoes of 'great night' and 'thank you' lingering in the street.

Abigail clicked the front gate closed and turned to gaze at her home. She took a deep breath in, releasing it into the tranquil night air. The home she and Luca had created would soon belong to someone else. She had no idea who the purchaser was, and it didn't matter. As the moon shone clear and bright and a soft breeze rustled through the trees, Abigail just wanted to snuggle up on the couch with Nigella, pour herself a weak whiskey and think about what it all meant to her. Then move on.

# CHAPTER TWENTY-SEVEN

'WELL, LET'S GET TO IT.' Brad's usual welcoming smile held a hint of smugness. 'I think you're going to be pretty pleased with how it's turned out,' he said to Abigail and Steph. 'First though, are you sure you don't need us to do a few more coats of paint on that large wall in Binalong?'

Abigail smiled. 'No, I'll be okay, but thanks for your concern.' She was itching to start her mural. The best part was that the image she held of it in her mind was so detailed it was as though the paint had already met its surface.

'Well, I'd like to come back and see what you've done with it then.' He shrugged. Steph's continued compliments on his workmanship quickly replaced his look of doubt, and with a broad grin he led them through the cottage. With each room, Abigail fell more in love with her home as it sparkled with newness and opportunity. From the front bedroom, or "the chandelier room" as Brad called it, which offered a light-drenched outlook to her future courtyard entrance, to the spacious hallway leading to the rear; from the high ceilings and ornate cornices to the polished floorboards. Her renovated kitchen boasted clean lines and neutral tonings whilst the dining area seemed to be just waiting to host raucous dinner parties. Abigail had decided on black steel and glass doors to offer the perfect indoor/outdoor connection to the rear courtyard. The steel gave a subtle nod to the period iron lacework that featured around the suburb. However, her courtyard with its rambling vines and the crumbling, weedy pavement still waited for its overhaul.

When they inspected the upstairs rooms, guest suite and restored fireplace, Steph took Abigail's arm and gave it a friendly squeeze. 'New beginnings, Abby.'

But Abigail was content; she didn't give a second thought to its original condition or what distressing secrets it had held. She no longer cared that Francesca had probably lived in the house at some stage.

Brad handed the replacement keys to Abigail as they departed through the front door. Giving the front yard a worried appraisal, he opened his mouth to say something.

Abigail held up her hand. 'It's okay. I'm organised for the gardens, thank you.' They both laughed.

Abigail slowly ran her hand along the rejuvenated exterior brickwork and down the wooden door of No. 66. She took a few steps back and inspected Binalong's clean lettering, but it was just the name of a building as Kate had said. She smiled as Brad and Steph waited for her enter first. Even without the full paint job the room was entirely different; spacious and filled with clean light. Abigail took herself back to when she had sat signing the purchase contracts, unaware that Liam was watching her in the dusty corner. Butterflies of excitement fluttered in Abigail's stomach – she had so much planned for this building.

'You still haven't told me what you have scheduled for here,' Steph said as if reading her mind. 'Presumably the artists' co-op has moved on with their objection.'

Abigail nodded. 'Actually, I heard about another studio that was empty and put the owners in touch with Patricia. Thank heavens it all worked out. I'll be painting a mural, but it's a surprise. You've been such a help to me with all this, Steph, but can you wait until I'm more organised before I fill you in completely?'

'Chill, Abby. Of course that's okay,' Steph replied.

As they headed up the stairs, 'chill' wasn't a word Abigail wanted to be reminded of. She trailed behind, waiting to feel a breeze, a sign Liam hadn't gone. Half of her hoped he had been fooling around on her last visit.

'Did you locate that draught, Brad?' she asked innocently.

Brad stopped and scratched his head. 'Bit of a mystery, that one. We couldn't find a source, and then it just disappeared. Hopefully it won't come back with a different wind direction, but let me know if you have any problems.'

'Oh, I'm sure it will be fine.' Abigail sighed. Disappointment washed over her as they reached the landing as her eyes searched for a coin or feather. A sharp bang came from downstairs just as she stepped through the doorway into the front room.

Steph extended a steadying hand to Abigail. 'Gosh, you jumped six feet!'

A voice echoed up the stairs. 'Hello? Abigail? Can we come up?'

It was Molly. Abigail muttered a quick 'sorry' and patted Steph's arm to show she was fine. She quickly retraced her steps to the landing. 'Molly. Tom. Please come up.' Abigail's heart, which had been happily nestled in her chest during the inspection, was now thumping against the railing. Surely her neighbours would feel it as they climbed the stairs.

They hugged, then Abigail led the way down the hall to join the others. She wasn't disappointed in Molly and Tom's reaction, both pouring out compliments and observations: 'Look at that beautiful ceiling. Oh, and that shelving – I have serious bookshelf envy.' 'You'll get a stunning view across the treetops from this window.'

Molly was running her hand over the rectangle of iron-work that was now housed within the window frame. Its restored, glossy tendrils and ivy leaves were full of life, reaching for the heavens. Abigail had an imaginary flash of Liam standing beside its former rusty state.

Steph had wandered off to the rear of the floor, and Tom and Brad were engrossed in conversation as Molly caught Abigail's eye. Neither needed to say a word; Abigail just knew her friend had intuited something had transpired in this room. To Abigail, all sensations of Liam had disappeared. She missed him.

Could she summon him back for just one more conversation, one more encounter? Her instincts told her that could never happen.

Sensing Abigail's sadness, Molly swiftly moved to her side, arms outstretched. She gave Abigail a brief hug. 'It's all good, Abby. This is a space that has seen wonder and emotion and extraordinary communication. Now it is in your universe. Can't you feel the love still here?'

Molly's words burrowed deep into Abigail's heart. Perhaps it *was* more a sense of peace and resolution that she was experiencing. Her spirits lifted, her determination firmly set to proceed with her idea.

'Molly, I need to brainstorm something with you. I hate to drag you away from Tom as he's heading off again soon but ...'

'Where am I going?' Tom interrupted, draping his arm around his wife.

'Abby would like to have a glass of wine with me tonight, Tom. Why don't you pick me up at six, Abby, and we can head down to Carpe Vinum.'

Seize the wine! Abigail laughed. 'It's a date!'

---

AS MOLLY STROLLED AHEAD of her into the wine bar, Abigail tossed her journal back onto the car seat. She needed to give Molly a snapshot of what she'd love to see be created, rather than overload her with details. She had no idea how her friend would react to what she had in mind.

They clinked glasses and settled in around the tempting

tapas selection. It didn't escape Abigail that she was finally able to reflect on Grappa's possibilities without feelings of remorse, even when faced with Luca's favourite food.

'Your renovations are wonderful, but you've still kept the bones and character of the properties. Well done,' Molly said.

'Thanks. The interiors needed to be timeless but I still wanted to keep some original elements and modernise other parts. I'm pretty excited.' Abigail popped a small roll of Spanish omelette into her mouth, procrastinating.

Molly waited, but when the silence stretched on, she said. 'Brad was telling Tom that, in his words, you insist on painting Binalong's downstairs gallery. I think he's fascinated by what you have planned. Is that for your mural?'

'Yes. Did you ever visit Binalong when it was an exhibition gallery?' Abigail asked.

Molly shook her head, her blonde curls springing back and forth.

'It was always a great space, and I just can't let go of creating something of mine there. Maybe I just need to leave my fingerprint on it somehow, to make sure that new memories are being born,' Abigail said. 'A mural is the best way I can achieve that, but I haven't quite decided on the exact style. I mean, it could be just sweeping patterns or a sky full of rainbows and birds, or it could be a still life of a table laden with a feast similar to the 17th century *Feast for the Eyes* paintings.'

Abigail paused to take a sip of wine. 'Or a vibrant botanical work featuring Australian plants and flowers.

Maybe a more formal trompe l'oeil that leads down a path to a fountain and hedges.'

Molly slumped back into her chair. 'Oh, yes. I like that idea. Jack said there was a fabulous leaf painting at the Thai restaurant you both went to.'

Unsure if Molly was hinting at learning more about what had transpired between her and Jack, Abigail agreed quickly. But she didn't want the conversation to veer off track.

'Molly, I want to run something past you. I'm just going to dump my idea on you, and it may be so far from where you are at that I'll shelve the idea, sulk and get on with something else with no hard feelings. I just think this may be something wonderful for us both.'

'Okay. I love surprises.' Molly smiled. She leant forward, obviously intrigued.

A warmth spread through Abigail as Molly's comment mirrored Jack's. How lucky she felt to have met the family at this time in her life.

'I think what I would like to do with the space in Binalong, the gallery space for a good description, is to utilise it on a commercial basis. I still need to be involved in the rest of the building, but I'll get to that bit.'

'Another glass, ladies?' the waiter interrupted. They nodded.

'And a bowl of those essential chilli fries,' Molly added. She turned back to Abigail. 'Like an office or a shop?'

'A shop. A garden shop. Well, not a garden shop, really,' Abigail said. Now that she was verbalising her idea, the words tumbled over each other as though trying to keep up with the images in her head. 'More like a bountiful, really lush botanical shop. Rustic but stylish. It could sell anything to do with plants – flower scents and essential oils, glamorous potting tools, seasonal buckets of flowers and plants, some succulents.' She ticked the items off on her fingers as she went along.

'And you could do your garden mural,' Molly exclaimed, a huge grin on her face. 'It could be like one of those European orangeries you see in home magazines. You know, with huge concrete urns that overflow with ... something. Oh, Abby, it sounds beautiful.'

Relief washed over Abigail.

Molly's face hinted at a cheeky grin. 'Do you suppose you could stock my herbs and maybe some plants? I could make them look really pretty, even do some bouquet garni or tussie-mussies. You don't have to if it doesn't fit your vision, but I reckon they'd suit your theme really well.'

Abigail laughed. 'Oh, Molly. I was hoping you would actually run it. Be the manager! I don't mean you have to sit behind a counter all day because I know how much you love the actual hands-on gardening thing, but we can do a list of Molly-Yes and Molly-No duties. I would need to be guided by you as to what to stock, so if tussie-mussies fit, whatever they are, so be it. Maybe they could tumble out of the urns.'

Molly laughed, shaking her head as a definite no.

Options and ideas ping-ponged between them as they nibbled on the fries. Abigail admired Molly for thinking through the different angles first and not rushing in too quickly but, as the minutes ticked by, she wished some kind of indication from her friend would be forthcoming. Would she be as interested in the profit and loss side as much as the creative garden side? Abigail was confident Molly would be completely capable at whatever she turned her mind to.

Finally, Molly looked firmly at Abigail and voiced her reservations. 'Okay. I love the idea and think it would be a fabulous addition to the area. I can just visualise how amazing it could look. I know you would have done all the initial machinations over the business plan and council side of things. You know, whether a garden shop would actually be profitable. I trust you for taking every detail into account. I appreciate your confidence in me as a gardener, and that I could handle the management. I agree it would work, so long as the stock and the ... the whole feel of the shop were unique, but ...'

'But?' Abigail bit her bottom lip. Her friend's initial reaction had been everything she had hoped for; positive and motivated. Abigail clasped her hands tightly together and waited.

'Well. I'm not wanting to steal your thunder or anything but, well, what if I rented the space from you? What if I set up my own business name and rent the space? I just know I could do it, and my mind is already so full of original ideas now that you've started me down that track. I'd like to run a few things past Tom but, well, what do you think?'

Abigail had already thought of Molly's option and, if she had to be honest, it would suit her perfectly. Molly was the one with the knowledge of flora, her creative flair was obvious and Abigail knew in her heart of hearts that she would be a dedicated, honest tenant. And it would give her more time to focus on what else she had planned.

'I love that idea, and I could work on the design plans with you. What?'

A veil of doubt had dropped over Molly's happy expression.

'Oh, I was forgetting about those extra costs. How much would they be, do you think?' Molly sighed.

Abigail flicked aside her concern. 'Don't worry about that. I would cover those costs once we know what you are going to do. We can design the layout and shelving once we have a rough idea of what products you will sell. I'm sure the council won't allow anything on the sidewalk, so it will all have to be contained inside, but with unique, eye-catching, external signage.'

Abigail saw Molly's face and entire body relax, as if she was being coated in fairy dust.

'You wouldn't actually pot anything in the shop though, would you?' Abigail asked.

'I doubt it. I have a full herb garden and potting shed at home. I'd do all the dirty work there and trundle it up the short distance. Oh, what fun, Abby.' Molly clapped her hands together.

'Would Rose help out during the holidays?'

'Mmm, well we'll see how the mood improves. But you know it might be good for her to earn some money over the holidays, and to give her some responsibility. At least I'd know where she was. What about upstairs?'

Abigail nodded. 'Ah, upstairs is my project. I want to do

something with the community. I'm thinking of using the front room as an education space; maybe small art classes, or yoga or lectures, or whatever is needed. But I'd like it to be for those who can't afford the normal high prices of learning.'

'Gosh. Good on you. Do you know how to set that up?'

Before she could catch herself, Abigail said, 'Sure. The Arpels company has a philanthropy division. I have a few projects I'm responsible for in New South Wales but I want to be more hands-on.'

Abigail hoped she wasn't blushing as much as she feared she was.

Molly reached out and put her hand over Abigail's. 'Jack told us all about the fundraiser in Sydney and the incredible work your mum and your family do. Forgive me, but I get the impression you are sort of embarrassed about it, and you shouldn't be. It's not like you wave your money under people's noses or brag about what you can buy. You're very modest.'

'Thank you,' Abigail said, relieved at her genuine friendship.

'I think it's fabulous that you can help others and that you do exactly that. You could spend your time floating the Mediterranean in your mega yacht and being incredibly shallow and useless. Oh, do you have a yacht?' Molly fluttered her eyelashes in mock mateship.

Abigail shook her head, laughing.

'What a shame. Tom loves fishing. But on a serious note, if we go ahead with this plan, I will not expect you to foot the bill for anything extra, okay?'

'Okay.'

'And if I'm late with my rent, you will be knocking on my front door the next day.'

'No, I'll send a terse solicitor's letter.'

They raised their glasses, grinning at each other across the table. Neither had to voice what they were both thinking – that a long-term business relationship was brewing. It would be another layer to the friendship and trust they already shared.

'Well, if we've decided one thing this evening, it's that your mural will need to include more leaves than clouds. Have you made any notes yet?' Molly asked.

'Just a couple of hundred pages completed in a journal,' Abigail hinted. 'Let's get together again soon and plot our path.' She couldn't wait for Molly to add her own personality and knowledge to the project.

How Jack would fit into the grand scheme of things, Abigail had decided to address when he returned. First, she had to move house.

# CHAPTER TWENTY-EIGHT

'YOU KNOW something is going on, don't you, girl. Don't worry, you're coming too, but you have to promise you don't upset Smokey. You need to be neighbourly.'

Nigella spread heavily across Abigail's feet, anchoring her to the spot. The conversation with the dog reminded her of the old woman. Where was she now? Certainly not hovering around Ferryman Road or roaming the streets any longer, asking Abigail if her dog understood her conversation. Here one moment, gone the next.

So much had happened during the last few months, as though her life was suddenly on pause until she sifted dreams from reality. And then, just as she had resurfaced, it had taken off again. Audrey always, mistakenly, had said, 'like a bull at a goat', which amused Abigail's sons no end. As exciting as it was, Abigail found it all somewhat daunting. She wasn't very good at the unexpected. But then, if a ghost and the stirring of her heart weren't excellent preparation for the unexpected, what was?

It was their last evening in the house before moving up the few blocks to No. 64. Abigail's much-loved water feature sprayed gossamer droplets across the deck, relaxing her into the next stage of her life. Abigail dislodged Nigella from her feet and wandered, her eyes taking in every corner of her home, confronting the memories that nestled there in ambush. She was confident she could compartmentalise the different areas of her life with Luca, and had unquestionably reached the point of letting the 'house' part go. Were they fading or just being pushed aside by the need to make new memories? Whatever it meant, she had to be ready.

Steph had offered to dispose of Luca's portraits. They had joked about doing a cleansing ceremony, to burn them and rid Abigail of all they represented. But in the end, Steph had taken them off the frames, rolled them and taken them away; Abigail suspected a Stanley knife had been involved in their demise.

'I have to let that heartache and deception go,' she had said to her friend. 'Otherwise I'll be forever going over everything.'

'Good idea, Abby,' Steph had agreed. 'Let Francesca float away like the red balloon caught on the wind. Over the rooftops of Paris she'll glide ...'

Laughing, Abigail said, 'Oh, shut up, Steph. But a moment later she realised that the book's story was a very similar scenario to how she had put Liam in a ribboned box. Hopefully this would be more successful.

'Are you serious about forgetting about Francesca? I hope so.'

Abigail had sighed. Her friend knew her too well, but

she wouldn't tell Steph about Liam or his comments about Luca's plan to return to her. 'My stomach churns every time I think about her and Luca together. No, I can't let it go completely, but I'm trying very hard. I'm not too sure what to do next. Maybe getting rid of the portraits will provide me with a more tangible closure.'

And Liam – how best to remember Liam? Many years ago he had wished her 'Luck. Love. Everlasting'. He had repeated it more recently just after Abigail had suddenly asked him to leave. The tenderness in his parting words showed how deeply his love for her went. Abigail accepted how lucky she had been to have had the chance, the incredible experience of speaking with him again. She gazed up at the moon and raised her glass.

'Cheers, Liam. And Luca. Whatever your decision about our marriage had been, who knows if you would have stuck with it anyway. Having seen Francesca's beauty, I doubt it.' Abigail's eyes misted, she took a deep breath and smiled as a shooting star streaked fleetingly across the velvet sky. Were those she'd been talking to waving back or perhaps silently saying goodbye?

---

'WELL, you had to choose one of the warmest days of spring to move, didn't you, Abby.' Kate puffed out a hot breath. She and Freddie had offered to man the house and Nigella while the packers did their job and Abigail waited at Ferryman Road to direct the boxes into their allocated rooms.

Molly had been mortified she wasn't there on moving day, but it was their wedding anniversary and Tom had booked them into a B&B at Daylesford for a romantic long weekend. Rose and Smokey were at a friend's house.

'I have to do something to help,' Molly agonised despite Abigail's assurances she had everything under control. 'I know, I'll give you our house key so you can make endless coffees, have access to water, and a bed if yours isn't ready. Feel free to come and go as you please. Moving house is no fun at all.'

As the day became warmer and exhaustion started to set in, Abigail appreciated the gesture. Even though she had sent anything that had sat unused to the Op Shop, she quickly discovered it was just as consuming to move a few streets away as it was to go interstate or across town.

The movers hoisted the last load inside as Abigail's body prickled with anticipation. She already loved her new home, even with packing boxes stacked in every corner.

She had missed a call from Jack, his message wishing her a stress-free move. It would have been marvellous to have him there beside her, but she hadn't asked and he was still interstate. At least he had been thinking of her.

She would return to the old house the following day to tidy up and leave the new owners a bottle of champagne and a food hamper to wish them well. Kate and Freddie had locked up for the night and delivered Nigella. They brought a bottle of bubbly to celebrate, propping a platter of dips and biscuits on an unopened box. Abigail was ravenous but it wasn't long before her eyes started to smart with emotion and tiredness. She stifled a yawn.

'Well, we will love you and leave you,' Kate said. 'We're so happy for you, Abby; it's all lovely and, I don't know, so *you*.'

Gratefully, Abigail wandered into Molly's spare bedroom. After a cool shower her head hit the pillow and she was asleep in no time. Nigella was happy to flop at their back door for the night, knowing that Abigail was nearby.

---

THE DOG DIDN'T MOVE FAR from her side the next morning, probably unsure which house was to be her new home. Abigail's car was in Molly's driveway, still full of those loose pieces that seem to magically materialise at the last minute whilst moving house.

A box of kitchen utensils had Abigail's bored attention when she heard a loud knocking, then the front door slowly open. She quickly followed Nigella down the hallway. Jack was striding towards her, balancing a takeaway tray of coffee cups, a brown paper bag and a bunch of daisies.

'Caffeine and buttery croissants!' he announced. 'And daisies. You know, you shouldn't leave your door unlocked with such shifty neighbours.'

Abigail laughed, thrilled to see him again. 'Thank you, thank you. Pull up a box.'

'Oh, and ...' he continued, reaching around to the back pocket of his jeans, '... an Allen key. Although something tells me there wouldn't be much from Ikea here.'

Jack searched her face, then within two steps he had reached her side. Holding the tray above her head, he ducked down and kissed her quickly and lightly, then waited for a second and did it again.

'Happy housewarming,' he murmured. The slight frown on his handsome face told Abigail he wasn't 100 percent sure of where he stood with her.

Abigail smiled. 'It's good to see you, Jack, and not just because of the flowers, although daisies are one of my favourites.'

'I had intended on surprising you yesterday to help you move, but I just couldn't get here. I'm sorry,' he said. He joined her on the floor, leaning against one of the larger boxes and stretching out his long legs. The gesture seemed as warmly familiar as if it was their nightly ritual.

Abigail waved aside his apology. 'Some friends were at the old house with Nigella while the movers did the rest.' She breathed in the strong scent of roasted beans. The coffee tasted like nectar from the gods.

'*Was* it okay?' Jack ventured. 'Moving out of your home, I mean?'

Abigail was touched by his thoughtfulness. 'Yes, it was fine. I've found my way home. I know all experiences add to the journey of life, but I'm happy to just sit for a while.' She nodded to reinforce her feelings.

'I'm glad to hear it.' Jack stood and held out his hand. 'Well, I'm here to work so crack the whip and tell me where I can be most useful. I have to split by five o'clock to meet a mate, but I'm all yours until then.'

Jack was clearly unaware of his inference, but Abigail felt a rush of warmth run through her anyway. She allowed him to pull her to her feet and into his arms. He brushed pastry crumbs from her chin, his eyes glinting cheekily.

'You know,' he said, 'I would have liked to have danced with you all night at that fundraiser. But you flitted off, leaving everyone in your wake.'

'Well, my mother ...' Abigail began.

Jack placed his finger on her lips. 'No, it wasn't your mother. She is amazing and I think she would have outlasted us all that night. It was something else. Something that I hope you will share with me at some stage because you seemed to be upset. Was it the drunk ex-husband?'

'You noticed?' Abigail was surprised and embarrassed.

'Of course. But I sense it wasn't totally that.'

Abigail gave a small shrug, confirming his suspicions. When she didn't offer anything further, Jack continued. 'But that is for another day, because we have a house to unpack!' He glanced around the room. 'If you have any idea where your speaker is, I'll hook up some music.'

'Of course I know. I label everything!' Abigail laughed, happy to be back on calmer ground. True enough, she headed for a particular box and quickly extracted her cylinder speaker, followed by a lamp base. While Jack cued the music, Abigail fitted her favourite tea rose shade to the base, setting it on the floor by the outlets. She couldn't help but pick up her pace and sing along to the list of upbeat tracks as Jack swiftly unpacked items for her to arrange later. He flattened and stacked the boxes, then took Nigella for a walk and returned with more coffee. The dog had been gazing forlornly through the back door all day, obviously unsure whether she should venture farther out into an unfamiliar courtyard.

Jack refilled the dog's water bowl then propped against the kitchen bench. He slid his hand across the natural stone benchtops and squinted through the glass doors. 'You'll need to give some thought to the layout and plants for the front and back gardens.' Slowly he moved the couple of paces to closer inspect what needed to be done.

Abigail studied his broad back as his body silhouetted in the doorway. She wondered if the tingles down her legs were from having crouched for too long or the attractive vision in front of her.

'I think timber decking for here, rather than stone pavers. I've got a few ideas for the gardens but I just need to know whether I've got the right plants in mind. I don't want anything high maintenance but I do want the gardens to be pretty with lots of fragrances. I'll have to think about garden lights, and some kind of water feature is essential. I love the sound of running water.'

'Just not when it's from a broken sprinkler.' Jack turned to face her. His smiling eyes held Abigail's, both of them locked in each other's gaze for what felt like minutes. 'That day seems like so long ago, doesn't it?'

When Jack flicked out his mobile and started to text, Abigail frowned. She retreated to the unpacked boxes.

Jack's fingers didn't pause in their frantic texting as he casually whispered, 'Where are you going?'

'You seem a little preoccupied,' Abigail replied.

Jack nodded at his screen. 'I'm just texting someone.

Which reminds me that you haven't met any of my friends. We'll have to fix that.'

Abigail didn't reply.

'I think it's polite to let someone know when you will have to miss an appointment. I've done a raincheck with Ben for a beer.'

'Really?' Abigail answered as she continued on her way. She ripped packing tape from along the top of the box, finding the sound comforting in amongst her uncertainty. Jack moved to her side.

'Uh-huh. I told him I was with a very important client and we would be discussing horticulture for some time.'

'Oh?' She paused, the tips of her fingers hooked under the next row of tape. A hint of a smile tempted the edges of her mouth.

'Uh-huh,' Jack repeated. He had moved behind her, his arms curling around her body. 'I told him it was an essential life skill to understand exactly what someone likes, to take your time, and to get the most satisfying result.'

Abigail grinned. 'That's a very long text.'

She eased around, feeling his hardness against her. Jack leaned her against the unsuspecting carton. His kiss was slow and demanding as his hands moved down her body.

A short intake of breath from Abigail made him pause.

'Maybe a shower?' she said, but the glint in Jack's eye suggested otherwise. 'Maybe not.'

She linked her hands behind his neck, urging him to continue as her pleasure fizzed like expensive champagne. Jack collected the corners of her T-shirt and drew it over her head. He quickly removed his own and tossed them in the corner.

Her body, arching with desire, allowed Jack to lift her onto the box. He unclipped her bra and slowly drew it down, following its path with hot little kisses. When Abigail fumbled at his belt, he helped her slide it through the loops of his jeans, while his lips continued down her skin. Her legs wrapped around either side of his firm body. She dropped her head back and smiled to herself. Who would have imagined she would view her new paintwork from that angle? Who would have thought that the body she had first admired as it stretched on Molly's front veranda would now be pressed against her? As Jack's mouth circled her nipple, Abigail drew him even closer to her. Luxurious sparks of sensuality rolled along her arms, down her body.

Sheer curtains were pulled across the tall windows, the heavier brocade drops still pushed to the sides. The early evening was quietly descending, enveloping them in gentle darkness. A pyramid of boxes blocked any view of the room from the street, but not from a visitor who happened to approach her front door.

'Jack,' she whispered as she kissed his heaving chest. He took a step back. Abigail shrugged as she glanced toward the window. Without a word he walked behind the box Abigail had been sitting on and dragged another box to either end. She heard scuffling, then a mellow glow appeared; Jack's hand stretched around the corner of the stack of cardboard, slowly beckoning her. Abigail's rose lamp was switched on and welcoming.

'Not quite what I had intended,' Jack said as he looked down at their nest of blankets and T-shirts.

He pulled her against him, then eased her shorts to the floor, shredding another layer.

---

THE MORNING SUN was an unwelcome wake-up call, Abigail blinking against it as she rolled to the centre of the bed. A small cough, soft as cottonwool, made its way across to her. Without opening her eyes, she registered Jack would be gazing at her from the other pillow.

A contented sigh escaped her lips. 'Good morning.'

She could hear a bird's trill welcoming the day as Jack's warm hand caressed her hip, pulling her toward him. Her breasts were cushioned against his chest as he sidled his warm naked body against hers. His arousal renewed her own longing. Yes, it was a good morning. Memories of their repeated lovemaking ignited her need for more, but something felt out of place. Frowning, she felt around her exposed body, her hand meeting loose, crumpled sheets.

'How ...?' she began.

Jack's eyes locked onto her own in teasing triumph. 'It was handy that there was a box clearly labelled Bed Linen Main Bedroom.'

Abigail could recall Jack's gentle touch increasing in urgency, her own peaks of ecstasy, the soft rosy glow that had enveloped their little nest, even Nigella's bark to be fed. Their move to the bedroom escaped her.

'Did you carry me?' she asked, embarrassed.

'No, you came of your own very free will.' He grinned impishly, his fingertip winding its way around her body.

'I do like a man who can make up a bed,' she said, then added, 'and one who can mess it up just as well. I'm sure it will come back to me in all its glory after a refreshing shower and breakfast. I ...'

Jack firmly rolled her onto her back and eased himself on top of her, devouring the rest of Abigail's sentence with his mouth. An aura of soft morning light curled around the cartons and across the room, settling on Jack and Abigail's own heated version of a house-warming.

THEIR BODIES MELTED against each other at a nearby café, unconnected to the outside world.

'What is it, Abby? Is there something on your mind? You've started to say something several times then stopped.'

She looked him straight in the eye, determined to be honest and upfront. 'Yes, there is, but I'm scared I'm going to muck it up. I have a question for you but I need to make sure you understand where it's coming from. Particularly after last night.'

'Okay,' was all Jack said, but his tiny frown couldn't be ignored. He eased slightly away from her.

Abigail squinted through the café's large window at the sky, at the trees, trying to find the right words.

'Is it about Nisha?' Jack asked outright.

Abigail jumped. 'Oh, why would you think that?'

He shook his head as if it had been obvious. 'Because of

your quick departure from the ball, because of the look on your face when she hung off my arm, because I sensed you knew each other or were sizing each other up or something. But neither of you were showing your cards. That's just my hunch. This is your dime, Abigail, so ask your question.'

It hadn't been said unkindly, but Abigail could still hear a hint of steel beneath Jack's words. She blamed her timing of bringing up the possibility of Jack having a girl-friend or a date or whatever, after the intimate night they had just shared. It probably hadn't been in her best interests.

'Last night was wonderful. You do know how I strongly I feel that, don't you?'

He waited, his eyes never leaving her face.

'I don't know her but, my question is ... was she your date? I mean, is there something between you? I ask because I need to know, after Luca, if there's a solid chance of you and me.'

Jack took Abigail's shaking hands into his own. 'Nisha does contract work for us, project management to be exact. I was as surprised as you at the way she behaved, but maybe that was all for your benefit.'

'I don't think so. She was all over you before she knew I was there.'

Jack raised his eyebrows. 'Oh? Were you watching me? I'm flattered.' Jack leant in to Abigail, kissing her lightly on the mouth. 'Are we sorted?'

Abigail smiled and nodded.

SEVERAL OF HER friends called by later that day to see how she had settled into her new home. Abigail felt very smug as her body reminded her how she and Jack had more than settled in overnight. Abigail was somewhat relieved he had already left for Sydney; although the temptation to physically revisit their glorious lovemaking had gone with him, she wasn't ready to explain their relationship to anyone.

Abigail felt restless to be alone with her dancing thoughts. Even sharing her plans for Binalong with them had seemed an unintended invasion. To distract the conversation, she had offered a challenge to name the cottage with many silly options being put forward before her friends departed.

Abigail lit a fragrant candle, relaxed, and hugged her recollections of the previous night's lovemaking. They had given in to each other's caresses and whims in a way she could only describe as being glorious. What was it about Jack Mattingley that encouraged her to live in the moment? She did recall her passing comment to him about two oldies making love on the floor, that they had survived it extremely well. Certainly there had been little room for any concerns about the lovely Nisha to needle their way into her thoughts. She was relieved her conversation with Jack that morning had further cleared the air.

---

ABIGAIL SUSPECTED that as soon as Molly and Tom returned from their weekend away, Molly would be in to see her. Sure enough, her neighbour was on the doorstep first thing Monday morning.

'Hello to my new neighbour,' Molly exclaimed, a grin from one ear to the other as she pointed down to her feet. 'If you don't like it, you can move it around the back and we'll never mention it again.'

A slim door mat tied with a big red bow, an elegant fleur de lis pattern gracing its surface, nestled against the step. It sat perfectly on the new period chequerboard tiling. 'I love it. Thank you. Can you come in?'

'I can't stay but I'll be back at another time soon.'

That evening Abigail sat on the kitchen doorstep and looked at her underwhelming courtyard and the stunning sky. Nigella's nose pushed her elbow aside. 'You know Nigella,' Abigail said as she happily pulled the dog in for a hug, 'it's the same sky as just a few nights ago, only a couple of blocks up the road. It looks the same, the air feels the same but it's not the same. Come on, you can sleep inside tonight.'

The next chapter of her life was sitting easily around her. Whether that would include Jack, only the heavens knew.

# CHAPTER TWENTY-NINE

HUGH FROM DECK the Halls Framing was helping Abigail allocate her artworks to their new positions. She was so grateful for every corner of her new home and now felt that perhaps Binalong and the cottage were supposed to come along in their own time after all. Thankfully, despite the disruption her builders had caused in the street, her other neighbours seemed not to bear any grudge and waved happily to her when passing. In fact, several had commented they were relieved to have new life being breathed into Binalong, and of course they were also free with advice as to its possible use.

Abigail was so absorbed in directing Hugh that she didn't note the caller when her cell rang. 'Hello?'

'Abby.'

'Adam, what a coincidence. I'm just about to hang the black and white seascape photograph you gave me for my birthday.'

'Abby!'

Adam's tone instantly flicked at Abigail's heart. All was not well. She held her breath, waiting.

'It's Mum. She has had a heart attack and she fell down a couple of stairs.'

'Adam?'

'I'm sorry but she died, Abby.'

Words wouldn't come for a moment as Abigail clutched the phone. Shivers then heat overlapped through her body. The room shifted as her limbs went to jelly, then tried to readjust. As her tears flowed, Hugh quickly dropped from his stepladder and silently led her to a seat.

The sun still shone through the window. Strains of Etta James still wafted around the room. Again, she was reminded that life went on. Abigail bit her bottom lip.

'I'll be on the next plane,' she told Adam, her words choked with sadness.

---

THE SANDSTONE CHURCH overflowed with mourners, a tribute that would have thrilled Audrey. She had planned the majestic music, the eulogies and the celebration down to the finest detail for when the time came. As per her instructions an abundant spray of white roses and foliage graced her casket, with donations to her various causes to be in place of other floral offerings. The heady scent of gardenias and lilies hung heavily over the mourners as it seemed many had still felt the need for a tangible remembrance, with bouquets scattered along the edges of the church. Martin and Christine had returned to the UK as soon as Christine's work in Australia was completed, but they had sent an elaborate cream and baby-pink floral arrangement which overwhelmed the church's entrance.

Abigail sat quietly and listened to her heartache. A porcelain shell had formed around her, threatening to crack and shatter at any moment.

She hadn't been in a calm enough space during Luca and Liam's gut-wrenching funerals to give in to too much reflection. There had been so much sudden grief and unanswered questions swirling around her; it had all been a blur. Luca's parents had sent her a note but that had been the end of their communication with Abigail despite her attempts to keep in contact. She had had no idea why, so she'd let it go.

Liam had shared his forlorn ignorance of his own funeral so Abigail presumed Audrey probably wouldn't be hovering, watching. But maybe it depended on how you died as to where you go and when? She sighed; it was all too difficult to work out.

Abigail had participated in one of the readings but had declined to speak further. Their mother-daughter relationship had often been difficult but she accepted that was just Audrey, a product of her upbringing and era. The fact that her mother had always given the benefit of the doubt to Adam no longer mattered and any hovering conflict had gone. Her own memories were only tugged back to the service when other mourners recounted their, often humorous, stories about Audrey. Abigail glanced along the pew to offer Scarlet a reassuring smile, but her niece sat with her eyes closed, her hands clutched in her lap. Adam was staring straight ahead, his jaw clenching. Georgia was inspecting her manicure. Abigail felt a cheeky urge to lean across and say, 'Don't worry, I have connections on the other side, Georgia'. But it slipped away as Abigail's sadness settled.

She could picture her late father waiting for Audrey, how happy they would be together again. He would be swaying nervously from foot to foot, a trait she had inherited. He would push his spectacles back up his nose, then wait for them to slide down again as he peered into the distance for his adored wife.

A silent tear slid down her moist cheek. Abigail yearned for a butterfly to flutter around her, but none came. Bereft, Abigail gave a silent request to Luca and Liam to look after her mother.

After the service the siblings shuffled behind the coffin, nodding and accepting condolences as they greeted the mourners. Audrey had organised her death as efficiently as she had her life, so all the processes had unfolded very quickly, but a planned brunch loomed ahead. Abigail was sure Adam would don his business persona and get through it heroically. Kate had flown to Sydney as soon as Abigail had called her with the news, and now walked behind her friend in protective support.

Molly had stepped in to mind Nigella as Abigail had left Melbourne on the first available flight. She had received gentle, heartfelt voicemails from Jack in response to her text, but she hadn't had the opportunity to return his calls.

And then she saw him. Jack was standing to the side of the mingling crowd, watching her with such angst that she couldn't help but offer a faltering smile. She left Kate's side and walked into Jack's arms, her emotions finally spilling over. He didn't say a word, just held her close to him, absorbing her sobs. When they quietened to shuddering breaths, he stroked her hair, whispering words of comfort. Abigail could feel his heart beating strongly against her. It felt good to rest her cheek against the softness of his jacket, to feel the slight roughness of his jaw rubbing her forehead.

'I've soaked your nice suit,' she apologised as she eased back from him.

'All in a good cause.' He smiled. 'I'm sorry, Abby. I didn't know Audrey well, but it was a lovely service for her.'

'You were there?'

'Of course. Standing room only up the back,' Jack replied gently.

Abigail nodded, his kindness overwhelming her with sadness again. 'Thank you. She would be so happy to know everyone remembered her in that way. Another person leaves my life, Jack.' As she gave a little sniff, Jack dug deep into his trouser pocket to produce a fresh handkerchief.

Abigail's heart hitched with a laugh. 'Mum would be so impressed that I know a man with a handkerchief.' She took it, quietly blowing her nose and wiping her eyes. She kept it, clutched in her hand. 'Are you coming to the brunch at the club?'

Jack frowned in apology. 'I needed to see you, and pass on my condolences to your family. I will come if you need me to, but that's who you probably need to be with at the moment. Are you okay?'

'I will be.' Abigail nodded and took a deep breath. 'Thank you so much for coming. Can we catch up when you're next in Melbourne?'

'Be careful what you ask for,' Jack said. 'I've decided I need to move down semi-permanently, for a couple of reasons.' His words elevated Abigail's hopes for them as he continued, 'I'll be at Molly's for a while, then moving into my place.' Jack glanced over Abigail's shoulder.

'I didn't want to interrupt,' Kate offered from a few feet away.

'Oh, come and I'll introduce you. Jack this is my friend Kate, from Melbourne.'

The two nodded and smiled at each other, Jack's hand never losing its protective touch against Abigail's back. He lifted her hand and placed a soft kiss on her fingers. 'You'd better head off,' he said.

Abigail could sense him watching her as she and Kate were enveloped by a sea of grey hair.

---

'I THOUGHT you would need to be in Sydney for a lot longer, Abby,' Molly said, passing Abigail a steaming hot cup of strong tea and a plate laden with scones, homemade jam and cream. Abigail appreciated her gesture of comfort food. A beautiful sheath of brightly coloured flowers sat beside her, a gift from Molly, Tom and Rose.

'There wasn't much to organise. We had a private

cremation. Mum and Adam had all her affairs in perfect order, and I only had to pass on any personal items she had instructed in her will.'

After Kate had returned to Melbourne, Abigail had kept herself busy by delivering the funeral's floral arrangements to the local hospital and cleaning out Audrey's wardrobe. Her mother's instructions had been to donate them to a women's refuge, which Abigail had fulfilled. Abigail had found her role as Father Christmas rather fun as she had delivered estate items to Audrey's friends, Pilates instructors and card groups. From cup, saucer, plate sets from her mother's vast Wedgwood collection to little antique ring boxes collected from all over the world, each accompanied by an embossed heart card. Abigail realised Audrey must have been putting items aside for months, not realising her passing was so close.

The reading of the will had been straightforward, with Adam and Abigail the main beneficiaries of shares and property. Georgia was already in possession of the diamond ring plus several items had been bequeathed to Scarlet, James and Scott. Valuable jewellery left to Abigail nestled in Audrey's opulent jewellery box, but she still couldn't shake her concerns about the whereabouts of her own chosen onyx earrings. It was such a small thing but their disappearance nagged at her.

Abigail continued to fill Molly in. 'We're keeping the apartment for a while for visitors to use, or I'll stay there when I go to Sydney, I guess, so there's no sale to arrange just yet. Adam's on top of things.'

The truth was Audrey's home had been eerily quiet

without her mother's vibrancy filling every room. Abigail also needed to retreat from the endless requests for coffee from her mother's wide circle of friends. A few gatherings had been compulsory but prying conversation always came back to the Arpels estate, a topic that Abigail refused to discuss. She had spent a full day meeting with her philanthropic beneficiaries instead, a commitment she felt was far more worthwhile. Another day in the company's offices to sign off on some of Audrey's legal matters, and then she told Adam she was returning home. Abigail hadn't crossed paths with Georgia again, even when she had dropped by their home to see how Scarlet was faring. The nanny had been the welcoming committee.

Molly reached over and patted Abigail's hand. 'Well, there's no harm in taking your time. And if you suddenly have to fly up there we'll look after things here.'

Abigail nodded in gratitude and took a sip of tea. Molly faltered, then said, 'If you want to take a raincheck on our business idea, I'll understand.'

'No, absolutely not, Molly. I'm thrilled you're on board and we need to finalise as much as we can as soon as possible. Now my house is finished, except for a name, I want Binalong to be completed as well. It needs the winds of change to blow through to bring it to life again. Oh, speaking of names, I thought of one for your business. What do you think of Floriade?'

Molly shuffled in her seat. 'I've thought of a name too. Not for your house, but for the business. Of course, Floriade is lovely.'

'It's your business, Molly. What's it to be?'

'Rose suggested "Molly's Mulch".' She paused, laughing at Abigail's shocked face. 'Don't worry, that's not it. What about The New Leaf? I thought it fit because it symbolises growth. And it's like turning over a new leaf for both of us.'

'It's perfect. It says so much.' Abigail couldn't help but raise her hand in a high-five.

'I've checked business names and there isn't another one registered in that category. That surprised me, to be honest. I've started the branding for it too.'

'Gosh, there's no stopping you! I'd better get my mural design drawn up.' Abigail settled, rolling the name over in her mind. 'The New Leaf. It's a marvellous name. Here's to your new business venture.'

Molly and Abigail, neighbours and now business associates, clinked teacups and beamed at each other.

# CHAPTER THIRTY

WITH A HEAVY CLOUD still over her from Audrey's death and the many details to be sorted for Binalong and The New Leaf, Abigail had renewed her resolve to ignore the distressing Francesca issue. She had gone over and over all the possibilities, all the scenarios she could imagine but, after all, who knew what was right, wrong, imagined or possible. Luca had obviously lied to her on many occasions.

Abigail had packed the subject away at the back of her mind, fearful it would consume her entirely. She was determined to fill her days with positive thoughts, with goals to move forward and not to dwell on the past and how much Luca had deceived her. She would never really know to what extent he had loved her, despite Liam's assurances. The first toe-tingling step in this new life was to embrace her feelings for Jack, to allow her thoughts to dance and wind around him.

But that was before she found what she would call 'the Camino note'.

When the movers had packed up Abigail's office, they had included a box of books that had belonged to Luca. Abigail had been meaning to take them to the Salvation Army store but she just hadn't got around to it. On top of the pile of John Grisham, John Berendt and Stephen King novels she saw a copy of Graeme Simsion and Anne Buist's book *Two Steps Forward* about walking the Camino. Abigail recalled one of their conversations after she had seen a documentary of the various options:

'Wouldn't it be great, Luca. We could really challenge ourselves to complete one of the routes.'

Luca had shrugged. 'Well, at least part of the way, I guess. Are there proper hotels and restaurants along the way?'

Abigail had been frustrated at his lack of interest and understanding of why people attempt the walk, then forgotten all about the idea. Why had he never mentioned he had a copy of the book? She set it on the floor and stared at it. It looked new, unread.

Perhaps she could attempt one of the expeditions on her own. Abigail picked it up and started flicking through the pages in search of a map.

Out fluttered a piece of card with a pretty watercolour of Spain on the front. The message inside wasn't as appealing, not for Abigail.

*My darling Luca. Thank you for my gift – you know my weakness for jewellery and they are divine. Like an adventurous walk, our beautiful future awaits. Together. F x*

There was no date, just Win Win scribbled in the corner in Luca's handwriting. Abigail's hands shook. She had no idea what it meant but tension hummed down her legs. She flicked the card with her fingers, then firmly folded it in half, then half again, then half again. Who had told her you could fold a square seven times? Liam. But Liam was no longer here, and she couldn't run to him for answers anymore.

Abigail sat, a gradual calmness covering her like warm oil. No salty tears came, no racing heart. She dropped the book into the box, then marched to her study and pulled up Josh's email. There it was. All the contact details for Francesca Lisi, including a Melbourne address. Hawthorn, where she had lived the fateful night Liam had collected Luca.

Despite all her previous attempts to let Francesca go, Abigail couldn't forget Jack's words either: 'You and I are similar, I think, Abby. We both need to have all the information, to tick all the empty boxes, if we can truly move on happily.'

Before Abigail knew it, she was in the car, hunched over the wheel like Cruella de Vil and heading to Hawthorn. Many times she told herself to turn around. *What's the point of confrontation? She won't be there. You told yourself you'd moved on.*

She had stabbed the address into her GPS, and when Siri told her she would be at her destination in fifty metres, Abigail firmed her jaw and her resolve and pulled over a few doors down from where she presumed Francesca still lived.

Without giving herself any leeway to back out, Abigail quickly paced along the sidewalk and up the path to the neat, single-fronted Edwardian house. She rang the brass doorbell, listening to the chime echo through the house. Like summoning the devil. It was followed by the echo of footsteps quickly clicking down a hallway.

Abigail took a step back, head held high, and waited, prepared to be disappointed if someone else appeared.

As Francesca swung open her door and saw Abigail, she gasped, her lips a perfect O. She had a leather handbag over her slim shoulder, obviously dressed for an outing.

*Meeting someone else's husband?* Abigail held back from uttering the pointed greeting. She was feeling more cocky than angry in that moment.

A steely flint came into Francesca's eyes as they swept down Abigail's body. 'Abigail. What are you doing here?'

'I know about you and Luca, Francesca.' Abigail wished she had prepared a better opening, something erudite and unforgettable. She also wished she had remembered to slip her shoes back on before leaving the car.

A few tense seconds of silence passed between the two women.

'Look, Abigail. I'm not going to stand here, in my home, and discuss, um, things with you. If you wanted answers you should have spoken to Luca, shouldn't you?'

My home. Abigail's eyes traced the elegant hallway over Francesca's shoulder. Luca would have sauntered down that hallway to a warm bed that was waiting behind one of the doors. Where he had made love to the woman standing in front of her. Abigail stood firm. She felt scrutinised, like a bug under a microscope.

Amusement came and went in Francesca's alert, green

eyes, openly reading every emotion that trawled across Abigail's mind.

'I'd ask you in, but you know.' Francesca shrugged. She gave her head a flick, her black, shiny bob falling back in perfect position. 'It was just a little game we played. Mind you, a very enjoyable game. A win-win.'

Abigail raised an eyebrow, unmoved. Having a tangible version of Francesca in front of her was strengthening her intention.

Francesca lifted her chin and continued, 'You may have lost Luca, but so did I.' Accusation, rather than commiseration, oozed between her words.

'We both lost him, apparently, but I wasn't playing games. It was our marriage.'

Abigail saw a shiver run through Francesca, quickly replaced with a concerted look of boredom. But had she just said 'win-win'? Abigail recalled that was Luca's scrawled note.

Abigail's dad had always said 'Don't ask the question if you don't want to know the answer', but she had to settle the mystery once and for all. She placed her hands firmly on her hips. 'One more thing, Francesca. Do you own a pair of onyx drop earrings?'

Francesca's obvious surprise at the question didn't quite hide the defensive tone that lingered behind her reply. 'I did. In fact, Luca gave them to me. He said they were a family heirloom or something. I sold them after he died.' Francesca paused. 'It would seem that I'm the only one standing here who valued Luca over his inheritance.'

What web of lies about his family had her husband

spun to Francesca? Abigail's stomach plummeted. Luca must have had her unsuspecting mother so wrapped around his finger that Audrey never thought to ask if Abigail had received the earrings. She sent a silent message to the heavens: *I'm sorry, Dad; I would have looked after your gift.*

The roar of a motorcycle shattered the silence. Francesca's beautiful eyes slid to watch it pass, then returned to her visitor. Her head tilted slightly as she gazed at Abigail as if seeing her for the first time.

'I watched you at Luca's funeral. I wanted to confront you, to tell you how much I was hurting at the loss of my love. He had only just left my home, my arms, when tragedy struck. Did you know that? If you had only released him out of your life, he wouldn't have died. But at his funeral you seemed so pitifully lost, so I let you be. I honestly felt sorry for you.'

Francesca's spiked words bounced off Abigail as steely determination took over her body, her mind. Deep down in her heart Abigail knew that in no way was she accountable for Luca's death. Who was then? Luca and Liam, yes. Francesca, possibly. But not her.

Abigail held her tongue. Francesca tried again. 'He sat for me, you know, to be painted. It was a wonderful, intimate experience.' She faltered, her eyes becoming misty. 'But one has to move on with no regrets.'

'So you left the canvases behind. No regrets. That was easy for you, wasn't it, Francesca.' Seductive images of them together floated inside Abigail's imagination. Her stomach clenched, her nails dug into the moist palms of her hands.

Abigail opened her mouth to share Liam's announcement that Luca had intended to leave Francesca and return to her. But, unlike Luca's lover, she didn't like playing games and knew it would only sound spiteful. She remained silent.

A warm breeze whistled around them, the gentle scent of eucalypts and flowers playing in the air. A passer-by would have presumed they were two friends parting after a shared cup of tea.

'If there's nothing else, you're holding me up from an appointment,' Francesca said. She turned her back on Abigail as she pulled her front door shut, then sauntered straight past her and down the path. Abigail was stunned at how quickly the woman had regained her composure.

A fleeting look back from Francesca was all Abigail needed: she had seen a flash of embarrassment on Francesca's face. Or was it sadness?

Abigail drove slowly home, taking all the backroads so her thoughts could drift a little. She felt gutted she had lost the earrings that had been promised to her and could well imagine how Luca had played up to Audrey to secure them. But not for his wife. Why had he chosen that particular piece of jewellery; because their absence would go undetected by Adam or Georgia? Because the black of the onyx perfectly matched Francesca's lustrous hair?

A Bluetooth call lit up Steph's number. Abigail recounted where she had been and why, omitting any reference to the earrings.

Steph roared with laughter, particularly the barefoot part. 'Good on you, Abigail. My God, I bet she got a shock seeing you standing at her front door. But what a nerve. I mean, she just walked away?'

'Yes, sauntered actually. I felt like one of those seagulls you see, you know, alone on a rock after all the others have flown off.'

'Maybe you could do the Camino together,' Steph teased.

'Hardly! And she needs a gardener. I got a bindii stuck in my foot from her grass.'

'But not *your* gardener.' Steph paused for effect. 'Yes, I have noticed references you have made to your neighbour, so I know I'm out of the running. Where are your shoes may I ask?'

'I was so focused on confronting her that I jumped out of the car without putting them back on.' Abigail laughed.

'I hope you feel well and truly cleansed now.'

Abigail wasn't so sure it was 'cleansed' that she felt but an emotional weight had been lifted from her shoulders. She felt a sense of release, as though invisible wings were pulling her up and away from Francesca forever. If her visit to Luca's lover had done nothing else, it had made her realise the extent of her feelings for Jack.

# CHAPTER THIRTY-ONE

SEVERAL LAYERS of paint had been lovingly rolled onto the interior feature wall of The New Leaf. Abigail was thrilled with how her mural was building: layer by layer, texture upon texture. She was on her hands and knees inspecting the base line when she felt a shimmer in the atmosphere, the merest wisp, like an angel had exhaled. She shivered, glancing along the wall, then saw it – a small brown speckled feather with white tips. It was caught, fluttering in the wet paint. Abigail wasn't surprised. She was feeling so inspired and driven with her artwork, as if someone was directing her paintbrush. Ghost or angel, she wasn't sure, but she had to accept that Liam's ghost had left her life forever. The random discovery of a beautiful feather did not mean he was back, unfortunately.

It was at that moment that Abigail knew in her heart that she needed to make a couple of modifications in the next stage of her design. Humming, she squatted down, easing the feather onto the wall and into the paint. Her whole body was awash with a calm feeling of achievement, of being exactly where she needed to be.

'Well, you sound happy,' said a deep voice from the doorway.

'Jack, I didn't know you were back.' Abigail jumped to her feet, her heart skipping at the unexpected sight of him. He pulled her close.

'Are you still my neighbour, or have you found somewhere else to live?' she asked.

'As luck would have it, a mate is off to Europe for a few months and offered me his apartment. It's just around the corner so it's perfect until I decide where to buy. But that's not important.' His handsome face became serious.

'Oh? What is so important then?'

'Well,' he continued, taking Abigail by the shoulders. Gently he brushed her lips with his own before turning her towards her painted wall. He crossed his arms over her chest, clasping her hands under his.

She felt his warm breath on her neck as he whispered, 'What's important is everything about this masterpiece. I want to know all about what you have in mind.'

'It's finished. Don't you like it?' Abigail kept any teasing tone out of her voice while she waited for Jack's response.

A moment's hesitation told her that Jack believed her before he quickly recovered.

'From what I know about you and your eye for detail, I doubt that very much.'

'To be honest, I've been thinking about that whole ticking of the boxes thing and whether it needs to be addressed. Is it so bad?' Abigail asked.

Jack nibbled her neck. 'Nope. Come on, tell me about your painting.'

Abigail moved through his embrace, wiping her hands on her paint-splattered jeans. She wandered across to the wall, conscious of Jack following close behind her. 'I'm inspired by you and Molly, actually.'

When she heard Jack huff out a breath of disbelief, Abigail half turned. 'It's true. The love you both have for nature is so open, plus there's a real story behind how you started down your path.'

She turned back to face the mural, her arms held wide. 'I'd like to recreate something subtle but with impact, so when customers visit they feel at home, whether they know about horticulture or not. The next layer will include all the botanical elements. You know, hah of course you know ... branches, leaves, buds, full-blown blooms, spindly nests and so on. More of these soft autumn colours, I think, with highlights of mint greens and maybe several patches of piercing blues, like a bower bird has just deposited a little collected treat.'

She paused, wanting to share one of her ideas with Jack. 'My stories will be reflected here as well. Hidden in there will be two little ladybird bugs, my boys.'

When the sound of silence reached her, she turned to Jack, anxious that she had rambled on too long. He was gazing at her, intent on her description. Then in two steps he was in front of her, his warm hands cupping her face.

'It sounds amazing, you are amazing. You've been away from the paintbox too long, judging by your excitement.

But then I always knew there was great passion inside you.'
Jack raised a suggestive eyebrow.

'If I'd known you reacted in such a way when talking
about art, I would have shown you my brushes a whole lot
earlier.' Abigail sensed he would support her no matter
what direction her dreams took, and it felt so good. Her
stomach flipped as Jack's kiss grew stronger, deeper. As one
hand disappeared into her hair, his other palm pressed
firmly against her lower back. His body was firm and
welcoming, his legs muscled as they stood guard on either
side of her answering body.

Gradually they eased apart. Abigail scanned the small
crinkles either side of Jack's eyes. Years of working
outdoors, and no doubt playing golf in wind and sun, had
weathered his features like a gentle etching. It was very
sexy.

'It's good to see you,' she said.

Jack caught Abigail's hand as she reached to flick back
her hair. 'Sienna?' he asked gravely, inspecting the
remaining daubs of paint on her fingers.

'Close. Yellow Ochre.' Abigail laughed.

Voices from the street grew louder as the front door
burst open. Brad didn't seem to notice them at first as he
held open the door for several large boxes to be brought in.

'Hi, Brad. Good lord, what's all this?' Abigail asked.

'The shop fittings,' he announced, clearly proud of his
delivery.

Steph had suggested keeping Brad on to source some of
the items, to install the shelving, the custom-made counter
and other fittings for The New Leaf. Molly had worked

closely with him to design a workable, appealing store. Abigail and Molly often laughed as either one of them said, 'thank heavens for Brad'. It was particularly true now when everything seemed to be happening at once, but Abigail had underestimated Brad's ongoing efficiency.

'But they're not due until next week!'

The disappointment on the builder's face made her backtrack. 'I mean, thank you for hurrying it up, but I haven't finished the mural and I can't have dust sticking to the paint.'

Brad held up his hand. 'No problem, Abigail. No problem. We can leave the boxes in the hallway here until you're ready. When will that be, do you reckon?'

'Well, you have some pieces for upstairs too, I think, so they can be taken up and unpacked now if that's okay.' She had ordered a new desk and chair, lamps and a rug for Liam's room. She was still planning on creating a shared space for a range of classes, but until the bookings came in, she wasn't sure what else she would need, so extra trestles and chairs would be kept in the storeroom. The shop was a firm priority but at the same time she was itching to get her other plans underway.

Once again, Jack seemed to be able to read her thoughts. Abigail had given him a rough idea of the direction she had wanted to take for Liam's room, but there just hadn't been further opportunities to go into detail.

'How are your plans for the lecture theatre shaping up?' he asked.

Abigail smiled. 'I told you it is hardly a lecture theatre, rather a more cosy, welcoming space. Okay. I think.'

'I'm sure it will all come together. You'll do a great job,' Jack replied.

'I'll just check where the counter is going, if you don't mind,' Brad said. 'It's pretty big, you know.'

'It has to be. We thought a long, simple oak table counter here in front of the mural would be essential. Packaging, racks of paper and ribbons all have to be accessible but out of sight, and we need space to wrap large items plus the money area ...'

'The money area?' Both Brad and Jack laughed.

'She means the cash interchange,' Brad teased, rubbing his fingers together.

Abigail placed her hands on her hips and smiled. 'You know what I mean. Anyway, this is where the counter is to be placed, on a bit of an angle.'

'Abby, I'll find Molly for you, and I guess you need to get on with your mural if it's all going to be finished before Brad wields his drill. Call me if you need anything else, but I'll be back tomorrow.' Jack casually gave Abigail a hug and kiss on her forehead, then left in search of his sister.

---

TWO MINUTES later Jack raced back through the front door, a stricken expression wounding his face.

'Rose is missing. Molly is frantic.'

Abigail tossed aside her brush. 'What? What happened?'

'They had a big argument, and Rose stormed out. She said she wouldn't be back. Molly went out to her potting shed and presumed Rose had gone to her room to let off a bit of steam. But she wasn't in the house when Molly went back in.'

Brad sauntered over and put his hand on Jack's shoulder. 'Oh mate, she's a teenager. She'll be back soon. Trust me, I had three daughters. She'll come home when she's hungry or when her phone battery needs recharging.'

'That's just it. Her phone is still on the kitchen bench. She never goes anywhere without that thing. Molly has rung all her friends nearby but no one has seen her.'

'Has she done this before?' Abigail asked.

'Yes, but does it matter?' Jack's retort stung, but Abigail knew it was just a reaction to his concern. And he was right. Sometimes only one hasty action could lead to disaster.

'When, Jack? When did she go?' Abigail gathered her belongings.

'It must have been hours ago.'

How long was too long for an angry teenager to be gone? Hopefully she was sitting in the park being stubborn or striding along the streets, venting whatever pent up emotions she was experiencing. But if she did need help, how was she to call anyone if her phone was at home? So many conflicting fears muddled Abigail's thoughts.

Jack and Abigail ran to Molly's house. They could hear the alarm in her voice as she spoke on the phone.

'Tom, she said she hated me. All I did was ask when she'd be around to help me with the house. She said she was going to meet this Lachie fellow no matter what I said and wouldn't be back.' Deep sobs followed.

As Jack took over the phone call to Rose's father, Abigail cocooned Molly in her arms and tried to sound optimistic. 'She'll be okay. She'll be home soon.'

'I wish Tom was here. He's always so far away and Rose, well, Rose and I have been arguing more and more. When she's home we don't seem to be able to talk about anything anymore. She just clams up.' Molly's voice hiccupped with worry. 'This boy she is supposedly seeing, Lachie, won't come and meet us. Why wouldn't he? Oh, Abby, I lost my temper. She looked so hurt ...'

Jack and Abigail's eyes met over Molly's head, both silently coming to the same conclusion.

Molly pulled away from Abigail, a look of relief spreading across her puffy face. 'Maybe she went to your house to hug Nigella.'

'I'll check but the house is locked.' Abigail gently shook her head, then led Molly inside.

'Jack and I will head out and look for her, but you have to stay here in case she calls from somewhere or comes home, okay? Just text us if she does.'

Molly nodded numbly as she checked her cell again for a text message that she knew wouldn't be there.

'Who's this Lachie?' Abigail quietly asked Jack.

Jack shrugged, frowning. 'We should split up. I'll take the car, but I'm sure she's okay. Just giving her mum a scare.'

Abigail knew him well enough now to recognise his confident tone being all show. He wouldn't stop until he found his beloved niece.

Abigail quickly tossed up whether to take Nigella as a

lure but decided the dog may be more nuisance than saviour. She carefully checked her backyard, but Rose was nowhere to be seen.

Abigail continuously glanced down side streets and into parks as she searched, the minutes ticking by. Where would I go if I was upset? she asked herself. You have been upset, Abigail, for heaven's sake. Your go-to hideaway is the beach.

No one had a clue where Lachie lived, so the beach it was. She couldn't presume Rose would think the same way as she did; she could only hope she would, as countless stories of young runaways living on the streets surfaced in her mind.

Abigail increased her pace, memories of James being lost in a shopping centre coming back. She couldn't remember how it had all come about, but the feeling of panic and remorse was still vivid in her memory as her young son had taken off down an escalator. He was out of her sight in less than a minute and remained so for what felt like hours. She'd had no idea where to look and was on the verge of calling the centre's security when she'd seen him sitting in the food hall. Relief, anger and confusion had ripped through her as she realised he was not in the least concerned, just being naughty.

Hopefully they were all overreacting. Abigail reached the foreshore and scanned the long expanse of sand. The beach was endlessly packed with people of all ages lying on the sand and heading for the water; indistinct sunbakers, walkers and kite flyers added to the mix. She searched in one direction and then the other.

A small figure, hunched over near the buffer wall, caught Abigail's eye. Despite Rose's attempt to be invisible, even at a distance Abigail recognised the neon pink T-shirt. Rose was alone. Perhaps the teenager's threat of taking off to meet Lachie had been just that. Abigail quickly sent texts to Molly and Jack with an instant text from Jack offering to collect them. Abigail replied that they'd walk home, but it would take a while. She wandered over to Rose, unsure of exactly what she was going to say.

Rose didn't look up as Abigail sat down next to her, she just continued to stab her finger into the sand. She may have whispered something but the wind was strong and whipped away any words that may have been muttered. Abigail waited a moment.

'I was just thinking about when one of my sons disappeared,' Abigail offered slowly. 'I've never been so worried. Parents don't always know what's going on in kids' heads ...'

'Well that's obvious.' Rose cupped her hands on either side of her tear-stained face and leant on her knees, blocking out any possible interference.

Clearly Abigail would need to try another approach.

'But we still worry. I don't need to know what happened, Rose, but your mum is super anxious.' Abigail paused. She had to tread carefully. She just hoped that Rose's sorrow, whatever had caused it, didn't run to a deep numbness. 'Can we go home?'

'Has she called Dad?' Rose demanded, glancing sideways through glistening tears. Her expression sat somewhere between confusion and defiance. She made no effort to stand.

Abigail shrugged, not wanting to give away anything. 'Rose, if there's anything I can do to help, you know you only have to ask. I'm right next door. Nigella is always happy to see you too.'

Rose peered towards the horizon, ignoring the offer. 'You seem to have it all together. Don't you ever make mistakes, or just get tired of waiting for something?' Rose asked accusingly.

Abigail shook her head. If only she knew! 'No, I don't have it all together. Not by a long shot. I don't know that anyone does actually.'

Rose turned to Abigail, as if making a decision. She glanced away, but continued in a whisper. 'Mum keeps nagging me about Lachie. Why doesn't she just respect my choice of a boyfriend? Anyway, she'd freak out if she saw his tattoo.'

'Why?' Abigail pictured a face covered in inked barbed wire.

'Because she doesn't like them, duh!' Rose retorted. 'I'm going to get one anyway. Lachie said he'd meet my parents when his body and mind are ready, and I respect that.'

Abigail wasn't sure how to reply, so she nodded at a waddling seagull.

'Anyway, I'm so bored. There's nothing to do and Mum just wants me to help around the house all the time. I bet it's just so I can't see Lachie. I mean, how am I supposed to know what I want if I haven't done anything else?'

Out of the mouths of babes. Abigail leant back on her elbows to give Rose space. She could just see glimpses of the shoreline through Rose's mass of windswept curls.

'Rose, I will have to let you and your mum work all that out together.' With no further comment from the teenager, Abigail took the plunge. She already knew the answer, but thought she would ask the question anyway. If nothing else, it was a distraction from Lachie.

'Did she mention the shop?'

Rose sifted sand through her fingers, releasing it into the wind gusts.

She probably wishes she could fly away with those little grains, Abigail thought.

'What about it?'

'Um, I've been thinking.' Abigail paused until she was sure she had the teenager's attention. 'If you want to, you could help me with my mural. I've got a bit of a timeline now.'

Rose squinted toward her, suspicion written all over her face. 'Why? You've already started it.'

'Because you said you would be good at it, and I only want someone who will be good,' Abigail said firmly. 'But you have to do your mum's jobs first, whether they're around the house or potting up plants for The New Leaf. But that's none of my business.'

'I guess,' Rose mumbled, still brooding.

'I expect a bit more dedication than "I guess",' Abigail goaded, nudging Rose's shoulder. 'And you have to run it by your mum and dad first. Come on, I'm getting cold.'

Abigail stood, reaching down for the teenager and not giving her any other option. She looked so lost and frustrated plopped in the sand, as though the whole world was against her. Abigail hoped she'd done the right thing in offering her young neighbour a painting job. She'd soon find out.

Rose was in no hurry. Abigail didn't want to rush her in case she fled again, so she matched the teenager's slow pace towards home. Neither spoke.

They could see Molly patrolling the front gate as they neared Ferryman Road, and Abigail felt Rose stiffen. Molly silently mouthed thank you to Abigail as she followed her sullen daughter inside their home.

Abigail let out a long, faltering sigh. It was only when the front door had closed behind mother and daughter that Abigail noticed Jack slumped in one of the veranda chairs. His face mirrored pure relief as he moved to her side, put an arm around her shoulders and led her next door.

'Thank you. I'll take you home,' he offered seriously. 'Did I snap at you earlier? I'm sorry. I was just so goddamned worried.'

Abigail smiled, and within a few steps they had reached their destination.

'Is she okay?'

'I guess, although I don't think she had any intention of going any farther than the beach or meeting anyone. Lachie's name did come up, but that's for Molly and Tom to talk with her about. I did say she could help me with the mural. Will Molly think I'm interfering?' Abigail asked, still unsure of her offer.

'She'll soon tell you if that's the case, believe me,' Jack reassured her. 'But now, I think that red wine and pizza are in order. Do you want to change and head down to Don Carmelo or get takeaway?'

'Definitely takeaway, if that's okay,' Abigail said, scraping thin ribbons of paint from her palms. 'I have wine.'

'And I will collect a couple of pizzas while you clean up or whatever,' Jack said. 'I'm not sure if that paint would go well with marinara. Oh, Brad left while you were looking for Rose, so Binalong is all locked up.'

---

ABIGAIL EASED a glass of shiraz across to Jack as he placed the pizza boxes on the counter. She wondered if Molly and Rose's conversation was still simmering, or if they had resolved it to any degree. Perhaps it hadn't even started.

'So how is the new kitchen working?' Jack asked. It seemed they had both decided not to go over Rose's disappearance.

'Oh, Jack, it's wonderful. I love the whole house. It feels like home and that's a big admission for me. Now I'm here and have all my paintings and bits and pieces around me, I'm feeling pretty settled.'

Jack glanced to the window sill and raised his eyebrows at the row of sea glass – little smooth blobs of soft blue and green glass that had been rolled and kissed by the ocean.

Abigail followed his gaze. 'My boys used to call all my collected finds "knick-knacks", and it wasn't a compliment.'

When Jack nodded in agreement, she shook her head. 'It must be a boy thing.'

'I have my favourite bits and pieces too, don't you

worry.' Jack smiled mysteriously as he bit into a slice of pepperoni. 'Whoa, this is hot!'

'Like what? Sports memorabilia?' Abigail teased, although she would dearly love to see how Jack's home reflected his personality.

'I'll have you know I own a couple of very sexy Norman Lindsay etchings. And a rather enviable signed cricket cap from ...'

'Ooh, I'll take the Lindsays over anything else you have.' Abigail stifled a yawn.

She was all too aware of the bedroom and her waiting bed. Her body yearned to climb under the sheets with Jack again, to feel his nakedness and lose herself in his fevered whispers and touch. But after a couple of glasses of red wine, combined with a full day of painting and the drama of Rose's disappearance, it wasn't long before her muscles started to ache and her eyelids drooped. She nestled into Jack's shoulder on her couch, enjoying the comforting rise and fall of his chest.

Gregory Porter sang his mellow 'Hey Laura', as Jack kissed her goodnight and saw himself out. She mumbled a reply and gave him a lazy wave.

# CHAPTER THIRTY-TWO

AS IT TURNED OUT, Rose's contribution to the mural worked perfectly for everyone. Molly was more than relieved to see her daughter happily occupied, and Abigail realised she had a lot to offer. She enjoyed instructing her young neighbour on what brushes to use for each section of the mural and setting challenges for her. The artwork was coming together quickly, but Rose's chatter and huge grin at Abigail's acceptance of her ideas was reward enough.

'So, are you and Uncle Jack together?' Rose asked, paintbrush raised. Abigail sat back on her heels, lost for words.

'I mean,' Rose continued, 'you don't have to tell me all the gory details or anything. It's just that I reckon he's pretty keen on you.'

'Really?' Abigail failed to concentrate on the dusty colours of a blooming rose.

'Yeah, he's hanging around a lot, even though he's not living with us anymore.'

All things are relative. Abigail hadn't seen Jack nearly as often as she had hoped as he was either in Sydney or out working on the Melbourne project. She needed to remember that Jack had a job, a responsible one in a very busy practice, but a few quick dinners, trips to the markets on Saturday mornings followed by an afternoon of lazy lovemaking weren't enough. When they weren't together, Abigail looked forward to their 'how was your day' chats every evening. Some of their calls to each other were just to touch base, whilst others meandered happily over several hours. They covered every subject imaginable, like teenagers not wanting to hang up.

'You've tied a string around my heart, giving it an irresistible tug when I least expect it,' Jack had murmured on one occasion.

Abigail longed for his caring face to be close to hers, to feel his arms around her at every opportunity. Nigella found her place each evening at Abigail's feet, welcoming the lonely pats from above.

Jack's designs for her front and rear courtyards had to be passed on to a gardener Jack knew; everyone was too busy with their own deadlines to accomplish any gardening.

Abigail and Molly were anxious to open The New Leaf as soon as possible. They knew they wouldn't be completely ready, but Christmas wasn't far away and they wanted to take full advantage of the early buying season. They had papered over the front window to prolong the surprise for curious locals including Sandy and Patricia, whom Abigail had seen with their noses pressed against the glass. The group had withdrawn their petition to disrupt the building plans, but when Abigail had approached the duo with a cheerful "good morning", they had scurried away like mice outrunning a flood.

While Molly was busy in her shed, Abigail's days were filled with preparing The New Leaf from Molly's list of instructions. Kate had used her exhibition skills to advise on lighting to bathe the whole shop in a welcoming glow and to highlight pockets of the mural. It had saved precious time when the job had been done purely from emailing a layout plan and rough sketch to Kate, then onforwarding her instructions to the lighting installer. Brad had worked miracles with the custom carpentry, including finding a local furniture maker to construct the oversized wood counter in record time.

Molly's logo for The New Leaf ran across the face of the counter. When she had shown her idea of the name in black italics on a white background to Abigail, Rose had interrupted: 'That's pretty boring, Mum. Why don't you add something like a flower or a leaf at the end.' After a few quick adjustments on the computer, Rose had added the flourish of a curlicue leaf at the end of the name.

'That's much better. Thanks, Rose,' Molly said. The threesome had nodded with pleasure when Brad erected the wrought iron sign outside the entrance. It was as though Binalong was being reborn, piece by emotional piece.

The fact that The New Leaf was Molly's business was always at the back of Abigail's mind, even though it was housed in Binalong.

'Are you sure I'm not intruding on your turf?' she had asked, referring to her mural.

'Absolutely not. Technically it's your wall and I love the hints you've given about what you are secretly creating. I'm busy enough keeping up with my end of things,' Molly had replied. Her space was soon overflowing with vast piles of greenery, wooden Christmas decorations and piles of patterned pots. It seemed she had previously undiscovered talents for sourcing suppliers, as more and more delivery boxes sat waiting to be unpacked.

---

ABIGAIL HAD ALWAYS ACCEPTED she wasn't a professional artist, but she did have to admit she was rather pleased with her creation. Nevertheless, she was still nervous about unveiling her mural to the community. Now, Jack, Molly and Tom were made to close their eyes until the last moment, then standing at either end of the painted wall, Abigail and Rose gave a big "ta-da!" Amidst gasps of approval and clapping, the mural came to life.

'Oh, it's like the Garden of Eden!' Molly exclaimed. She had insisted on not peeking behind the temporary rattan screen until the mural was complete. 'It's so abundant and beautiful.'

Thick tendrils of textured vines wound their way through a lush landscape: huge rose blooms in ivory, copper and dusty pink intermingled with oversized leaves and foliage in every shade of green, from mint through olive to emerald. Deep-red bunches of berries, tiny insects and wispy ivy burst from the depths of the virtual garden as though there had been an explosion of all the seasons at once.

'You can almost smell those flowers, and the mossy branches, and look at those pops of blue. It's wonderful, girls.' Molly pulled Rose in for a hug.

Abigail could sense Jack searching for her hidden secret, her touchstone. His face broke into a smile as he found the two bugs, James and Scott.

He pulled her to his side and whispered, 'It's a beautiful wall of possibility, isn't it.'

Abigail couldn't agree more. In a quiet moment, Abigail planned to show him the two butterflies she had painted deep within the layers of foliage. At first she had painted two angels, but it didn't seem right. This would be her tangible way to respect the past, but welcome the future. So she had overpainted with butterflies – the angels would always be there.

Unpacking and stocking the shelves began in earnest, amongst laughter and swearing and endless lists of forgotten tasks. Molly and Abigail had insisted on doing the bulk of the setup themselves; Jack, Steph and other friends who offered to volunteer were relegated to clearing away packaging or fetching coffees and snacks.

'We've decided this Jack fellow is a keeper,' Kate and Steph declared one day.

'Well, I'm glad you like him,' Abigail had replied smugly. 'I think you might be right.'

'YOU KNOW, ABBY ...' began Molly early one morning. She was getting frustrated by an assemble-it-yourself wooden holder for their greeting cards. With a giant sigh she abandoned the project and started to unwrap packets of cards instead. Images of Australian native flowers fluttered over modern Marimekko style illustrations of daisies, and soft botanical watercolours hand-painted by a local artist. Boxed card sets featuring paintings of famous European gardens were a nod to Abigail's love of art history.

When nothing further came from Molly, Abigail stretched up from unpacking a box of essential oils. 'Mmm?' she prompted. She picked up the discarded template and clicked the sides into place.

Molly shook her head in wonder, then continued. 'Don't you feel it, Abby? Don't you feel everything just falling together, and I don't mean that darned wooden thing. It's like, I don't know, like ...'

'... like someone is here just nudging us forward.' Abigail nodded. 'I know, I feel it too, and it makes me so happy and content, like a cat who has finally found its favourite cushion. I was saying to Jack the other night that I was worried for a while that I wouldn't be able to move on from what Binalong had always stood for; Luca, our restaurant and everything, but I have.'

Abigail recalled the conversation with Jack had actually been more focused on Liam than on Luca. They had been curled on his couch when she had felt an urge to share more of herself with this man who was playing such a large part in her life. She needed to fill in some gaps.

Aspects of her marriage to Luca had been laid bare,

from the dream to convert Binalong, to Luca trying to infil-
trate the Arpels estate. Jack had silently listened, interrupting with his own questions only occasionally. He
stroked Abigail's shoulder while she shared how Luca had
drifted from her and that she would never be sure if
Francesca had been his only diversion. When she
recounted her visit to Francesca's home, he gave a hearty
laugh and raised his glass to her courage. She had felt him
relax when she promised that it didn't matter anymore.

Then, when she had turned her story to Liam, Jack
admitted to nearly asking her on many occasions how she
was faring with her ghost.

'Why didn't you ask me, Jack?'

'It wasn't from lack of interest or that I didn't believe
you. I knew you would reach out to me again when the
time was right. You had to work through it all yourself first.'

How well he knew her.

'I can look back on being with Liam in Binalong as a
privilege now,' she had ventured. 'I was angry at him, and
scared, and thought I was losing my mind. Now, I miss him.
I still can't believe it, really.'

'But if he hadn't come back, then you wouldn't have
been able to fill in so much of your story with Luca.'

Abigail nodded. 'I did thank him at the end but now I
don't think it was enough. I hope they're okay. You know,
wherever we all go.'

'I only hope you'll be there with me.' Jack had sealed
his wish with a deep kiss.

Abigail had snuggled into his body, unsure if her next
question was too personal.

'Have you ever wondered why your brother Sam has never come back to visit you?'

Jack paused for a heartbeat. 'Maybe he did, but I missed it.'

Abigail nodded, recalling very similar words from Molly.

'I remember you saying that you can smooth out bad memories, but do you ever truly move on from them?' she asked without thinking. She felt Jack edge away from her.

'Abby, some things need to be in the past. You can still value them, turn them inside out but ...'

Abigail sat up and leaned away. 'You don't think I can? I don't agree.'

'Well, you've said you're happy, so I can only hope that's the case.'

It had been a tense moment between them but Abigail had acknowledged Jack had been saying what she had been fearing anyway. He had just shone a light on it.

The pieces of her life jigsaw were falling into place now and she was mighty pleased with how it was coming together. She knew now that any longing for the way life might have been had gone. That place in her heart had been happily replenished.

Molly's voice brought Abigail back to The New Leaf. 'I'm so excited. Thank you, Abby.'

'No, thank *you*. You've got a great little business, my friend. Oh, and thank you also for having such a sexy brother.'

'Who's got a sexy brother?' Rose's voice floated from the staircase. 'Are you talking about Uncle Jack again?

Listen, the upstairs storeroom is getting pretty full of boxes. And I just saw a truck pull up with a load of something. I'll go and see what that's about if you're too busy chatting.'

Molly and Abigail giggled at hearing Rose sound so responsible.

The little shop on the corner in Ferryman Road nestled in and took shape. Tom continued his return trips from their shed with trolleys of Molly's tiered terracotta herb pots; she had been working around the clock to have as dramatic a display as possible. One whole wall was layered with brilliant red poinsettias in green tubs, tables were laden with other beautiful Christmas gift ideas, some pre-gift wrapped in eco paper and giant raffia bows – another of Rose's ideas.

'People get busy at Christmas and this means the wrapping is done for them,' she had informed Molly and Abigail seriously.

Molly had mumbled 'no kidding' but gave her daughter a thumbs up.

When Abigail had put forward the idea of a 'soft opening' instead of a grand event, Molly had looked at her blankly.

'It's totally up to you, but we're both so busy. We can always have celebration drinks in the new year,' Abigail explained. 'By then people will know the shop and we can do a VIP list or open house or something. In the meantime, I thought we might just string up a few fairy lights, open the doors and welcome our customers on the first weekend with a little gift. Maybe one of those sachets of seeds or a

Christmas gingerbread cookie if we can source some quickly.'

Molly let out a sigh of relief. 'Perfect. I couldn't quite get my head around being a glamorous hostess at the moment.'

———

ONE MORNING, as Molly was visiting her suppliers at the central flower market and Abigail was crouched down behind the counter searching for her labeller, the front door opened. A rush of warm air billowed through the space.

'Damn it, I thought I'd locked that,' she cursed.

She stood up, rubbing her knees. Her hands flew to her mouth. 'Scott, James! What are you doing here?'

Abigail couldn't reach her sons fast enough. Arms outstretched, she pulled her grinning boys to her, then kissed them on both cheeks. They had been the missing cogs in her new adventure wheel and now they were here in her world. She thought her heart would burst with love.

Another figure appeared through the doorway. 'Gee, it's hard to park around here.'

'Adam. Did you arrange all this?' She tried not to show her surprise at her brother taking the time to visit her. She moved to give him a hug, noticing his quick appraisal of the space before pulling his attention back to her.

'No, it was the boys' idea. They wanted to visit you before Christmas. I am merely the Australian contact, and I had to be in Melbourne for a conference anyway. Plus, I wanted to visit your new venture. It looks pretty good. All organised?'

James shook his head in disbelief as he looked at Adam. 'As if Mum would let a stone go unturned.'

'"What doesn't happen doesn't happen" is my new motto,' Abigail said. She gathered her laughing sons in to her for another hug.

---

'I WANT TO PROPOSE A TOAST,' Abigail announced that evening as she stood at the end of her dining table. Jack, Molly, Tom, Adam, James, Scott and Rose raised their glasses in unison, waiting for what Abigail had to say.

'I'm probably going to stumble a bit,' she began, her voice already shaky.

'Can we do the toast first, if this is going to take a while?' James joked.

'I second that,' Scott said, and they all took a sip then put down their glasses.

Abigail looked around the table at all the people she loved the most in the world. She cleared her throat and continued softly. 'I guess what I want to say is thank you. Such simple words, but in my heart they mean so much. Molly, Tom and Rose – thank you all for your friendship and acceptance of this new kid on your block. Thank you for being here, Adam, but with a little empty space of sadness that Mum and Dad aren't.' They raised a glass to the heavens.

'Thank you to my darling boys for coming all this way and for showing interest in what your old mum is doing.'

She paused, locking eyes with Jack. 'And ... oh, is it my imagination or did it suddenly become very quiet in here?'

Laughter echoed around the candlelit room but Jack's attention on Abigail didn't waver. Abigail placed her hand over her pounding heart. 'Thank you, Jack, for your companionship and belief in me.'

His wide grin drew her in like a bee to honey.

Abigail's sons groaned loudly.

'And to you all for bringing dinner,' Abigail quickly added. She sat down, then jumped to her feet again.

'Not more.' Rose sighed.

'I meant to tell you that my new home has a name. I now proclaim this property formerly known as No. 64 as Feather's Rest.

# CHAPTER THIRTY-THREE

JAMES AND SCOTT had returned to London, via a few beach days in Byron Bay, in time for a white Christmas. They had each mentioned new girlfriends they were eager to return to, but their visit had still been nurturing food for Abigail's soul, and she'd spent as much time as she could with them. She was thrilled when they'd both told her how much they liked Jack and given the thumbs up to their obvious relationship. Adam had scurried back to Sydney straight after his conference, in time for him to join Georgia and Scarlet on a flight to Aspen for a skiing holiday.

The opening weekend had been a huge success with the community's word-of-mouth publicity living up to its reputation. Jack had arrived during the Friday afternoon bearing an oversized basket of fruit. His card read: 'Abby & Molly: I would have sent flowers but guess you already have some. Good Luck and Congratulations on The New Leaf. Jack. X.'

He was promptly given the job of finding some nice

rope to drape across the staircase so no one ventured up the stairs, but was waylaid by an early shopper. Abigail and Molly broke down in a fit of giggles to witness the sheer look of terror when he was asked to gift wrap her many purchases, but pleased when he offered to carry them to the customer's car for her.

Now, the festive season at The New Leaf had arrived like a freight train and had steamed ahead without stopping at any stations.

'Well that was a day' had become Molly's daily exclamation after she had farewelled the last customer.

'You're doing such a great job, Molly,' Abigail had reassured her. 'I don't know how you keep up with all the plants and herbs you're selling. I can hardly get my head around all the other merchandise that's walking out the door.'

'It is the silly season, and Tom has been a huge help moving things around,' Molly replied. 'But thank heavens people are loving it. Imagine if no-one came or if the tussie-mussies went brown, or I had to throw out bunches of wilting flowers.' Molly's eyes had grown wide at the thought.

'I'll turn my mind to longer-lasting pieces when things settle down, but that flower fridge was a must,' she added.

'There will be quieter times, no doubt. Probably in winter when no one wants to walk around the block in the rain for a card,' Abigail said.

'Mmm. The rent might be late for a few months then.' Molly gave her landlord a sidelong glance.

'I've already decided to cut off the shop's lighting if the

summer quarter wasn't paid.' Abigail tried to keep a straight face. 'Maybe we should each get a tattoo saying *The good times always return* or something.'

'Who's getting a tattoo?'

Without turning, Abigail could feel Rose glaring at her, and hoped the teenager didn't presume she'd told Molly about Lachie's body art.

Unaware of any suspicion, Molly replied, 'We're thinking of getting a tattoo each to remind us of the manic times at The New Leaf.'

'Yeah, right. As if you'd do that. Anyway, you're nearly out of tissue paper,' Rose said as she headed for the door. 'Just saying.'

'Ah, where are you going, Rose?' Molly asked carefully.

Rose paused then half turned. 'Lachie is taking me for a coffee. I'm meeting him at the café.'

Molly flinched.

'Then we might come back to our house. Okay?' Rose said.

'Sure. No problem.' Molly smiled as her daughter had already skipped out the door.

---

ABIGAIL WAS LOOKING FORWARD to a deliciously quiet, cosy Christmas Eve at Jack's apartment. The New Leaf had closed early, giving Abigail time for a quick shower and change, and to wrap Jack's present. A fizz of excitement, her constant companion when meeting him, overflowed as she approached his gate. She laughed to see him leaning over the second-floor balcony, frosty champagne glasses in one hand.

'Come on, hurry up. I can't wait to see you,' he called.

A passing couple glanced up, then back at Abigail and grinned. 'Merry Christmas.'

'And to you,' Abigail replied. Christmas carols drifted on the gentle breeze through the trees, and she realised there was nowhere else she would rather be in that moment.

She rummaged in her handbag, trying to suppress the obvious joy that spread across her face. She knew Jack's door would be open in welcome while he put the champagne on ice. She quietly stood in the doorway and waited.

'Abby?'

As he appeared around the corner of the hallway, she whipped out her sprig of mistletoe and held it over her head. Abigail heard his approach; she could sense the intensity of his eyes even though hers were closed. Silence, but she resisted opening them. Cool, sweet lips touched hers as though they were coming from thin air; then her body was encircled by strong arms and gathered in. The mistletoe dropped to the ground as Jack gently guided her inside and kicked the door closed.

'That's a nice Christmas welcome,' she whispered.

''Tis the season.' Jack nodded, his lopsided grin and twinkle in his eye suggesting so much more. 'Hungry? For food, that is.'

'Ooh, yes. I didn't realise how hungry until you mentioned it. And thirsty. You did say not to bring anything, didn't you?'

Jack led her through to the terrace, where iced platters of shelled prawns with mountains of pineapple, coconut and bok choy salad were waiting. Jack brushed several leaves from a chair with instructions to relax as he fussed with their drinks. As the sun set on the balmy day, the sky exploded in a tangerine wash, creating a backdrop worthy of any romance book cover.

They took their time grazing through the delicious seafood, then sat back in easy silence. Jack's knees balanced Abigail's tired feet, his strong finger massage coaxing little purrs from her.

She nodded at the thick eucalypt branches that were propped in a giant vase on a side table. Flickers of street-lights and festooned trees were reflected in the dozens of shiny, silver baubles that they supported. 'Very creative.'

'It's my standard Christmas centrepiece for all festive occasions.' Jack laughed. 'We could have wandered into the gardens to listen to the local choirs. Although you do look pretty settled right here,' he added.

'And I feel very settled. Nigella is having a sleepover with Rose, so you have me for the whole night.' Abigail winked, her wine-soaked laziness not outweighed by a wonderful sparkle of contentment.

---

ABIGAIL AND JACK uncurled from each other's bodies early on Christmas morning. They were hosting Brad and his family for an early glass of bubbly and croissants at Feather's Rest as a thank you to Brad. She had asked Steph,

Kate and Freddie to join them but they were tied up with their families' Christmas celebrations.

Then it was on to lunch at Molly and Tom's house where, in true Australian style, a large table under a market umbrella had been set up in their backyard. The days were increasingly hot, so Molly had cooked the evening before, leaving Christmas day free to relax and enjoy copious salads, cold turkey and ham and antipasto platters. Abigail was responsible for bringing the traditional plum pudding, custard and brandy sauce, and Rose had made trays of rum balls. Jack was in charge of keeping everyone armed with chilled mineral water, margaritas and wines.

Laughter and snippets of conversations drifted across the neighbours' fences throughout the afternoon, as surely as their bonbon popping and silly jokes made their way back. Tom insisted on having the soundtrack from *Love Actually*, his favourite movie, on repeat in the background.

The summer day eased into a beautiful, clear evening, the predicted thunderstorm not having eventuated. The coloured party lights Rose had looped around the yard popped on, balls of red, green and white bobbing in the welcome breeze. Abigail and Jack were shooed away whilst the others cleared the tables. They wandered hand in hand, an unusually docile Nigella ambling at their side. Abigail suspected Rose had passed too many secret snacks to the dog under the table.

The streets had settled, except for the occasional echo of happy voices. Abigail and Jack sat close together on June's bench, Nigella plopped at their feet. Someone had had a spurt of festive cheer and tied a length of sparkling green tinsel around the seat's timber slats. Abigail's mind drifted. It seemed so long ago that the old woman had stopped and spoken to her there. Little had she known the unforgettable events that would soon unravel in her world. Abigail squinted up at Liam's window, now dark and empty.

A young girl, staying up late to master her new bike, teetered past as her dad clung to the seat. Jack's thumb gently rubbed the back of Abigail's hand as she rested her head on his shoulder and watched them go. She loved how easy it was to be with him. His mere presence transformed her from feeling like a cork being tossed around an ocean to a petal floating along a stream.

For Christmas he had gifted her a beautiful champagne-coloured blouse, as sheer and light as a spider's web. She had laughed at the packet of Turkish Delight that had been wrapped separately. 'For old times' sake,' Jack had said. Her gift to him had been sterling silver cufflinks, one a tree and the other a spade. Everyone had been spoilt with their presents, but when a smile had lit up Rose's face, Abigail knew she had been spot on with the teenager. Abigail had inscribed in the front of the red leather journal: 'For Rose, who can do whatever and be whoever she dreams of. Love, Abby. X' Rose had raced to show Molly, who mouthed a grateful thank you to Abigail.

'I'm so happy, Jack. To have spent today with you and your family, to be included.' She gave a little hiccup as a single tear escaped.

'I hope they're happy tears.' He wiped her cheek.

She tried to laugh it off but Jack continued to study her face.

Abigail took a deep breath. She fingered the strands of tinsel 'I wish ... I wish you could have met my dad. He loved Christmas. Mum would always have the most beautiful Christmas tree, perfectly decorated in that particular year's colour theme. She would go from full on silver and gold glamour one year to mauves and pinks the next. One year we were amazed to see the tree smothered in wooden figurines, hand painted of course. Dad would go and buy really tacky little decorations and hang them on the branches together with drawings Adam and I had made at school. Mum would get cross at him every time, but maybe she actually loved his gesture. He could do no wrong in her eyes.'

She paused, squinting at the star-spangled sky. 'He would have liked you, and he would have been happy for us.'

'I'm glad. I'm sure he was a special man because, well, I might be biased, but he has a pretty amazing daughter. She's strong even though she doesn't think so, she's smart and kind and generous. Damned good in bed too, although I wouldn't tell her dad that.' Jack kissed her gently, eased back, then kissed her smiling mouth again. It was a double dose of deliciousness Abigail was happily getting used to.

# CHAPTER THIRTY-FOUR

THE NEW YEAR saw the first tutoring class held in 'Liam's room'. It was to be a trial run, with Abigail promoting the full program after the summer holidays.

She had found herself talking out loud as she set up the tables and chairs. It should have felt silly but it didn't, as she shared her thoughts and plans with Liam. She knew in her heart that Liam would never appear to her again, that he had disappeared when she had told him to go, or perhaps when the old woman had joined him. But she also sensed that a welcome murmur of him remained. How could she ignore an out-of-place item or a door suddenly ajar, the very faint hint of Tic Tac peppermint on occasion or the discovery of a welcome feather on the stair?

Her ghost now nestled in a special corner of Abigail's life. Luca rarely featured and she was perfectly happy with that. Perhaps she had been affected by Liam's love for her more than she had realised. Hopefully, somewhere, he could hear her.

'I've brainstormed lots of ideas with Molly and Jack and this room will be a hub of learning. You might pick up a few pointers, Liam. So far, we've planned tutoring in literacy, yoga and relaxation classes and Network Knitting for lonely old folk. I know you'd hate to miss that last one.'

Abigail glanced around the room, and sighed. 'I'm so grateful that the Arpels Trust will provide full sponsorship. There has been so much more work than I anticipated to gain approvals, find competent tutors and cull hopeful participants. But I've done it all Liam, and you won't be surprised to know I have many spreadsheets to prove it. It's all coming together and, just between you, me and Jack, I'm rather proud of what the program will become.'

'HELLO, EVERYONE,' she said. The chatter didn't subside but Abigail didn't mind. By the level of laughter and enthusiasm already bouncing off the walls, the ten young class members were already enjoying themselves.

She had expected the participants to be quiet, wary of expressing themselves or interacting with strangers. They had all gone through a life-threatening illness; Abigail wasn't keen on the word 'survived' but it was probably apt for many of their experiences. Kate had sowed the seed one day as she told Abigail about a successful gallery tour she had conducted for recovering cancer patients and their families. Abigail had tracked down an experienced art therapy teacher and the Life through Colour class was born. She hoped this would be the first of many to give kids the opportunity to express themselves through colour and drawing.

They turned and found themselves a seat as the therapist introduced herself.

Abigail propped herself beside the window, running her finger along and around the ironwork's curving branches. A whisper of air curled across the group. A green pastel rolled off a table. The little leprechaun strikes again.

---

ABIGAIL AND MOLLY met frequently to plan activities for both areas: Upstairs Downstairs they called it. Rose had reluctantly returned to school with Molly promising her more work in The New Leaf during school holiday breaks and weekends.

'It's so handy living literally next door to our work, isn't it? No peak hour traffic or public transport to contend with, and we can be home in no time,' Abigail said.

'And I can quickly go back for whatever it is I've forgotten, which is often. I don't know if it's age, exhaustion or this darned heat,' Molly replied. She was fanning herself with a seedling brochure, little blonde curls stuck limply to the sides of her shiny face.

Despite the humidity, Abigail was actually enjoying relaxing in her renovated courtyard. She had asked the landscaper to use mature plants, eager to be surrounded by lush greenery as well as providing Nigella with stretches of shade. Australian summers could be brutal. Her new fountain tinkled nicely in the corner, but she agreed that some small breeze would have been welcome to move the sticky air.

'Do you want to move inside into the air conditioning?' Abigail asked.

'No, I'm an Aussie girl. I can handle it.' Molly laughed as she took a sip of her long gin and tonic. 'Was that Sandy, the notorious Patricia's friend, I saw yesterday?'

Abigail laughed. 'Yes. I asked her take a look at the space upstairs. Apparently she volunteers at one of the unemployment centres and I thought there might be a need for an interview room. You know, somewhere private. She seemed very keen.'

'Good on you. Speaking of jobs, did Jack mention that his company might have a position for Tom?'

'No. But we haven't had a chance to talk at length about anything lately. It's frustrating actually. When Jack said he'd be staying in Melbourne more I thought it would mean just that, but he seems to be in Sydney just as much as before.'

Molly nodded. 'Tom said they've just got a huge contract up there, but his job would be in Melbourne. Jack might have to ...'

Abigail frowned, but Molly's focus had been diverted to catching an ice cube at the bottom of her glass. Abigail felt hot prickles climb her back and knew they weren't from the summer heat. Was Jack moving back to Sydney? If that was on the cards, why hadn't he shared the news with her? She told herself not to jump to conclusions, but a niggling doubt had wormed its way into her mind.

'Well, hopefully he'll mention what he has planned

tonight. His flight was delayed, so we're having a late dinner. Heavens, look at the time. I'd better go and get ready.'

She needed space to think. The possibility of permanently living interstate from Jack had devastated her. They had both been so busy over the summer and now she hoped they hadn't wasted precious time.

---

'YOU'RE QUIET, ABBY,' Jack said as he took her hands in his across the table. 'You know that I was joking about it being too hot for meatballs, don't you? I love that you remembered how much I love them.'

'It's just that, well, Molly said something about your work and warned ...'

'Really? Well, there's proof she listens to my ramblings. Was that about Tom? I'm sorry I hadn't got around to mentioning it, but I think I've secured him an HR position with my firm. He'll have to be interviewed, of course.'

Abigail frowned, suddenly impatient. 'No, not about Tom. About you and your job. And Melbourne. And me. No, about you and me ...'

Jack eased back in his seat, a frown creasing his forehead.

'Hang on. Molly *warned* you about me?' he asked, a hurt edge to his words.

'No. It wasn't like that. Jack, are you moving back to Sydney to live?'

'What? Don't you think I would talk to you if that was a possibility?' Jack stood and moved to the kitchen. He poured them both a long glass of iced water, then silently sat back at the table.

Abigail shrugged, foolishness stamped on her forehead. She pushed a meatball deep into the spaghetti as if trying to bury her concern.

Jack didn't satisfy her with a quick reply, but rather took his time twirling spaghetti around his fork. Finally, he said, 'I wonder where Molly could have heard that.'

'Maybe I jumped to conclusions,' Abigail muttered. She waited.

'I was thinking of travelling, but moving to Sydney? No.'

A tense cloud threatened. Jack shuffled forward. A sly smile escaped his lips as he mumbled, 'But I am very flattered by your reaction.'

'Jack, I'm serious because, well, I have something I wanted to ask you, but if there's an inkling that ...'

'I'm planning a trip to London.' He took a sip of wine and paused, obviously anticipating Abigail's reaction to his announcement. When she shot upright in her seat he seemed immensely satisfied, like a preening feline.

'Really? When?'

'Whenever you're free. It's years since I've been there and I figured you'd be needing to touch base with your boys again soon. I'd like to spend time with them too, to get to know them a bit better, but if you're too busy talking nonsense with Molly then maybe it isn't such a good idea.'

He shrugged, settling back in his seat. His eyes twinkled with delight at his offer.

Abigail felt she may explode with excitement. 'Let's go before the summer crowds. Oh, Jack, it would be wonderful.'

'What about the classes?'

'The next few terms are sorted. I don't really need to be here.'

'I thought a relaxing stopover at someone's private island resort on the way home might also need to be on the itinerary. My treat. I met a guy a couple of years back, a sculpture who did some amazing metal wall installations for one of our projects. I think he lived on an island up near Nautilus Cove in Queensland. I don't suppose you know anyone with an island we could call?'

Abigail shook her head. She groaned with delight as she visualised them together, nestled in the sand on a deserted beach somewhere. 'Sadly no, but that sounds like heaven on a stick. Tropical nights soaked in the scent of frangipani, nothing to do but eat and float around a pool.'

'And lie in bed,' Jack added. They both chuckled and clinked their glasses.

'What did you say earlier, Abby? That you wanted to ask me something, or was that more about the unfounded accusation of me moving to Sydney? Why would I leave my best friend?'

For a moment Abigail wondered if the holiday should also be a testing ground for their relationship, to check whether the zing she felt in his presence would remain when they were together day after day, night after night. Could it be possible that the frisson she felt in her stomach whenever he walked into the room could disappear; that the deep security she welcomed whenever she was wrapped in his arms would weaken?

*Yes, good idea, Abigail. Wait.*

Then, between a sip of wine and a search of Jack's handsome face, Abigail felt something pass over her. She recognised happiness and a sense of belonging. A glint of something caught her eye through the window and there, balanced upright on the arm of the deck chair was a coin. A sign.

Her lips tweaked with the beginnings of a satisfied smile. She turned to Jack. He was watching her, his intense gaze never wavering from her face.

'You're my best friend, Abby, and a best friend is like a four-leaf clover. Hard to find and lucky to have.' He faltered as Abigail's eyes glistened with unshed tears. 'It's an Irish proverb,' he added.

'No, it's another sign,' she smiled and began laughing.

She cleared her voice. 'You don't have to answer straight away. You know, maybe after our holiday. But for the first time in a long time, I feel I have a real purpose. I feel a part of something new and wonderful and you're a big chunk of that. Sorry, chunk is the wrong word, but I was going to ask you something.' She paused. 'I'm hoping that you would like to move into my home with me. We could be together.'

Jack slowly put his fork down.

'I'd like that so much,' she added.

The world eased away as Jack pushed back his chair and moved to her side. He lifted Abigail to her feet. 'Abigail Croucher, you are on my mind morning, noon and night. I would love to live with you. And Nigella. In a house called Feather's Rest at 64 Ferryman Road.

**What do you pack to pursue your dream, and what
do you leave behind?**

Marnie Fawkner just wanted to escape the demands of adult
children, job hunting and selling her house. So when Marnie's
sister, Libby, asks her to mind her house and dog, Marnie jumps
at the chance. Who would knock back a couple of easy weeks in
Nautilus Cove, a popular coastal town in sunny Queensland?

She never expected a simple favour would change her life.

When Libby delays her return, Marnie reluctantly steps in to
manage Libby's homewares store, Whimsy. What could possibly

go wrong? Marnie finds that Nautilus Cove is offering her more than just a temporary escape – an intriguing sculptor called Harry Mitchelton for a start. It is here, whilst tackling personal change, welcoming new friends and second-chance love, and embracing the chance to start over, that Marnie confronts what she needs to pack to pursue her own dreams.'That Summer in Nautilus Cove is a heart-warming sea change story of self-discovery. It may even prompt you to research coastal real estate.'

**Available Now**

# ABOUT THE AUTHOR

Julie has worked in many industries: from advertising to travel, education to public relations. She dabbles in painting and photography, writes inspirational verse and is a prolific reader. Julie grew up in Melbourne, Australia before making a sea-change to the beautiful Sunshine Coast in Queensland where she writes and, with her partner, owns an art and homewares store (Hearts and Minds Art).

Her contemporary fiction novels focus on mature women who are faced with life changing choices, with emotions, family and location all playing important roles. Her stories are warm, humorous and inclusive.

Her first novel, That Summer in Nautilus Cove, was published in 2021 and her third book is due in 2022.

Reader Review for That Summer in Nautilus Cove (Canada):

"I could feel the sand between my toes and the warmth of change shining through Marnie's life. A great read."

To contact and follow Julie, please visit: facebook.com/juliehollandauthor